THE
DESTROYER
OF
WORLDS

THE DESTROYER OF WORLDS

OF

WORLDS

A RETURN TO LOVECRAFT COUNTRY

MATT RUFF

HARPER

An Imprint of HarperCollinsPublishers

THE DESTROYER OF WORLDS. Copyright © 2023 by Matt Ruff. All rights reserved. Printed in the United States of America. No part of this book may be used or reproduced in any manner whatsoever without written permission except in the case of brief quotations embodied in critical articles and reviews. For information, address HarperCollins Publishers, 195 Broadway, New York, NY 10007.

HarperCollins books may be purchased for educational, business, or sales promotional use. For information, please email the Special Markets Department at SPsales@harpercollins.com.

FIRST EDITION

Art by Morphart Creation/Shutterstock, Inc.

Library of Congress Cataloging-in-Publication Data has been applied for.

ISBN 978-0-06-325689-7

23 24 25 26 27 LBC 5 4 3 2 1

for Nisi,

who wanted more

Then Joseph took an oath from the children of Israel, saying, "God will surely visit you, and you will carry up my bones from here."

—*Genesis 50:25*

"Now I am become Death, the destroyer of worlds."

—*J. Robert Oppenheimer, quoting Vishnu*

THE
DESTROYER
OF
WORLDS

THE LAST TEMPTATION OF SIMON SWINCEGOOD

◆

He kills the dogs before he runs.

Simon has heard the ignorant whispers of other slaves plotting escape. How they will wash away their trail by wading in rivers, or mask it with some stronger scent: Peppercorns. Vinegar. Turpentine. Horse piss. He knows it's all foolishness. Even an ordinary coonhound can track a man through water, or tell a fugitive's sweat from the staling of a horse. And Master Swincegood's hounds *aren't* ordinary. Bred from Egyptian stock, they are descendants of the hounds of Pharaoh, survivors of the debacle of the Red Sea. Nothing on foot can elude them for long.

Hecuba, the midwife, claims that she can fly. Each night she casts her soul aloft, above the reach of dogs or men. She's been to the North many times, she says; and to the future, and the lands of the dead, and to other, stranger places. But it profits her nothing. However far she travels, she remains tethered to her body by an unbreakable cord that each morning reels her in, to wake once more a slave.

Other slaves, lacking even a temporary power of flight, have sought more earthly means of emancipation. Ezekiel, who was keeper of the hounds before Simon, tried to mail himself to freedom. He packed himself in a trunk with one of Missus Swincegood's ball gowns that was bound for a party in Delaware. But the wagon that was to take the luggage to the train depot was late; Ezekiel began to suffocate, and prematurely pulled the stopper on the air hole he'd drilled for himself. The hounds, already suspicious about his absence, were on him in seconds.

Master Swincegood gave Ezekiel fifty lashes and sold him away south. When Master made Simon the hounds' new keeper, he warned him not to repeat Ezekiel's mistake. Simon took the words to heart. He cannot say how his own bid for freedom will end, but he knows how it must begin.

He enters the barn just before curfew. He finds a lantern and lights it, and goes to the pen where the dogs sleep. Four pairs of amber-colored eyes look up at his approach, watchful and curious. They're smart animals: they know it's not time to be fed, and if they were needed for a hunt, a white man would be coming for them.

Simon doesn't give them time to think about it. He opens the gate and points at Little Boy—at fifty pounds, the runt of the litter. "Follow," Simon says.

He crosses the barn to the stall of Adolphus, the mule, and takes the shoeing hammer from its peg on the wall. He side-eyes a warning at Adolphus as he does this; the mule, adept as any slave at playing dumb, stares back vacantly. I don't see nothing, boss.

Leaving the lantern in the barn, Simon leads Little Boy to the old well out back, the path lit by a nearly full moon. In the shadow of a tree near the path's end, Simon pauses. "Set," he says. Little Boy sits obediently. Simon squats beside him. He cocks his right arm and points with his left and says, "Look there." Little Boy looks. Simon swings the hammer. The back of Little Boy's skull gives way with a wet crack and he drops, lifeless.

Simon stands up and begins removing the boards from the mouth of the well. The well was covered after Simon's younger brother, Luke, had his accident. Simon's other brother, Peter, had been teasing Luke, telling him there was a tunnel at the bottom of the well that led all the way to Canada. Luke knew that was nonsense, and said so, but Peter kept insisting it was true, adding that it didn't really matter, anyway, as Luke was too much of a coward to see for himself. It was that last part that proved fatal, for while Luke didn't mind being thought a fool, he couldn't bear to have his bravery questioned. So he tried to climb down, and fell, and hit his head, and drowned. Now the well is tainted.

Go on, drink, Simon thinks, tipping Little Boy headfirst into the well shaft.

When Simon goes back to the barn, Whitefoot has pushed open the gate to the dog pen and is looking out. Volunteering to be next. Simon crooks a finger at him.

After Luke died, Peter ran away. The hounds tracked him to a neighboring plantation and treed him in a hundred-year-old oak. When Peter wouldn't come down, two white men climbed up after him. Peter climbed higher. He was eighty feet off the ground when he found the branch that wouldn't hold his weight.

"Look there," Simon says. Whitefoot looks; the hammer falls.

In the dog pen, Caesar and Cleo have started putting two and two together. When Simon tells Cleo to follow, she doesn't obey; she barks at him. Simon gives her an openhanded smack on top of the head and says, "Mind." That stops the barking, but she still doesn't want to come with him. He has to drag her out by the scruff.

Simon's sister, Rachel, was thirteen years old when Master Swince-good's cousin Charlie took an interest in her. Rachel went along the first few times because she didn't know what else to do, but finally she had enough and stole a knife from the kitchen. She got in one good slice that left a flap of cousin Charlie's cheek hanging off his face. Then Charlie took the knife away from her.

"Look there," says Simon, and Cleo turns and snaps at him. Distracted by a vision of his sister lying bloody on the ground, Simon is caught off guard and drops the hammer. But he recovers quickly. He grabs the back of Cleo's head with one hand and clamps the other around her muzzle and *twists*, hard. The curfew bell rings.

He returns to the barn. Caesar is backed into a corner of the dog pen with his teeth bared. Out of siblings, Simon thinks now of his father. When an overseer tried to rape Simon's mother, Simon's father beat the man to death. He made no attempt to run, afterwards; just waited for his punishment, which was swift and brutal. Master Swincegood tied him to a post and made the other slaves watch as he doused him in turpentine and set him on fire. Simon was barely old enough to walk at the time, but he recalls that day quite clearly. It is his earliest childhood memory.

Caesar growls. It occurs to Simon that time has come round; in this situation, *he* is the master. He nods in recognition of the fact and then lifts his chin up, exposing his throat. Caesar springs, and meets the hammer. The first blow only stuns him, but Simon follows him to the floor and plants a knee in his rib cage and goes to work. The hammer rises and falls in a blur.

When it's over, Simon lets go of the handle, swipes blood from his face, and gets up slowly. He feels like his chest should be heaving from exertion, but he's not even breathing hard. Just a little light-headed, is all. He wipes his hands on his shirt and steps back out of the dog pen.

"Nigger."

Jeff Trumbo, the overseer who replaced the man Simon's father killed, is standing in the barn doorway. Trumbo was never kind, but in the past couple of years, as Simon has gotten bigger, he has gone out of his way to terrorize Simon and so discourage him from following in his father's footsteps. The conditioning works: at the first sight of the overseer Simon is gripped by a paralysis of the will. He doesn't even think about going for the hammer in the dog pen. He just stands there, his attention evenly divided between the fury in Trumbo's eyes and the revolver on Trumbo's hip.

"Past curfew," Trumbo says. "What you doing out here, nigger?" The words are slurred. Simon belatedly notes the bottle in Trumbo's fist. Trumbo is drunk most nights, but tonight he must be blind drunk—that, plus the fact that Simon is backlit, the lantern on the floor behind him, explains why Trumbo's gun is still in its holster.

Instinct takes over. "Caesar's poorly," Simon says. "Master Swincegood told me to check on him before I turned in."

Trumbo says nothing to this, only glares, and Simon fears that the blood on his shirt is visible. But then Trumbo tilts up the bottle and drinks. His eyes lose focus and he goes off in his head, seeming to forget that Simon is even there. On any other night, Simon would be fine with that, but if Trumbo passes out in the barn, someone more sober may come looking for him. So Simon prompts him, gently: "Master Trumbo?"

Trumbo blinks himself back to something resembling consciousness. "Get done," he tells Simon. "I come out here again, I better not catch you."

Simon bows his head. "Yessuh." When he looks up, Trumbo is gone.

Now Simon's chest heaves, as relief mixes with rage at the departed overseer.

No time for that. He finds some burlap to wrap Caesar's remains in, dumps the body down the well with the others, and replaces the boards. Returning to the barn for a final time, he scatters fresh straw in the dog pen to cover up the blood. Before blowing out the lantern he shoots another warning glance at Adolphus, who responds with a fair imitation of Simon's "Yessuh" nod. *I still don't see nothing, boss.*

Out into the night. The route back to the slave cabins takes Simon past the main house. He keeps his head down and walks quickly, staying in the shadows as much as possible, but as he comes in view of the front porch another voice calls out to him: "Simon!"

It is young Master Daniel, Master Swincegood's six-year-old son. Up past his bedtime, alone and bored. He is delighted to see Simon, whom he regards as both playmate and plaything.

Simon turns towards the boy, conscious once more of the blood on his shirt. Conscious, too, of the hammer, which he has brought with him. The handle lies flush against the inside of his forearm; the head, still sticky with blood and dog fur, is cupped in his hand. As he contemplates the deadly weight of it, his rage comes bubbling up, bringing with it a dreadful temptation.

He meant to run away. But there is another way this night could end.

A dozen strides will bring him onto the porch, where a swing of the hammer will crack the boy's skull as easily as any dog's. Then in through the front door, turning right off the hall into the parlor where Missus Swincegood and her daughter, Patsy, will be sewing or reading. A hammer blow for each of them, and another for the house slave, Elsbeth, if she dares to interfere.

Then up the stairs, on a collision course with Master Swincegood, who, alerted by his family's screams, will come running from his study, wielding the pistol that he always has with him. He'll probably shoot Simon dead before Simon even makes it to the top of the staircase. But maybe not. Maybe, carried along by bloodlust, Simon will shrug off the first bullet and resist the urge to freeze up in the face of a man more terrible than any overseer. Maybe he'll do unto Master as he did unto Caesar.

He'll still die, afterwards. Trumbo will come with the other white hands, bringing more guns, and Simon's choice will be to surrender and perish slowly by torture or to resist and be shot down instantly. Either way, his life will end.

And it is this, more than any desire for revenge, that tempts him. Simon is only fifteen, but already he is old and careworn, unable to recall a time when he was not afraid. Even if he escapes, he knows he will never truly be safe. A fugitive's existence must be better than a slave's—it cannot be worse—but fear and uncertainty will dog him all the rest of his days.

To end it all now; to join the rest of his family underground, and feel nothing anymore—that is a powerful temptation, more seductive than anything the devil offered Christ on the mountaintop. It tugs at Simon's soul and he wavers, teetering on the brink, while away up in the future all the children and grandchildren and great-grandchildren he has yet to engender wait to see if their existence will be sacrificed, forfeit to a moment's weakness.

His body decides before his conscious mind does. Simon's left hand—the one without the hammer in it—comes up, and waves. Whatever facial expression accompanies this gesture starts the little master laughing. Daniel waves back. "Simon," he says, "come here!"

But Simon doesn't come. He turns away and walks on without a word. If Daniel were even a year or two older, he would never tolerate such a thing—a slave turning his back—but the boy is still young enough, just, to be unsure of his power. He stamps his foot but he lets Simon go.

At the slave cabins all is quiet. No lights burn in the windows. Simon has told no one what he is planning, but tonight the others have all decided to turn in promptly at curfew anyhow. He senses them lying awake in the dark, rehearsing their alibis for tomorrow. I didn't see nothing, boss.

He enters the cabin that he shared until recently with his mother. From its hiding place he retrieves a sack, already filled with supplies for his journey: Food. Some rope. A knife. Other items and bits of contraband. He adds the hammer and slings the sack over his shoulder.

When he goes back outside, Hecuba is standing in the moonlight waiting for him. She cannot be mistaken for any other slave. Her left leg is shorter than her right, and her left foot is twisted out to the side. She stands at a lean, perpetually on the verge of tipping over.

Simon approaches her warily, wondering whether this is Hecuba in the flesh or merely her soul on its nightly peramble. Up close, she looks solid enough: a white-haired, crippled old woman. "What you want?" he asks, keeping his voice low.

She pivots. Slung over her shoulder is a sack like his. "Coming with you."

"No you ain't."

Hecuba lowers the sack to the ground. Then, to Simon's astonishment, she reaches up and tugs down her top, exposing a pair of sagging and wrinkled breasts. Her other hand shoots out, catching Simon's wrist and drawing it forward until his palm is pressed firm against her bosom. He hisses in disgust and snatches his hand back, but not before he feels the lump underneath the skin.

He knows what it is. His mother had a lump like that, on her lower back; for months she had Simon track the progress of its growth, all the while swearing him to secrecy. Cancer is a death sentence, but white people are always experimenting with cures, and Simon's mother was terrified that if Master Swincegood found out, he'd sell her to a doctor. So she suffered in silence, and when the pain got too bad she had Simon gather ingredients for a special tea. Now she lies in the earth with Simon's father and his brothers and his sister.

Hecuba covers herself up again. "It's all through me," she tells him. "I can feel it in my marrow and my gut. I ain't got long." She looks up. "This my last full moon in this body."

Simon stands back, rubbing his palm furiously on his shirt. "So why run, then?"

"Because it's time," Hecuba says. "I tried when I was your age, more than once. Last time I got caught, that's when they did my leg like this. Told me if it happened again, it'd be my neck got twisted. So I had to decide, stay or die, and I wasn't ready to die, not then. But now . . ." She nods in the direction of the main house. "They stole my life. They won't have my bones. When I lie down, it's gonna be in a place of my own choosing."

Not my problem, Simon thinks. He tries to say it aloud, but his tongue won't cooperate, the paralysis this time caused not by fear but sudden shame, his mother admonishing him from the grave to respect old age and the horrors endured to reach it.

"You pick your free name yet?" Hecuba asks him.

Simon feels himself nod.

"Well?"

"Turner," Simon says. "I get free, I'm gonna be Nat Turner."

Hecuba grins in the moonlight. Nat Turner! The great boogeyman, leader of a failed slave rebellion that a quarter century later still gives white people nightmares. The story goes that after Turner was hanged, they cut up his body and buried the pieces in separate graves, just to be sure. "Nat Turner," says Hecuba. "Hah! You'll need to do some mighty deeds, to be worthy of *that* name."

"You don't need to worry yourself about me," Simon assures her. "I—"

A train whistle interrupts him. It's a faint sound, carried for what must be many miles on the night air, but Simon reacts as if a siren had gone off in his ear. He looks past Hecuba towards the moonlit horizon. When the whistle comes again, a slight change in the sound's bearing tells him that the train is southbound.

Southbound. But they go north, too. That's how he's getting out.

"It's not that easy," Hecuba says. "It's farther than you think, and there's patrols up and down those tracks. But I know the way to go. I been over it many times."

"Yeah? What you need me for, then?"

"I don't, to get *to* the train. But to get *on* it . . ." She touches the thigh of her twisted leg. "For that, I'm gonna need help. You do that for me, I'll see you get your new name."

Sure you will, Simon thinks. Rather than waste more time arguing, he takes the path of least resistance. "You tag along if you like," he says. "But don't expect me to go slow for you. You fall behind, I'll leave you."

The old woman laughs. "You be careful *you* don't fall behind," she says. Then she picks up her sack and takes off.

Hecuba's gait is as peculiar as her resting stance. She pitches and weaves like a scarecrow teaching itself to walk. She stays upright, though, and she's faster than she has any right to be. By the time Simon gets moving, he actually has to run to catch up to her.

A north-south carriage road marks the edge of the Swincegood property. On the far side is a line of trees, bright moonlight on top, dark shadow underneath. Simon has been in those woods before, but tonight he feels like he's racing towards terra incognita; if the ground were suddenly to fall away beneath his feet it would scarcely surprise him.

No longer Simon Swincegood, not yet Nat Turner, he steps off the edge of the world and follows Hecuba into the trees.

PART I

CARRY UP
THE BONES

THE KING IN YELLOW

⊰⊱

One hundred years later, in the summer of 1957, Nat Turner's great-grandson Montrose Turner, and Montrose's son, Atticus, drove from Chicago to North Carolina. Their plan was to visit the former Swince-good plantation and mark the centennial of their ancestor's escape by retracing the route he and Hecuba had followed into the Great Dismal Swamp. They got more than they bargained for.

Montrose and Atticus left Chicago two days before the anniversary, taking an indirect route that was intended in part to keep them above the Mason-Dixon line for as long as possible. Of course the North wasn't especially friendly to colored people either, but they were prepared for that: Montrose's half brother, George Berry, was the publisher of *The Safe Negro Travel Guide*, a quarterly that listed hotels, restaurants, and other establishments where they could be sure of being welcomed, and warned of sundown towns and other hazards best avoided; they brought a copy with them. Montrose had hoped that George and his son, Horace, would come on the journey as well, but Horace already had plans to travel out west with his mother, and George begged off at the last minute.

Atticus would have liked to beg off too. His relationship with his father had often been difficult, and while they'd been getting along better the past couple years, he expected this trip into history would bring out all of Montrose's worst tendencies. There was also the fact that in his day job as a scout for *The Safe Negro Travel Guide*, Atticus spent far too much time in Jim Crow country already; he had no desire to vacation there. But his father wanted him to come, so he came.

They stopped the first night in Philadelphia. In the morning after breakfast they drove around South Philly, searching for an address that no longer existed.

Family lore held that Great-grandpa Turner had joined a maroon colony in the Great Dismal and lived there for six years, subsisting on feral hogs and other wild game, and occasionally raiding white settlements along the fringes of the swamp for other necessities. In 1863 he'd emerged from hiding and enlisted in the Union Army, rising to the rank of sergeant by war's end. By 1870 he'd gone out west to Indian Territory, where he would remain until his death in 1886.

His whereabouts in the years immediately after the Civil War were harder to pin down; he'd moved around a lot, looking for work that paid well and seldom finding it. Through a genealogical society he belonged to, Montrose had obtained a copy of a letter Sergeant Turner had sent to another Negro veteran in April 1868, giving the address of a Philadelphia boardinghouse where he'd spent the preceding winter. Around the turn of the century the street had been renamed and renumbered, but by comparing old and new maps, Montrose thought he'd identified the lot where the boardinghouse had once stood.

Finding it was harder than it should have been. Montrose insisted on driving, and ignoring Atticus's navigational suggestions he made several wrong turns, at one point nearly crossing the river into Camden. After forty-five minutes of circling and doubling back, they arrived at the lot, now occupied by an undistinguished row house. Montrose took a photograph of it, then stood on the sidewalk looking up at the second-floor windows as if he expected Great-grandpa Turner to stick his head out and say hi. Atticus tried to appear interested, but he was mostly just glad they weren't in New Jersey.

They got back in the car and drove south. They ate lunch in D.C., at a restaurant across the street from another house where Great-grandpa had briefly resided after mustering out of the Army. As Montrose and Atticus finished dessert, the front door of the house opened and a Negro family came out: father, mother, two sons, and a daughter, all dressed up as if for a special occasion. The sight of them seemed to genuinely lift Montrose's spirits.

The mood didn't last. On their way out of the city they stopped at a red light beside a charter bus that must have been on its way to a Civil War reenactment. Men in Confederate uniform were laughing and joking in the windows, and a few of them, noticing Montrose and Atticus, began making rude comments. Atticus braced himself for a fight, but Montrose didn't even look up, just tightened his grip on the steering wheel; when the light changed, he let the bus go on ahead, ignoring the impatient honking of the cars behind them.

"You all right, Pop?" Atticus said.

Montrose turned and regarded him with the expression he reserved for the stupidest of questions. "No, I am not all right," he said. But then he sighed and put the car in gear. "It's good to be reminded where you stand, I guess."

They crossed Virginia without incident. By early evening they had reached their destination, a small city in North Carolina some thirty miles from the old Swincegood property. They had reservations for the night at the Royal Hotel.

After a quiet dinner they retired upstairs. Their room, on the top floor, had a narrow balcony that overlooked the street. Montrose propped open the balcony door to let in some air. He sat on his bed and spread out a surveyor's map that he'd hand-marked with dotted lines and various other notations, studying it like a general preparing for battle. A few feet away in his own bed, Atticus tried to read one of the books he'd brought with him, but he had trouble concentrating, and kept sneaking glances at his father. The third or fourth time he did this, Montrose said without looking up, "Is there something I can help you with?"

"No, Pop, I'm fine."

Montrose reached for a pack of cigarettes on the nightstand behind him. "What you reading, anyway?"

Atticus turned the book so that his father could see the cover.

"*The King in Yellow*," Montrose said. "What's that, a Fu Manchu story?"

Atticus shook his head. "It's about a play that makes people crazy," he said. "Something about the way the second act is written—if you read even one line, it hooks you, and you start to take leave of your senses."

"*Read* one line," said Montrose. "But it's a play? How could you perform it if just reading it makes you crazy?"

"I don't know, Pop. Maybe the actors are all crazy too."

"Foolishness," said Montrose. He got up and went out on the balcony to smoke.

Atticus turned back to *The King in Yellow*, but then he heard his father chuckle. "Come out here," Montrose said.

Atticus joined him on the balcony. Montrose pointed up the street to a boulevard that marked the divide between the white and colored sections of downtown. On a corner on the far side stood a movie theater called the Commodore. Atticus had glimpsed it earlier but had somehow failed to register the words on the marquee:

TODAY ONLY

D.W. GRIFFITH'S CLASSIC

THE BIRTH OF A NATION

"*The King in Yellow*," Montrose said, nodding at the line of white people stretching away down the block. He took a draw on his cigarette and blew smoke into the evening air. "Like I said, it's good to be reminded where you stand."

WELCOME TO NEVADA

⧗

Two thousand miles to the west, the sun had not yet set. As Atticus's aunt Hippolyta cut across Arizona on U.S. 91, the light reflected off the silver skin of the trailer attached to the back of her Buick Roadmaster.

The trailer had been her husband George's idea. George had a new client, Fred Tunstall, who owned a number of Airstream dealerships in Chicago and Detroit. Mr. Tunstall believed that Negroes represented an untapped market; in exchange for buying a year's worth of ads, he'd gotten George to agree to run an article in *The Safe Negro Travel Guide* touting the virtues of the travel trailer lifestyle. Mr. Tunstall had offered the loan of a top-of-the-line Airstream for research purposes, and George, upon learning of Hippolyta's trip to Las Vegas, had passed the research duty on to her.

She wasn't happy about it. Though a seasoned driver, Hippolyta's only experience with towing involved a small box trailer she'd once rented to help her mother move to a new apartment. The Airstream was a monster, thirty feet long and weighing more than two tons. Coming over the Rockies, she'd been terrified of jackknifing on the mountain switchbacks; in populated areas, she feared collisions and vandalism. Mr. Tunstall had told her that the Airstream was insured, but he was clearly vexed that a woman would be driving, and Hippolyta guessed that any damages—whether her fault or not—would cause no end of grief.

Here in the open desert with no traffic around, she had the leisure to turn her mind to other worries. She tilted the otherwise useless rear-view mirror so she could see into the back seat, where her fifteen-year-old son, Horace, lay stretched out with his big feet propped up in the passenger-side window, toes sampling the breeze. The dog-eared book in his hands had a mushroom cloud on its cover, and the title, with its many exclamation points—*THE ATOM SMASHERS!!!!!*—promised an exciting read. But Horace didn't look excited, he looked sullen and angry—his default expression, these days.

Hippolyta had been hesitant to bring him on this trip. She had business to conduct in Las Vegas that she didn't want him involved in. But she'd decided he'd be safer with her than running around the streets back home unsupervised—and *much* safer than he would be traveling south with his uncle and his cousin. She'd sooner drive blindfolded across the Himalayas than let Horace loose in Jim Crow country in his current state of mind.

While Hippolyta eyeballed Horace, her friend Letitia Dandridge, riding shotgun, kept up a steady monologue: "—and so finally after last week's service the reverend asked me, 'Hey, how come we never see Ruby in here anymore? I hope she didn't get bored with my preaching.' And you know, truth be told, his sermons *have* been a little dry since his wife ran off with that guitar player, but of course I didn't say that, I just made up a story about how Ruby's pulling double shifts at this new job. 'Don't worry, though, she'll be back to church regular once things slow down.' And he gave me this look like, 'You know it's a sin to fib to God's servant, right?' but I just smiled and walked out . . ."

It was the second time Letitia had told this story since they'd left Chicago. Hippolyta didn't mind; she knew the repetition was just her friend's way of working through her own feelings. And Letitia was an undemanding speaker, requiring no more than an occasional nod as confirmation that she hadn't been completely tuned out.

"But now I'm like, OK, what *is* Ruby up to? So I go by her apart-ment, and this woman I've never seen before answers the door. And I say, 'Where's Ruby?' and she says, 'Ruby who?' and I say, 'Ruby Dan-dridge. My sister. She lives here.' And this woman says, 'No she doesn't. *I* live here.' So long story short, it turns out Ruby moved months ago, didn't tell me, didn't tell any of our friends, and when I try to get a forwarding address, this woman shuts the door in my face."

They passed a sign saying LAS VEGAS, NV—84. Half a mile ahead was another, larger sign marking the Nevada state border. Just beyond it, a Nevada State Police cruiser sat parked on the road shoulder facing the highway, two uniformed white men in the front seat. Letitia saw the cruiser at the same time Hippolyta did. She abruptly stopped talk-ing and dropped her feet from the dashboard to the floor; Hippolyta checked her speedometer. Both women adopted looks of respectful indifference meant to communicate that while they were aware of the police, they had no reason to be concerned by them.

Naturally it was Horace who didn't follow the playbook. When Hippolyta told him to get his feet inside the car and stay down, he sat up and stuck his face out the window instead, just in time to lock eyes with the cops as they drove by. Hippolyta sighed and raised her own eyes to heaven.

"They're pulling out behind us," Letitia said.

Hippolyta glared at her son in the rearview. "You sit up *straight*, now," she told him, her tone brooking no contradiction. "Eyes forward and hands up on the back of the seat in front of you. Do not *speak* unless spoken to. Do not *move*. Do not give them an *excuse*."

A siren began to wail behind them. Mindful of the trailer, Hip-polyta eased off on the gas without braking. She found a wide flat spot on the shoulder and pulled well off the road. The cruiser came in alongside them and parked by the trailer's back end. Hippolyta watched in the side mirror as the driver got out. He was an older man, thick gray hair visible under the brim of his trooper hat, and as his gaze swept the length of the trailer, Hippolyta could see that his expression was cheerful, which experience told her was either a good sign or a very, very bad one. She found Horace's eyes in the rearview again, gave him one last warning look.

Then the trooper was there beside her, leaning down to look in her window. Smiling.

"Hello," he began. "How you folks doing today?"

"Fine, officer," Hippolyta said, Letitia nodding agreement. "What can we do for you?"

"I'd like to ask you some questions, if you don't mind. Could you step out for a moment?"

"You want my license and registration?"

"No, that won't be necessary. Just come out here."

Hippolyta opened the door and got out slowly. She stood six feet tall, which some men had a problem with, but the trooper, a comfortable six four, didn't seem to care; by the time she'd risen to her full height he had turned and was walking back towards the trailer. As Hippolyta followed him, she saw that the other trooper—younger and far less cheerful—had gotten out of the cruiser and was leaning back against the front hood with his arms crossed; she also noted, with no small alarm, that he had drawn his gun and was holding it with the muzzle peeping out from behind his left elbow.

"I wanted to ask about your Airstream," the gray-haired trooper said. "This is that new King of the Road model, isn't it?"

"Yes sir," Hippolyta said. It was actually the Sovereign of the Road, but she saw no need to correct him. "I've got papers for it, if—"

"How do you like it?"

"How do I . . .?"

"Like it. Is it a good trailer?"

"It's all right," Hippolyta said cautiously. "I suppose it's a bit much for me, if I'm honest."

"What's the interior like?"

Hippolyta took this as a request for a tour—a request she'd ordinarily feel compelled to grant. But thinking of the black case hidden in one of the storage compartments, she decided to risk playing dumb. "Sitting room and kitchen up front," she said. "Sleeping compartment with twin beds in the middle, and bathroom in back. Bathroom's got a little tub and a shower, and a thirty-gallon water tank. Septic tank, too."

"Gas lighting?"

"The lights are electric. Battery powered. The water heater and refrigerator use gas, and the stovetop and oven of course."

"Self-sufficient. I like that," the trooper said. "My brother, Richard? He bought a trailer that doesn't even have a water tank. It's got a shower, but to use it you have to park somewhere and attach a hose. Didn't seem practical to me."

Hippolyta nodded. This was, of course, one of the main reasons Negroes had not rushed to embrace the travel trailer lifestyle: trailer parks, which offered convenient hookups for water and electricity, were typically whites-only. Mr. Tunstall thought the Airstream's self-sufficiency would be a key selling point: all of the onboard appliances ran on bottled gas, and the battery that powered the electrical system was recharged by the car's engine.

"How much did it run you?" the trooper wanted to know.

"I have it on loan," Hippolyta said, resisting the urge to offer her papers again, "but I think the list price is somewhere between five and six thousand, depending on the options."

The trooper let out a low whistle. "Hey Cal," he addressed his unsmiling partner, "I may need you to help me knock over a bank later."

From behind her, Hippolyta heard the creak of a car door opening. The younger trooper stood up straight and uncrossed his arms. The older trooper turned his head. "Hello there, young man," he said.

The desert heat vanished, replaced in an instant by a nightmare chill that bloomed from Hippolyta's marrow as she too turned around. Horace had gotten out of the back seat and stood beside the Roadmaster with a look of naked rage on his face. He was still holding his book, Hippolyta saw, gripping it as you would a brick that you meant to bash in someone's head with.

"Horace," she heard herself say, "you get back in the car, now."

He ignored her, focusing his fury on the gray-haired trooper: "You got no right to stop us like this."

"Excuse me?" the trooper said.

"Horace! Get *back* in the *car*!"

"My mother didn't do anything wrong!" Horace protested, nostrils flaring. "You got no right to pull her over and interrogate her like, like—"

"Horace!"

"Hold on there, Calvin," the gray-haired trooper said, and his partner, moving forward with his gun raised, stopped short like a dog hitting the end of its lead. Then the gray-haired trooper said to Horace: "Young man, I don't know what's troubling you, but people in my line of work get nervous when folks look at us the way you're doing right now. So before this goes any further in a direction we're liable to regret, I'm going to ask you take a deep breath and calm down a bit." Nodding at the book: "I also need you to empty your hands for me."

Horace just stood there, chest heaving.

"For God's sake, Horace," Hippolyta pleaded. "Drop it."

Maybe it was her words. Maybe it was some shred of sanity reasserting itself. Horace's hand didn't so much open as convulse; the book dropped to the ground.

"Thank you," the trooper said. "Now ordinarily at this point I'd ask you to put both hands on the roof of the car, but I imagine that metal's pretty hot, so instead I'm going to have you lace your fingers together behind your head, all right?"

Horace swallowed hard. He still looked angry, but doubt had crept in—a belated realization that he wasn't quite as eager to jump off this particular cliff as he had thought. He slowly raised his arms and pressed his hands to the back of his skull.

"OK, that's good," the trooper said. Without taking his eyes off Horace, he added an aside to his partner: "Calvin, why don't you holster your weapon and step back a few paces."

Reluctantly, the younger trooper did as he was told.

"Now," the older trooper continued, "Horace, is it? Why don't you explain to me what's got you so worked up."

Hippolyta spoke up before Horace could put his foot in it again: "I'm very sorry, officer. Horace is a good boy, really he is, but he hasn't been himself lately. A friend of his back in Chicago got shot to death, not two weeks ago."

Horace's eyes widened in a look of betrayal. *"Mom."*

"You *hush UP!*" Hippolyta yelled. Her voice dropped back to a conversational register and she went on: "It was a young girl, Celia Fox. My friend Letitia, in the car, she's a landlady, and Celia and her father were her tenants. Everybody who knows them is heartbroken by it."

"Shot to death," the trooper said. "By the police?"

"Yes sir. They say it was an accident. They were shooting at someone else, but a bullet went astray."

The trooper nodded. "That does tend to happen." He thought a moment, then looked Horace in the eye and said: "You seem like a brave young man. It's good to be brave; sometimes, it's good to be angry, too. But if you live long enough you learn that bravery and anger aren't sufficient. Power is what matters. Without power, bravery and anger will just get you hurt, or killed."

The trooper held up his right hand, turning it so that both Horace and Hippolyta could see that he was missing most of two fingers. The little finger was gone entirely; a single joint of the ring finger remained, the stump capped with an ugly knot of scar tissue. "I was a brave young man too, once. And one day I got angry at a man who'd mistreated my mother. He was bigger than I was. Stronger. Meaner. But I was mad as hell and I knew I was in the right, so I thought that would carry the day for me. I paid dearly for that mistake." He lowered his hand to his side again. "Now, I meant no insult to your mother. As for pulling you over, regardless of whether I have a legal right to do that, the fact is, out here, I have power. If you were foolish enough to set yourself against me, you'd lose, and no one would care which of us was in the right. I think you're smart enough to know that's how it is, but because you're mad you're trying to pretend it's not so, and doing that puts both you and your mother at risk.

"Now, I'm not going to hold this outburst against you. I do care about what's right, and like I say, I remember what it's like to be young. But this is a long highway, and there's other men out on it—men with power, with guns—and most of them won't think twice before they make you pay for stepping out of line. Please nod your head if you hear what I'm saying to you."

Horace swallowed again. No longer visibly angry—just miserable—he bowed his head.

"All right, then," the trooper said. He turned to Hippolyta. "Ma'am, I apologize for interrupting your journey."

"Thank you," Hippolyta said. "Thank you, officer."

The trooper smiled. "I do envy you that trailer. Have a safe journey. And keep an eye on your son. He'll be a good man if he makes it that far."

And incredibly, that was it. The trooper and his partner got back in the cruiser. Watching them go, Hippolyta was giddy with relief, but as the cruiser was turning around she saw the younger trooper staring out the window and the chill came back, as she considered how differently the last few minutes might have gone if *he* had been the one in charge. After that she didn't breathe again until the cruiser was well on its way.

When at last she turned around, Letitia was climbing out of the Roadmaster like someone emerging from a storm cellar. "Praise Jesus," Letitia muttered, then said laughing: "Welcome to Nevada, huh?"

Hippolyta didn't laugh. Her gaze fell on Horace, who looked, finally, as scared as he ought to be.

"Mom—" he began, but got no farther, Hippolyta swooping towards him with her own right hand raised high.

UNION OF PAST
AND PRESENT

⊰⊱

The trouble began when they saw the slaves.

Early the next morning, Atticus waited in front of the hotel for his father to bring the car around. In the night he'd dreamed he was running through the woods with Great-grandpa Turner and Hecuba; Great-grandpa had seemed oblivious to his presence, but the old woman had addressed him by name and admonished him repeatedly to keep up. He'd awakened with sore legs and sore feet.

No report survived of the events on the Swincegood plantation the morning after the escape. As a boy, Atticus had liked to imagine that it was Trumbo who'd discovered Simon's and Hecuba's absence; the thought of the overseer, head still pounding from last night's drunk, forced to go before his employer and confess the loss of two slaves—not to mention the death of the precious hounds—had filled him with gleeful satisfaction. As an adult, he understood that any humiliation Trumbo suffered would be revisited tenfold on the other slaves, and for their sake Atticus now hoped Master Swincegood's reaction had been calm and businesslike: Send for fresh dogs, Trumbo. Start the hunt.

Montrose pulled up. Atticus put the bags in the back trunk and got into the front passenger seat. They drove out of the city. Atticus held one of his father's maps open on his lap and traced the route to the plantation, which was simple enough: East twenty-one miles. Turn right onto a slender ribbon of blacktop that a hundred years ago had been an unpaved carriage road. Go south until the present meets the past.

The countryside they drove through was a patchwork of small farms and fields broken up by stretches of pine woods. Montrose, ordinarily a lead-footed motorist, kept the car's speed at a leisurely forty miles per hour. Neither of them spoke. Montrose watched the road ahead, while Atticus stared at the passing farms, taking silent inventory of things that would have been anachronisms in Great-grandpa's day: Tractors. TV antennas. Power and phone lines.

At the carriage road junction stood a dilapidated cabin that, but for the Confederate flag hanging over its front porch, might easily have been there in 1857. The flag seemed a double anachronism, though, its bright new fabric contrasting sharply with the weathered wood of the structure. Montrose idled the car for a full minute as he tried to burn down the cabin with his eyes. But it failed to ignite, and at last he put the car back in gear and made the turn.

The carriage road ran straight south for two miles, then snaked to pass between a pair of shallow hills. Just beyond this S-curve, on the right side of the road, several acres of pine wood were in the process of being cleared. The cut trees had already been hauled away, and now a dozen colored slaves watched over by two armed white men were laboring to remove the stumps that remained.

The colored men wore striped uniforms, which to many passersby would have carried a different connotation. But Atticus, as Montrose's son, knew the words of the Thirteenth Amendment by heart and was all too aware of the loophole they contained: *Neither slavery nor involuntary servitude, except as a punishment for a crime whereof the party shall have been duly convicted, shall exist within the United States, or any place subject to their jurisdiction.*

The men toiling in the field were not volunteers. They could not refuse to work or demand a fair wage for their labor. If they made trouble, they could be beaten or even killed with impunity. They were slaves.

And yes, they were also convicts. Atticus would have liked to take comfort in the belief that they were hardened criminals, murderers or rapists. But the Thirteenth Amendment said nothing about felonies: if the state or the county wanted your servitude, a simple charge of vagrancy would suffice. One of Atticus's high school teachers, a gentle man named Mr. Fish, had lost six months of his youth to a Georgia chain gang after falling asleep on a park bench.

Since turning onto the carriage road, Montrose had been driving even more slowly. Now he brought the car to a full stop and his eyes once more filled up with fire. "God damn it," he said. "God *damn* it."

Atticus shifted his attention from the slaves to the white men guarding them. One sat atop a horse, holding a rifle upright against his shoulder. The other had set up a lawn chair near the edge of the clearing and was stretched out reading a newspaper and drinking from a thermos. There were several anachronisms here, but the one Atticus zeroed in on was the horseman's rifle: an M1 Garand semiautomatic, more accurate and much deadlier than anything a nineteenth-century overseer would have carried.

"We can't be sitting here, Pop," Atticus said. Trying to keep his tone reasonable, as if that would make a difference.

Montrose ignored him. "A hundred goddamn years . . . a hundred goddamn years, and they're *still* . . ."

"Pop!" As Atticus turned his head towards his father, he caught a flash of movement in the rearview mirror. A white Studebaker, speeding around the curve behind them.

The Studebaker's driver slammed on the brakes, but it was moving too fast to stop. Atticus managed to brace himself for impact, but Montrose, who like Atticus wasn't wearing a seat belt, was caught completely unprepared. The force of the collision whipped his head back and then forward, to connect solidly with the rim of the steering wheel.

Atticus was shaken but uninjured. When things stopped moving, he looked first to his father. Montrose was slumped forward, bleeding from a cut above his eye. He appeared to be unconscious, but when Atticus touched his shoulder, his eyes blinked open and he frowned and shoved Atticus's hand away roughly. A good sign.

Of the two cars, the Studebaker seemed to have gotten the worst of the collision, its front hood now crimped into a snarl. Through the web of cracks in the front windshield, Atticus could make out the pink blob of a face. A white driver: of course.

In the field, the guard who'd been sitting in the lawn chair was on his feet now, pointing a shotgun at the slaves, who all had their hands in the air. The horseman had wheeled about to face the road, his rifle still aimed skyward for the moment. Atticus thought about the revolver in the hidden holster under his seat and wondered how much extra trouble that would cause if the car ended up getting searched. But there was no way to get rid of it now.

He opened his door and got out slowly, showing his own hands, open and empty, for the benefit of the man with the rifle.

The driver's door of the Studebaker creaked open. Atticus looked around to see a white man in his late forties with a bull neck and a military brush cut climbing out of the car. As the driver turned to face him, Atticus was startled to realize that he knew the man, and not in a good way. The last time they had met had been at three in the morning in the Sabbath Kingdom Wood in north central Massachusetts, a few miles outside the village of Ardham.

The recognition did not appear to be mutual, and Atticus would have liked to keep it that way. But his own tongue betrayed him, speaking unbidden, as if under a compulsion.

"Sheriff Hunt?" he said. "Sheriff Eustace Hunt?"

The driver of the Studebaker stared at him in a daze. Then a light came on somewhere back in his head, a long-suppressed memory stirring and waking from slumber. His gaze hardened.

"*You,*" Hunt said. He took a step back, reaching for something on his hip, Atticus ducking as the big muzzle of a .44 swung up into view.

As the sound of the gunshot echoed across the field, all of the slaves dropped to the ground. The horseman let go of the reins, steadying the horse with his knees, and brought the rifle to firing position.

Atticus had been a soldier at war. His combat reflexes took over now. Crouched beside the open passenger door, he reached around for the gun under the seat, noting peripherally as he did so that the driver's door was also open and his father was no longer in the car.

A rifle bullet struck the window of the rear passenger door, shattering it. Atticus cocked the revolver and fired back. It was a long shot for a handgun and he aimed instinctively for the horse, the larger target. He was never sure if he hit it or just panicked it, but at the second pull of the trigger the horse reared up and threw the rifleman from the saddle. As the horse galloped away riderless across the field, the other guard started to take aim, but Atticus snapped off two more bullets in his direction and he dropped the shotgun and dove down cowering beside the lawn chair.

Montrose slid back into the driver's seat with blood on his knuckles. "*Get in,*" he said, tossing Sheriff Hunt's .44 onto the floor in front of the passenger seat.

The engine was still running. Atticus climbed inside and Montrose hit the gas before he'd gotten the door closed. As the car started to roll, the rifleman popped up and continued firing. Atticus heard several bullets punch through the front fender but the car kept moving, and Montrose pushed the accelerator all the way to the floor.

They roared off down the road, leaving the field of slaves behind them.

By the time they reached the old Swincegood plantation, a mix of steam and smoke was trailing from the speeding car like a rocket exhaust plume.

Montrose nursed the overheating engine along for another quarter mile. Up ahead he spied a ramshackle house with its doors and windows boarded up and a weathered FOR SALE sign nailed to a tree out front. The house had a detached garage set back from the road, its open doorway like the mouth of a cave. Montrose swung a hard left and drove straight in. As he brought the car to a stop the engine seized up completely; he switched off the ignition and waited to see if the engine would burst into flame. It didn't.

Atticus sat dazed in the passenger seat, waving away smoke. "You're bleeding," he said, after a moment.

"It's not the first time," Montrose replied. He reached over and got a screwdriver from the glove box. "Come on."

They got out and went to the back of the car. While Atticus kept watch on the road, Montrose knelt and got to work removing the rear license plate.

"Who was that guy?" Montrose asked.

"Eustace Hunt. He was sheriff of Devon County that time George and I came looking for you."

"The one who walked you into the woods at gunpoint? I thought Braithwhite put a hex on him. Wiped his memory clean."

"He did," Atticus said. "But I guess seeing my face broke the spell."

"Yeah, and how does *that* happen?" Montrose sounded accusatory. "We're a long way from Massachusetts. What's he doing here?"

"Hunt was originally from North Carolina. He was a drill sergeant at Camp Lejeune. The camp's not that far from here, so maybe he's back to visit his Marine buddies. Or maybe he's got a family reunion over in Fayetteville."

"The same day we're here. That's a hell of a coincidence." Montrose yanked the license plate free and stood up. "All right," he said, "I'm going to get the other plate. You start getting the gear together. We can leave the suitcase with our spare clothes behind, but we need to make sure there's nothing with a name or address on it."

"And where are we going?" Atticus asked.

"Where do you think? Train tracks aren't more than ten miles as the crow flies. And I got my maps—we can figure a way that keeps us off the roads as much as possible." Blood still seeped from the cut above Montrose's eye, and his expression was grim, but Atticus thought he detected a note of satisfaction in his father's voice, as if some part of him were pleased that things had come to this pass.

"I got to hand it to you, Pop," Atticus said. "You really know how to throw a vacation."

RED PAWN

◆⧖◆

Hippolyta woke to the sound of children screaming. By the time her eyes were open, the screams had become a chant of "Cannonball! Cannonball!," which was followed by a loud splash, and laughter.

Letitia snored softly in the opposite twin bed. In the trailer galley, a box of Frosted Flakes stood open on the cold stovetop, and there was a cereal bowl and spoon in the sink. In the sitting area in the trailer's front end, the divan where Horace had slept was empty.

Hippolyta got dressed and went outside.

The motel was called the Desert Ocean. Hippolyta's car-and-trailer rig occupied one of two extra-large parking spaces; these were more commonly used by the tour buses of Negro performers, who could work in the white casinos and hotels but had to return to West Las Vegas to sleep. The wall behind the Desert Ocean check-in desk was covered with photos of famous guests; according to the clerk, they'd missed meeting Eartha Kitt by only a few hours.

The "ocean" part of the motel was at the end of the parking lot farthest from the street: an above-ground swimming pool surrounded by a raised wooden deck. As Hippolyta mounted the steps, she scanned the bobbing heads of the children in the water. Horace wasn't among them.

"You looking for your boy?" A dark-skinned woman stretched out on a lounge chair looked up from the crossword she was working on. "He's over there." She indicated a table in a corner of the deck that was shaded by an enormous umbrella. Horace was sitting with a chubby-faced girl of about twelve. He was showing her one of the photographs in *THE ATOM SMASHERS!!!!!*, but it looked like she was more interested in him than the book. Horace was bare-chested and wearing his swim trunks, while the girl, Hippolyta noted, had on a baggy long-sleeved dress that looked out of place at poolside.

"That's my Maisie," the woman in the lounge chair said. "I'm Tilda, Tilda Jackson."

"Hippolyta Berry," Hippolyta said. "Your daughter doesn't like the water?"

"She likes it just fine, she's just a little shy about how she looks in a bathing suit. Her brothers like to tease her." Mrs. Jackson nodded at two of the bobbing heads in the water. "Not to worry, though—she'll be over it as soon as the sun gets a little hotter."

"I hope Horace isn't bothering her."

"Your boy? No, he's fine. I'm surprised she's talking to him—she's shy with strangers too, usually—but it's good to see her making friends . . . You folks staying here awhile, or just passing through?"

"Staying a couple days. I have some business to take care of downtown. And Horace came along because he wanted to see the A-bomb test tomorrow morning."

"Yeah, my husband was talking about that. That's for real? They set off atom bombs right outside the city?"

"Not right outside. The test site is about an hour away by car. But you'll be able to see the explosion from here. And the mushroom cloud, after."

"An hour away in which direction?"

"Northwest," Hippolyta told her. "Out past Indian Springs."

"Northwest." Mrs. Jackson nodded knowingly. "So if something goes wrong, it's closer to our side of town."

"Well, that's true, but I don't think—"

"No surprise there," Mrs. Jackson said. "No surprise at all."

✿   ✿   ✿

You want me to come in with you?"

Five minutes before noon, Hippolyta and Letitia sat parked across the street from a downtown Vegas shop whose awning bore the words **RED PAWN**. They'd left Horace and the trailer back at the Desert Ocean. Hippolyta had intended to leave Letitia behind as well, to watch Horace, but Mrs. Jackson had volunteered to keep an eye on him.

"I should go in alone," Hippolyta said. "He's only expecting one person. And if there's trouble—"

"If there's trouble, I'm coming in after you. I brought something." Letitia removed a velvet bag from her purse, loosened the drawstring, and drew out an ebony wand that was capped at one end with a miniature silver dragonfly. The wand of sleep and forgetting, she called it: a souvenir from a previous adventure.

"You kept it," Hippolyta said.

"Of course I kept it."

"It still works?"

Letitia shrugged a shoulder. "Not like there's a meter on it to tell you how much charge is left. But it worked just fine the last time I tried it."

"When was that?"

"A few months ago. I was out dancing, and there was this grabby-hands boy who wouldn't leave me alone. I could have got the bouncers to throw him out, but I felt like teaching him a lesson, so I led him around behind the bandstand and dropped him." She grinned, turning the wand in her hand, taking care not to bring the dragonfly anywhere near her skin. "Of course, the problem with teaching him a lesson that way is he wouldn't actually remember what happened, once he woke up. But it was satisfying, watching him go down. Like knocking a tree over with one finger."

❧ ❧ ❧

At noon, Hippolyta got out of the car and crossed the street, carrying a small black case marked with the initials H. W. and the icon of a half sun peeking over the horizon.

H. W. was Hiram Winthrop, heir to a textile-mill fortune and one-time leader of the Chicago chapter of a white sorcerers' cabal called the Order of the Ancient Dawn. Winthrop's chapter of the Order had come to a bad end a couple of years ago, but his own misfortune dated back further: in the summer of 1935 he had been murdered by an associate named Samuel Braithwhite. Dead but not gone, Winthrop's spirit endured inside the walls of his old mansion, which Letitia now owned and ran as a boardinghouse.

Hippolyta accepted all of this with a surprising matter-of-factness. She still struggled, occasionally, with her role as Winthrop's emissary to the outside world. There was a piece of information he'd possessed, a set of celestial coordinates that she'd hoped to trade a simple favor for; but when she'd gone to strike a bargain with him, he'd offered her something better, something too tempting to pass up. The price had been steep: not one favor but a long series of them, of which today's errand was the culmination.

She couldn't help wondering about the provenance of the case and its contents. Most of her errands had involved some sort of delivery or pickup. She had, for instance, mailed a number of letters for him—Winthrop being unable, in his current state, to make use of the telephone. The letters didn't trouble her; it made sense that a man who'd designed his home to be a soul-catcher would also take care to stockpile useful items like money and stationery. But some of the other objects she'd been tasked to deliver were harder to account for through foresight alone. Hippolyta had come to suspect that in addition to a large storeroom, the subbasement of the Winthrop House contained a workshop equipped with tools that a ghost could operate. And that raised the question of what else Winthrop might be building down there with the things Hippolyta brought back to him. Sometimes at night when her conscience was bothering her she'd lie awake and try to fit the pieces together, to see if the finished puzzle was something she could live with.

The door to the pawn shop was locked and there was no one visible inside. Hippolyta read the sign painted on the door glass:

RED PAWN

Angus Rutherford, Proprietor

HOURS Noon to 6 PM, Daily

RING FOR ADMITTANCE

She shifted the case to her left hand and pressed the buzzer. After a few moments, a white man emerged from the shop's back room. He was short and muscular, dressed like a mechanic in overalls and a light work shirt. His eyes were green behind thick spectacles, and above his broad, freckled forehead was a shock of white hair that might, in his youth, have been red. He came up to the door and looked out at her with his lips pursed.

"Mr. Rutherford?"

"You're in the wrong part of town," he said, his deep voice muffled by the glass. "The nigger pawn shops are all north of Bonanza."

"I'm not here to pawn anything." She held the case up so he could see the monogram and symbol. "My name is Hippolyta Berry. Hiram Winthrop sent me."

"*You're* Winthrop's courier? His letter didn't say anything about sending—"

"I know."

Rutherford shut and locked the door behind her. "I wasn't expecting you until tomorrow," he said, sounding reproachful.

"I'm sorry if I caught you off guard," Hippolyta lied.

"You have my coins in there?"

"Yes sir." She recited from memory: "Two gold aurei from the reign of Nero. A silver tetradrachm from the court of the Spartan King Areus. Rarest of all, a bronze medallion, struck in ancient Minoa right before the civilization was destroyed by the eruption of Thera."

"Give it to me." She handed him the case and he set it on the nearest counter. But when he tried to open it he was frustrated: the case was secured by three latches, each with its own lock. "Give me the keys."

"I don't have them." As he glanced up sharply at her: "They're in an envelope, being held by a friend of mine. Once I've collected what I've come for and I'm safe away from here, I'll put that envelope in the mail to you."

"Once you're away . . . And I'm just supposed to trust you, am I?"

"No sir, you're supposed to trust Mr. Winthrop. If he could be here in person, he'd trust you, too. But since you're dealing with me, he was worried you might be tempted to do something greedy." She paused. "You understand, Mr. Rutherford, I'm following Mr. Winthrop's instructions here. I mean no insult to you personally."

"No?" He crossed his arms, reminding her of the younger trooper on the highway. "And what if I decide to take offense anyway? You think I can't get this open without the keys?"

"You might be able to," Hippolyta allowed. "Mr. Winthrop said you were the most gifted engineer he ever worked with. But that Minoan medallion, that's one of a kind, and if you don't open the case just right, you won't get anything out of it but acid fumes."

Rutherford shook his head and sighed. "Winthrop," he said, his tone suggesting a long litany of complaints. But he relented, ducking down to retrieve an urn from behind the counter. It was about a foot tall, cast of bone-white porcelain, and lidded—the kind of thing, Hippolyta thought, that a rich person might use to store grandma's ashes.

Rutherford placed it on the counter beside the case. "Stygian transfer vessel," he said. "Untested, but I couldn't find any visible defects."

It looked fragile. "Do I need to wrap it in something?" Hippolyta asked.

"Not unless you don't like the aesthetics." He splayed a hand above the lid and mimed a counterclockwise turn. "The cap locks in place to create an anti-entropic seal, which, among other things, renders it effectively shatterproof. Just don't drop it when it's open."

Hippolyta nodded. "All right." Then, trying to keep the excitement out of her voice: "What about the other item?"

Her long-awaited prize was sitting on a workbench in the shop's back room.

It was the size of a cash register, and might easily have been mistaken for some sort of tabulating device; its slanting brass face featured an eight-by-eight array of three-digit number displays, each of which currently read 001. Resting in a slot at the top of the machine was a palm-sized chrome disk with a clicker-button on it, like a faceless stopwatch.

"That's the transport unit," Rutherford said, indicating the disk. "You set the target coordinates you want in the base unit and load them in by pulling this side lever. Then you remove the transport unit from its dock." He lifted the disk out of the slot and curled his fingers around it, with his thumb poised above the button. "Grasp it firmly, like so. One click transports you to the target coordinates. A second click returns you to the vicinity of the base unit. Repeat as desired. Got it?"

"I think I can remember that," Hippolyta said dryly. She nodded at the base unit. "What does that red button underneath the lever do?"

"Resets the number array to its home position." He returned the chrome disk to its slot. "But the transport unit will retain whatever coordinates were loaded into it last, so if you want to clear it as well, you'll need to pull the lever again."

"What about the projector?" The original, much larger version of this teleportation machine had been installed inside a concrete dome. Like a planetarium, it was capable of displaying a panorama of the target destination—an essential safety precaution, since the vast majority of possible destinations were inimical to life.

"There isn't one," Rutherford said.

"What do you mean, there isn't one? What good's the machine if I can't see where I'm going?"

"Mind your tone with me," he cautioned. Then: "Scaling down the optics was a pain in the ass. I *could* have made it work, but it wasn't worth the trouble. I came up with another solution." He pointed to a line of pyramid-shaped crystals—one green, three red—that were set into the top of the base unit beside the transport unit's dock. "These signal lights. If you press this test button, here, the base unit extends an extradimensional probe to the target location and samples the environment. The results of the test are indicated by the flashing of one or more lights."

"Green light means safe?"

"Green light means breathable atmosphere, temperature between minus-forty and plus-fifty Celsius, and gravity no more than one-point-four Earth normal. The probe checks for other hazards too, but there are some, like microbes, that it can't detect."

"Microbes," Hippolyta said. "And animals? Predators?"

"Bring an elephant gun if you're worried."

"What about the red lights?"

"Degrees of lethality," Rutherford said. "One red light indicates an environment that won't support human life but isn't instantly fatal. Not that I'd recommend it, but you should be able to survive for at least ten or fifteen seconds without suffering any lasting harm. Long enough for a quick look around."

"Can you give an example?"

"Deep space is the obvious one. You can survive brief exposure to vacuum as long as you're not too close to a star. But again, I wouldn't recommend it."

"What about two red lights?"

"Theoretically survivable," Rutherford told her, "but both you and the transport unit will almost certainly suffer permanent damage." For the first time since he'd let her in the shop, he smiled. "And it voids the warranty."

"And three red lights, that's what, a one-way trip?"

He nodded. "The surface of a star, or the heart of a gas giant. Dead before you can feel it."

She studied the device, looking for other buttons or switches that he hadn't yet explained. "What about power? Does it have batteries that need charging?"

"It doesn't actually use much power. And what little power it does need is provided by a prime-matter resonator. As long as you don't go poking at it, that should be good for several decades without requiring replacement." He looked at her. "This is really for you, isn't it?"

"Does it matter?"

"I'm just surprised."

"That I'd want it?" Hippolyta said. "Or that Mr. Winthrop would give it to me?"

"Both," said Rutherford, "but more the latter. Do you have any notion how much a device like this is worth?"

She didn't, but the question made her think of Winthrop's workshop again, and of the long-term project she'd been helping to gather components for. She considered asking Rutherford outright: What is a "Stygian transfer vessel," anyway? Does it have something to do with moving souls between the worlds of the living and the dead? And if it does, what else is Mr. Winthrop going to need to complete the transfer?

But she didn't ask that. Instead she looked down at her new portable home teleporter and said: "Can I have a box to carry this in?"

* * *

He stood impatiently holding the door open as Hippolyta carried the teleporter out to the car and returned to get Winthrop's urn. As she exited the shop for the second time she expected him to remind her about the keys, but he only stared at her. She quickened her pace, cradling the Stygian vessel in her arms as if it were as delicate as it looked.

Rutherford shut the door but didn't lock it. He watched her drive away. When the Roadmaster had turned the corner at the end of the block he opened the door again and stepped out onto the sidewalk, rummaging in one of the pockets of his overalls. He held up a closed fist and opened it to reveal a mechanical scarab beetle nestled in his palm. He raised the beetle to his lips and spent the better part of a minute whispering instructions to it. When he'd finished he stretched out his arm in the sunlight. The noonday glare highlighted the fine lettering etched into the beetle's brass carapace.

With a tick of fine gearwork the carapace sprang open. The beetle deployed wings of gold and took flight. Rising quickly to the level of the rooftops, it headed off in the direction that Hippolyta's car had taken.

THE TRAIN

⚔

The countryside was more heavily populated than it had been when Great-grandpa Turner and Hecuba had made their escape. Montrose's surveyor's map of the region, printed in 1946, showed some of the changes to the landscape but not all of them. Half a mile into the woods behind the house where they'd abandoned the car, they came upon an unexpected clearing containing a pair of trailer homes. Fortunately the owners of the property were away, but the Doberman chained to the front of one of the trailers nearly strangled itself trying to get at them. They gave a wide berth to another, larger housing development that was on the map, this and other detours adding a couple of extra miles to their journey. But no one saw them, and by eleven o'clock they had reached the railroad tracks.

The tracks ran through a field on the east side of a two-lane road. The field offered no cover, but on the road's west side they found a spot beneath a billboard, surrounded by bushes, that allowed them to remain concealed while watching for oncoming traffic in both directions. They settled in to wait for a train.

Noon came and went. They shared a candy bar from Atticus's backpack and drank sparingly from canteens they'd filled at a stream back in the woods. Around one o'clock, clouds appeared on the eastern horizon.

Traffic on the road was light, but about a quarter after one, a white man with a walking stick came hiking along the road shoulder just beyond the bushes. Montrose and Atticus lay back flat on the ground, staring up at the Wonder Bread ad on the billboard overhead, not making a sound. The man passed by without noticing them. Ten minutes later they heard a siren approaching from the direction the man had gone, and worried that he'd seen them after all; but the vehicle that appeared seconds later was a fire engine that raced past without slowing.

By two o'clock the sky was completely overcast. It wasn't raining yet, but the cloud cover darkened to the east; they could see distant flickers of lightning, and a haze below the clouds that suggested a heavy downpour. Atticus knew that even a hard rain might not wash away their scent trail completely, but it would certainly make it harder to follow. And dogs didn't like lightning. Hurry up, Atticus thought, watching the storm approach, and if you see a train, tell it to hurry too.

Montrose meanwhile had opened up his own knapsack and pulled out another map. This one showed a region of southeast Virginia as it had looked a century ago. Between the cities of Suffolk and Portsmouth, a railroad line identified as the Seaboard & Roanoke cut across the north-ernmost fringe of the Great Dismal Swamp. That section of the railroad had been circled in pencil and an arrow drawn pointing south into the swamp's deeper reaches. Beside this, in Montrose's hard-to-read script, was the legend "Maroon sigil on tree next to tracks."

Atticus did his best to ignore this. As far as he was concerned, to even daydream about continuing their pilgrimage into the past was flat-out crazy. If they were lucky enough to make it out of North Caro-lina, they should make a beeline for home and start praying that Sher-iff Hunt's recovered memories didn't include a recollection of Atticus's name.

He felt a drop of moisture on his cheek. "Rain's here," Atticus said, unable to resist adding: "You might want to put that away now."

Montrose side-eyed him archly, but whatever retort he might have made was preempted by the sound of a train whistle. They both tensed, heads cocked, listening. The whistle came again. From the south.

"Northbound," Atticus said. "Hallelujah. Now just cross our fingers that it's got a boxcar we can climb into."

"It will," Montrose said, hurriedly folding his map up and stuffing it back into the knapsack. "That's our ride."

Atticus rose to a crouch. He was about to step out of the bushes when his father grabbed his elbow. "Wait. Listen."

From the north, partially masked by the sound of the wind blowing across the road, came the low growl of a motor. Atticus peered through a gap in the bushes and saw a gray pickup truck approaching, moving no more than fifteen miles an hour. Sheriff Hunt was standing up in the truck bed holding a rifle, one hand braced on the roof of the cab. A uniformed policeman was in the truck bed as well, and as the vehicle rolled closer Atticus saw a black-and-tan coonhound with a chain on its collar.

The truck had almost reached their hiding spot when the wind picked up and the dog began to bark. The driver brought the truck to a stop directly beside the billboard. Sheriff Hunt and the policeman turned and looked out at the side of the road, Hunt with his rifle at the ready.

But they were looking towards the open field to the east, not at the bushes.

"Just a rabbit," the policeman said after a moment. Then, as the dog continued to bark: "Knock it off, Sam."

Hunt thumped his hand on the roof of the truck cab. The truck started moving again. As it pulled away, the sky opened up, rain descending in a sudden downpour, as if God had opened a sluice somewhere. Atticus and Montrose were soaked through instantly, and the truck disappeared behind a curtain of water that obscured everything but a brief flash of its taillights. Good, Atticus thought, as the taillights vanished too. You head on back to the klavern now and dry yourselves off.

The train whistle sounded again, very close. Shielding their eyes against the rain, they peered across to the field, and all at once the train was just *there*, materializing out of the downpour. An ancient locomotive, coal-fired, its rain-blurred silhouette recalling something from a child's toy set.

"Come on," Montrose said, slipping the knapsack onto his shoulders.

Breaking from cover, they ran out onto the road, its surface slick from the deluge. They were halfway across when the lightning bolt came down, striking somewhere close on the shoulder behind them, the boom like a mortar round exploding. Atticus jerked his head around at the sound and his feet shot out from under him, flipping him onto his back and knocking Montrose down in the process.

As Atticus fought to get back up, the weight of the backpack impeding him like a tortoise's shell, the rain slackened abruptly and he saw taillights again. The pickup truck was stopped a hundred yards down the road, and the parting water curtain revealed Sheriff Hunt standing at the back of the truck bed.

The sheriff pointed and shouted something and then he raised his rifle to fire. Atticus felt Montrose's strong hands grip the straps of his backpack, hauling him upright even as the rifle cracked. The bullet skidded off the asphalt where he had been lying.

Another bullet zipped by close overhead as they dashed into the field. The locomotive had already passed them, and the consist it pulled behind it was short, just a coal car and two wooden boxcars. The doors of the second boxcar were wide open.

Sprinting ahead of his father, Atticus unslung his backpack and pitched it through the open boxcar door. He hoisted himself aboard and then turned to help Montrose.

Montrose started to take off the knapsack to toss it inside, but had only gotten the left strap off when he heard a growl and glanced back to see the coonhound coming up fast behind him. He cursed and lunged for the boxcar door, arms outstretched, Atticus reaching with both hands to haul him aboard. Montrose's feet were off the ground, his body half in, half out, when the coonhound leapt up and clamped its jaws on the dangling knapsack. The sharp tug of the strap on his right shoulder pulled Montrose back and yanked his right hand from Atticus's grasp.

The coonhound was being dragged now but it hung on fiercely, even as Montrose, his own feet dangling inches from the track bed, tried to kick at it. Atticus, holding tight to Montrose's left arm, attempted to use his free hand to slide the strap off Montrose's other shoulder, but Montrose, infuriatingly, resisted, shouting, "My maps!"

"The hell with your maps!" Atticus shouted back. With a final tug he freed the strap; it slid down Montrose's arm, Montrose trying to grab it with his hand, but slick with rain it slipped through his fingers. Dog and knapsack fell away tumbling, and Montrose swung his right arm up again, a look on his face like he wanted to fight Atticus right then and there, Atticus more than half inclined to oblige.

A rifle bullet struck the edge of the open boxcar door, splintering the wood. Atticus looked to the road and saw the pickup truck running parallel to the train, fishtailing slightly on the wet asphalt. Sheriff Hunt was kneeling in the truck bed, the policeman acting as a human anchor, gripping the back of Hunt's belt to steady him as he took aim with the rifle. For the second time that day, Atticus and the sheriff locked eyes.

The lightning came again, practically on top of them, the instantaneous thunderboom eclipsing the sound of the rifle shot. Atticus felt the bullet buzz past his cheek. The truck's fishtail worsened and then it was hydroplaning, Hunt losing the rifle over the side and nearly going with it as the pickup spun out.

Atticus pulled Montrose into the boxcar and collapsed, exhausted. As the track curved, taking the train away from the road, the rain picked up again, turning the passing countryside into a wet and blurry dreamscape.

LIGHTS OUT

❧❧

Evening at the Desert Ocean. Letitia had gone out in search of a poker game. The Jacksons had gone out as well, hoping to do some dancing.

Hippolyta was in the trailer, sitting cross-legged on her bed. Mrs. Jackson had asked her to keep an eye on the children; through the open window beside her she could see the two boys on the pool deck, hunched over a Monopoly set in the fading light, and hear the splashing of Maisie, who'd finally overcome her shyness. But the lion's share of Hippolyta's attention was on the teleportation machine in front of her, as she laboriously entered a set of numbers into the array from a sheet marked **TERRA HIRAM COORDINATES**.

Mr. Winthrop hadn't wanted to give her the planet's address, preferring to withhold it until she returned to Chicago with his prize. Hippolyta had insisted that she needed it, to test that the machine actually worked. Mr. Winthrop hadn't liked that idea at all, for while Planet Hiram might have gravity and a breathable atmosphere, it was nevertheless a dangerous place: the beach that served as a landing site was patrolled by a monster named Scylla. There was also the matter of Ida, Winthrop's former maid, who was stranded on a promontory overlooking the beach; Ida had tried to kill Hippolyta on her previous visit, and she still had Hippolyta's gun. But Hippolyta thought she could reason with Ida, and in fact hoped to rescue her. And as for Scylla—well, she'd be careful. I'll just take a quick look around, she'd told Winthrop. And even if something does happen to me, Letitia will see that you get your magic urn.

From the sitting room at the front of the trailer came the steady scratch of a pencil on paper—Horace, hard at work on a project of his own. Hippolyta hadn't told him about the teleporter, fearing that he too might object to her using it, in terms that would be harder to argue with. Just a *quick* look around, she repeated to herself. In and out—he won't even have time to notice I've been gone, nobody will. But I need to know it's real, that I've got what I've wanted for so long. I *deserve* that.

The last number ticked into place. Hippolyta pressed the test button and frowned as two red lights flashed. She picked up the paper with the coordinates and began to recheck her work. A big fly buzzed outside the window. In the third row of the array, she spotted a mistake—a pair of digits transposed. She fixed them, and pressed the test button again.

Green light.

"OK," Hippolyta whispered. She pulled the lever to load the coordinates into the transport unit, then lifted the disk from its slot and clutched it firmly, thumb poised over the button. "OK . . ."

In the front of the trailer, Horace coughed. Hippolyta's ears pricked up and she leaned sideways, listening for the telltale wheeze that would indicate Horace's asthma had come back. He hadn't had an attack in some time, and she'd begun to hope that with puberty he'd grown out of it. But you never really knew, and the condition was no joke; Horace's grandfather had died of it.

This time, the cough was just a cough. The scratch of pencil on paper continued uninterrupted.

Hippolyta turned her attention back to the teleporter, but her resolve to use it had weakened, overcome by a sudden pang of maternal responsibility. What if something goes wrong and you don't make it back? she thought. What happens to Horace then? She sat wrestling with herself for several moments before reluctantly returning the transport unit to its dock. Then she stood up, stretched, and walked forward into the trailer's sitting area.

A drop-leaf table was attached to the wall beside the divan. Horace was seated there, hunched over a sheet of sketch paper that had been marked off into panels. At his mother's approach, he pursed his lips and bent farther forward, signaling his desire to be left alone. Undeterred, Hippolyta came and stood beside him, her own lips curving in a frown as she saw what he'd been drawing.

The panel Horace was working on covered half the sheet—a full page of the comic book it was destined to become. The scene was of a city bus stop. A Negro man who bore a striking resemblance to Letitia's tenant Mr. Fox was down on his hands and knees, peering under the passenger waiting bench, while a young girl—spitting image of the late Celia—stood over him. The dialog balloon above the girl's head hadn't been filled in yet, but from her expression, it was clear that she was urging the man on.

"What's he looking for?"

Horace sighed in exasperation and put down his pencil. Then he said: "Evidence." He nodded at the girl. "She got murdered. Her father knows it, and he knows who did it, but he's got no proof, and he can't rest until he finds some."

Looking more carefully at the drawing, Hippolyta saw that the girl was transparent from the neck down; what had at first appeared to be a pattern in the fabric of her blouse was actually the slats of the bench, visible through her torso. "So she's a ghost."

Horace gave a little shrug. "That's not for me to say."

"What do you mean, it's not for you to say? It's your story."

He sat back and seemed to consider the question more seriously. "She could be a ghost," he allowed. "It'd be nice if that were true. Or not nice, but not all bad—at least she'd still *be* somewhere, even though she's dead. And maybe once she gets done helping her dad catch the guy who killed her, maybe she'd get to go on, to heaven or wherever. Maybe she and all her friends could meet up there again someday.

"But maybe that's not true," he said. "Maybe she's just, gone. Maybe her dad only thinks she's a ghost, because he can't live with the idea she's nowhere at all. That she lost everything when she got shot."

"And you don't know which it is?"

"Nobody does." He looked at her with a frank open expression that dared her to contradict what he was saying. "That's the point of the story: nobody *can* know, until they're dead too—and even then, only if being dead *is* something. But I'm still here, so." He shrugged again. "It's not for me to say."

"Horace," Hippolyta said. "We need to have a conversation."

"I know," he said, nodding. "But can we do it tomorrow? I want to finish this up and turn in early, so I'm awake for the bomb test in the morning."

If there'd been a hint of sullenness in his voice, she might have forced the issue then and there, but he actually sounded reasonable. Like his old self. "All right," Hippolyta said, after a moment. "Tomorrow. But it's going to be a real talk, you understand?"

She went back to her bunk and stood looking down at the teleportation machine. Tomorrow, she thought.

She picked up the paper with Terra Hiram's coordinates and opened one of the storage compartments above the bed. A thin sheet of plywood covered the floor of the compartment; Hippolyta lifted this up and tucked the paper underneath it, then retrieved a small envelope that contained three keys. The envelope was already stamped and addressed to Red Pawn.

She closed the storage compartment and sat down on the bed, setting the envelope on the mattress. She pressed the reset button on the side of the teleporter's base unit and watched as the number windows in the array all ticked back to 001. Then she placed her hand on the lever that would reset the transport unit as well, but she didn't pull it.

Come on now, she chided herself. If you leave it loaded, you won't sleep a wink tonight for temptation.

Her fingers drummed on the lever. Impulsively, she reached over and lifted the disk from its slot. She nestled it loosely in her palm, her thumb stroking the button.

In the front of the trailer, Horace made an odd sound. Not a cough this time, but a funny sort of grunt—one that in a comic book might be transcribed as *OOF!*

"Horace?" Hippolyta called out. "You all right?"

No answer. She stood up, still holding the transport unit, and went into the sitting area.

Horace was slumped forward with his head on the table, as if he'd fallen asleep in the middle of drawing. His mouth was open but Hippolyta couldn't hear him breathing, and as she came closer she saw a welt rising on the back of his neck, tinged red by the fading sunlight coming through the open window beside him.

"Horace?" She grabbed his shoulder and shook him. His arm slid off the table and dangled limp at his side. *"Horace?"*

A loud insectile buzz behind her. Something landed on the back of her neck, a ticklish sensation followed immediately by a sharp sting that made her eyes water. She raised a hand to slap at it, but the sting seemed to have robbed her of her coordination and she ended up just spinning herself around. She stumbled sideways into the kitchen, caromed off the refrigerator, and fetched up against the sink, just barely managing to get a grip on the edge of the counter.

Her vision was narrowing, the world seeming to recede before her. Hippolyta found herself staring as if down a long tunnel at the open box of Frosted Flakes that still rested on the stovetop. Even as her conscious mind struggled to make sense of what was happening, some older and more instinctive part of her brain took action. She watched, fascinated, as her right arm came up and extended itself, reaching down the tunnel to deposit the transport unit in the cereal box. As the chrome disk dropped out of view, she felt a brief moment of satisfaction. Now go hide the rest of it, she thought, the words echoing meaninglessly inside her skull.

Then her other hand lost its grip and the trailer revolved around her. By the time her head hit the floor, she was already out cold.

GO DEEPER IN

⊰⧓⊱

But for the fact that it was moving, the parlor might have been mistaken for a room in Master Swincegood's house. Simon, who had never been on a train before and had no expectations of what it should be like, took in the lavish decor matter-of-factly—the silk wallpaper, the oriental carpet, the seascape oil painting that hung above the little mahogany bar. The rocking of the car unnerved him, though, and whenever the train jolted over a rough spot in the tracks he clutched the arms of the chair in which he sat and glanced at the drapes covering the windows, wishing he could see out.

Hecuba, sitting opposite him with her bad leg propped up on an ottoman, was considerably more at ease. In the bar, she'd found a cut crystal decanter filled with an inch of whiskey; as she sipped from it, the flame of an oil lamp on the bartop made the decanter facets glitter and put a twinkle in her eye.

Atticus, who in this dream was a disembodied spirit, floated midway between the floor and the ceiling, able to shift his gaze but otherwise frozen in place, and mute. His ancestor remained unaware of him, but Hecuba side-eyed him knowingly, at one point extending the decanter in his direction as if to offer him a drink.

"We in the North yet, you think?" Simon said.

"We ain't even out of Carolina yet," Hecuba replied. "We got one more stop, at a place called Weldon. We gonna change trains there."

Simon clutched the arms of his chair again. "You mean get out?"

"No. This car we in belongs to a rich man, who's having it shipped to a city called Portsmouth. In Weldon, they gonna stick it on the back of a different train."

"How you know what they gonna do?"

"I can feel it," said Hecuba. And she could: even as her body reclined in the chair, a portion of her soul dangled like a live wire beneath the train's undercarriage, brushing the passing ties. They spoke to her of routes and timetables, train consists and their destinations, the information like a Morse code message shooting up into her spine. Atticus could feel it too.

Simon felt only fear and frustration. He was helpless and he knew it: if Hecuba was crazy, they were doomed. "Then what?" he made himself ask. "After they put us on the new train, we keep going north?"

"East," Hecuba said. "Towards the sea. But we ain't going to the end of the line. Along the way, we gonna pass through this swamp, and that's where we get out."

"Swamp?" Simon said. "What *swamp*? You didn't say nothing about—"

"Calm yourself," said Hecuba. "You done all right by me, and I'm gonna keep my word to you. But you're gonna have to listen to me now, and trust me, because I've seen all the paths ahead, and there's only one that leads where you want to go. You try to walk across Virginia on your own? Or hop another train? You won't make it. There's slave catchers on every road you might think to take. You want to live? Before you get out, you gonna have to go deeper in."

"To a swamp."

Hecuba grinned. "It won't be forever," she said. "It'll feel like it, at first, because you're young, but you'll learn patience. And you won't be alone. There's other people there, free men and women. I'll tell you how to find them. They'll teach you how to survive. And in time, when you're ready—when you've earned the name Nat Turner—you'll come out again, and walk free in the wider world."

He stared at her, lips pursed. "Happy ever after, huh?" he said.

The old woman laughed. "If I promised you that, you'd know I was lying . . . But you will walk free, and your name will live on after you."

The train hit another bump. This time Simon didn't tense up, just rocked and rolled with it. "What about you?" he asked her.

"I told you: I'm gonna find a place to lie down. Rest my bones awhile. A long while. And after that—"

"*After* that?"

"After that," Hecuba said, "it gets interesting." Then she raised the decanter to her lips and drank down the last of the whiskey, looking straight at Atticus as she did so.

THE BOMB TEST

⚜

Mom.

Hippolyta stood on a darkened plain beneath a starless sky. A big insect buzzed around her, the clatter of its wings inscribing patterns in the darkness, shapes of letters from some long-forgotten alphabet. She tried to string them together to form words, but the meaning eluded her.

Mom wake up.

A trumpet sounded. Light flared on the plain, illuminating the skeletal form of a derrick tower; suspended within it was a sphere composed of interlocking metal plates that had been bolted together. As the trumpet's note stretched into a siren-like wail, the sphere began to glow, and steam jets hissed from the joints. Hippolyta put up a hand to shield herself from the inevitable explosion.

"Wake up, Mom."

She opened her eyes. She was in the trailer, lying on her back on the floor between the twin bunks. Horace was crouched down over her, his face filled with concern.

"Horace!" she gasped. "Oh thank God—" She slung an arm around him in a clumsy embrace, but when she tried to lift her head, a sharp pain at the nape of her neck made her wince.

"Easy, Mom . . ."

"Horace . . . Horace, are you OK?"

"I'm alive," he told her. "But we're in trouble." Cradling the back of her head with his hand, he helped her into a sitting position.

The trailer had been ransacked. Hippolyta's teleporter and the envelope with the keys were gone, and her mattress, stripped of its sheets, now lay askew. Letitia's bed was heaped with clothes and other personal items. Tilting her head back carefully, Hippolyta saw that the overhead storage compartments were open.

"Help me up," she said. Horace wrapped his arms around her and lifted, his strength still a surprise to her, even though she knew he wasn't a little boy anymore.

Her own strength was taking its time coming back. She swayed unsteadily on her feet. Leaning on Horace for support, she gripped the edge of the compartment over her bed and peered inside. The plywood sheet looked undisturbed; she lifted it, and was thrilled to discover that the paper with Terra Hiram's coordinates was still there. So they didn't find everything, she thought.

Hippolyta took the paper from its hiding place and then, still leaning on Horace, made her way forward to the kitchen. Here she was disappointed: the cereal box lay on its side, and Frosted Flakes were scattered across the stovetop and in the sink. "Damn it."

She bent to the window above the sink. It was dark outside, but what little she could see had her doubling back to her dream. She turned to Horace. "Was there . . . Did I hear a siren?"

Horace nodded gravely. "Fifteen minute warning, I think." He pointed at the clock built into the stovetop, which said that it was eleven minutes to five.

They exited the trailer and found themselves on a sidewalk in front of a row of three identical ranch houses. All three houses had lights on inside, visible through drawn curtains, and the sky behind them was pale with early dawn. Staring straight ahead, Hippolyta briefly wondered whether they might actually be in a suburb of Las Vegas. But the illusion collapsed as soon as she looked around. Past the rightmost of the houses, the sidewalk abruptly ended, and the paved street on which the trailer was parked became a dirt road that stretched off into the desert. To the left, the sidewalk extended a bit farther before butting up against a concrete tower, a slit window near the top like a Cyclopean eye focused on the houses.

Hippolyta's Roadmaster was still hitched to the front of the trailer, but the keys weren't in it, and a quick check under the hood showed that that didn't matter anyway: the distributor cap had been removed.

Across the street from the houses was open desert. The sky in that direction was still dark, but Hippolyta could sense, somewhere out in the gloom, the real-world analog of the bomb derrick from her dream. "What are we going to do?" Horace asked beside her.

"Find a way to call for help."

As they went up the front walk of the center house, the illusion of suburbia took hold again, coloring Hippolyta's bomb anxiety with a more familiar strain of dread: approaching a white stranger's home in the dark was a good way to get shot. But she quickly pushed the thought aside. They were in Doomtown, not Levittown, and this close to zero hour the house would be unoccupied. There might be a working telephone, though, or a radio. Something.

The front door wasn't locked. Hippolyta went in first, starting at the sight of the three white mannequins posed in the den to the right of the entryway: Dad with his pipe, sitting in a Barcalounger; Mom standing next to him, holding out a tray with two martini glasses; and cross-legged on the floor in front of the TV, little mannequin Junior.

To the left of the doorway, set partly into the wall, was a concrete bunker with a slit window, squat cousin to the tower outside. A camera lens was visible behind the thick glass in the slit. "Hey!" Hippolyta shouted, waving her hands in front of the glass. "Hey!"

But Horace said, "They can't see us. I read about this in my book. It's a movie camera. They start it by remote control just before they set the bomb off, then come get the film after things cool down."

"Well there's got to be some way to let them know we're in here . . ." After another quick glance around the den, Hippolyta went down the hall towards the back of the house.

In the kitchen two more mannequins—Grandpa and a little girl—sat at a Formica-topped table, grinning vacantly at a box of Cracker Jacks. Looking past them, Hippolyta spied a phone on the wall beside the kitchen sink. She lunged for it and snatched up the receiver. "Hello?" she said. "Hello?"

The line was dead. Hippolyta looked out the window above the sink, hoping there might be more buildings back there, maybe even a command center with real people inside it. But beyond the backyard fence she saw nothing but more desert, streaked with shadows in the dawnlight.

Turning back around, she focused next on the concrete bunker poking through the kitchen's side wall. "What if we climbed in there?" she said. "If it's strong enough to protect the camera from the blast . . ."

"Yeah, that might work," Horace said. "*If* we can get inside. I don't know if they lock it."

It seemed like their best option. Hippolyta took a last desperate glance around the kitchen, to make sure she hadn't overlooked anything. Her gaze snagged on the Cracker Jack box, the sight of it now triggering a childhood memory of her brother Apollo, impatient to get the toy surprise inside, dumping out the whole box in a pile on the kitchen table.

In a pile, Hippolyta thought.

"Mom?" Horace said, his voice edged with fear now. There was a clock on the wall above the kitchen sink, and its hands stood at three minutes to five. "Mom, what is it?"

"We need to get back to the trailer," she replied.

Less than a minute later, they were in the trailer galley, Hippolyta staring at the spray pattern of Frosted Flakes on the stovetop with the intensity of a detective studying a crime scene.

A spray, she thought, not a pile. The cereal box hadn't been dumped out; it had fallen over, probably while the trailer was moving.

Which didn't mean Angus Rutherford hadn't found the prize inside.

With shaking hands Hippolyta picked up the cereal box and tilted it. The transport unit came sliding out, faster than she expected, and in her effort to grab it without clicking the button she very nearly dropped it in the sink. But at last she had it firmly in hand.

"What is that?" Horace said.

"No time to explain." The clock on the stove said a minute to five. Hippolyta opened her arms. "You hold on to me, now," she said. "Hug me tighter than you ever have." And Horace did.

GREAT DISMAL

When Atticus opened his eyes, the boxcar was on its side, half buried in muddy peat soil, the door through which he and his father had boarded now a roof hatch framing the morning sky above him. Vines curling over the rim of the opening gave testimony to the fact that the boxcar had been lying here for some time, though this evidence was contradicted by the splintered bullet hole, clearly visible in the wood, that had been made by Sheriff Hunt's rifle less than twenty-four hours ago.

Something small and many-legged crawled across Atticus's face. He swiped it away and sat up, brushing more crawling things from his shirt and trousers. He stood and poked his head out and saw a raised gravel track bed running alongside the derailed boxcar. His father was sitting on the tracks, eating an apple from the backpack. Montrose nodded at him, and Atticus nodded back, as if this were a perfectly ordinary way to start the day.

According to his watch, it was just past nine a.m., but the humid air was already growing hot. He used the sun to orient himself. The tracks ran roughly east and west; the train, which had been eastbound when it derailed, lay in a ditch along the tracks' south side. The other boxcar had been smashed to pieces against the coal car, and the broken smokestack of the locomotive jutted up at an angle beyond them, festooned with brambles and poison ivy. Extending south from the ditch was a mixed forest of pine and hardwood trees with a fantastically dense undergrowth of reeds, bushes, and tangled vines.

Atticus climbed carefully out of the boxcar. As he joined his father on the tracks, he heard the drone of automobile traffic from the north, and glimpsed, through a narrow screen of trees, cars and trucks moving along what appeared to be a highway.

"U.S. 58," Montrose volunteered. "There wasn't any road at all here, a hundred years ago. Back then, you wanted to drive from Suffolk to Portsmouth, you'd have to take your horse and buggy and circle around further north."

"So we're in Virginia," Atticus said. Not really surprised. He turned back to face the forest to the south. "That's the start of the Great Dismal. And this is the spot where Great-grandpa and Hecuba—"

"Where they got off the train, yeah," said Montrose. "Or near enough."

Atticus nodded at the boxcar. "What about this here? It's not—"

"The same train? Nah. That locomotive is pretty old, but I doubt it's been running since before the Civil War. And this wreck is recent."

"But it's a wreck. A ghost train," Atticus said, just to hear the words aloud. "We rode here on a ghost train."

"We were *brought here* on a ghost train," Montrose replied.

Atticus knew what that meant, but tried to pretend that he didn't. "So if we go out to that highway, what do you suppose our chances are of hitching a ride?"

"I think we'd have better luck following these tracks into town and looking for a ride there—*if* we were leaving."

"Pop . . ." Atticus sighed, then made one last attempt to appeal to reason. "Unless you've got a machete, I don't see us making a lot of progress through that." Gesturing at the jungle of vegetation beneath the trees. "And we don't have your maps anymore either, remember?"

"Oh, I remember all right," Montrose said, fixing him with a hostile stare. "But we ain't going to need a map." He tossed the apple core aside and stood up. "Follow me."

They walked east along the track bed. Beyond the wrecked locomotive, a gap appeared in the foliage. As they came abreast of it,

Atticus saw that it was the start of a path that had been carved through the undergrowth and wended away south through the trees.

It had not been made with a machete. The vegetation was broken and crushed flat, as if something very heavy had rolled or been dragged over it. Atticus might have guessed it was the work of a bulldozer, but there were no vehicle tread marks, and the path was too narrow to have been made by a conventional earthmover. "Did a bear do this?"

"Yeah, sure," Montrose said. "A big old bear, crawling on its belly." He placed a hand against the trunk of a pine tree that grew beside the opening. A glyph had been scratched into the bark at eye level. It resembled a letter Y, though it could have been a forking path.

Or a serpent's tongue. Atticus had a sudden image of a giant anaconda, broad as a grizzly, forcing its way through the undergrowth. Not long ago, either, he thought, noting that the crushed leaves and the tips of the broken branches were still green. Who knows, if we hurry, we could still catch up to it.

"Here." Montrose shoved the backpack into Atticus's arms. "You carry. I'll lead."

POKER ROOM

⌘

"You really flew yourself here?" Letitia said to the man sitting across from her at the poker table. "In your own plane?"

"I did indeed," he replied. Smiling: "Why? Don't I look like a pilot?"

He looked, Letitia thought, like the gospel singer Sam Cooke, on an especially fine day. "I'm just thinking about the airport. White folks let you land there?"

"Landing's not usually a problem. Control tower can't see me over the radio." He lowered his voice, assuming a passable white Texas drawl: "I say there, Las Vegas, this is Anthony Starling, out of Houston, requesting clearance." Letitia laughed, and he continued in his normal voice: "Once I'm on the ground, it can get dicey, sometimes—one reason I prefer being up in the air. But I flew recon in Korea, and between the U.S. Air Force, the South Koreans, and the Communists I was actually supposed to be fighting with, I learned how to look out for myself."

"*Excuse* me!" This from the other man at the table, who reminded her of a brimstone preacher from her childhood, the one her brother called Pastor Popeye for the way his eyes bulged when he ranted about the wages of sin. "*Excuse* me, are we here to play *cards* or tell *war* stories?"

"Sorry," Letitia said. Which she wasn't in the slightest, though under other circumstances she'd have felt some sympathy for the man, who'd been having a bad run of luck at her expense.

It had started about an hour ago, when the bartender had announced a free round of drinks for anyone who cared to go up on the roof and watch the A-bomb test. A new hand had just been dealt, and most of the other players had responded by folding and leaving the table, but Popeye, busy looking at his cards, didn't even seem to hear the bartender's offer.

Letitia, sensing an opportunity, had checked her own cards. She'd been dealt three nines, ordinarily a hand she'd be happy to play. But sometimes, you just got a feeling . . . She folded instead, turning her cards over so that Popeye could see what she was giving up. This action had the desired effect. After Anthony the pilot quietly folded his own hand, Popeye blew his top, shouting "God *damn* it!" and exposing his own hand: four jacks and an ace.

On the very next hand, Letitia was dealt a pat flush, which Popeye refused to believe she had. He bet into her with a pair of kings, continuing to reraise her raises even after his hand failed to improve on the draw, his reaction at showdown echoed by the distant rumble of the bomb blast. From there, they were off to the races, with Popeye making bad play after bad play, letting his emotions rule him. He lost all his chips, bought in again, lost everything again, and on his second rebuy suggested they switch from limit to no-limit.

All of which had led to the present moment, with Letitia and Popeye heads-up, Letitia holding a pair of aces, and Popeye, who'd drawn a single card, opening the post-draw betting by pushing all his chips forward. This all-in bet was an obvious bluff; Popeye, ignoring all evidence to the contrary, still thought that he could bully her. The thing she'd been trying to puzzle out, under the guise of bantering with Anthony the pilot, was what exactly Popeye was bluffing with: a busted flush or straight draw, or a weak two pair? Given the pot odds, a mistaken call would be needlessly expensive, and as Letitia's father had taught her, there's no shame in waiting for a better spot.

But sometimes, you just know. "Call," Letitia said, and showed her aces. Popeye made a strangling noise in his throat and balled his hands into fists. Anthony the pilot took his own hands off the table and slid his chair back, preparing to intervene if Popeye turned violent. But there was no outburst this time; Popeye stood up without a word and stalked out of the building with his fists hanging loose at his sides. Anthony watched him go, only relaxing when the exit door had swung shut behind him.

"Another hand?" Letitia said, raking in her winnings.

Anthony smiled, looking down at his own much-diminished pile of chips. "I think I better quit while I'm behind," he told her.

He offered to buy her breakfast. Letitia was tempted, but she could tell from his expression that he had more than just a meal in mind, and while that was a little tempting, too, she'd promised Hippolyta she'd be back at the motel in time for an early checkout.

She did accept his offer of a cab ride, though. When they reached the Desert Ocean, he handed her a playing card with the name of his hotel and his room number written on it, and invited her to call him later if she felt like seeing Las Vegas from the air. "Careful I don't take you up on that," she said, and kissed him on the cheek.

She crossed the motel lot in a happy daze, and was almost to the trailer's parking spot before she realized the trailer was no longer there. She stared at the empty space and then turned to look back across the lot, wondering if Hippolyta had had to move for some reason. But the trailer was nowhere in sight.

The door of a nearby motel room creaked open. A young girl in a baggy long-sleeved dress came out. "You looking for Horace and his mom?" she asked.

"Yes, I am," Letitia said. "You know where they went?"

"Not exactly. But a white man came to the motel last night, right after the sun went down, and drove off with them."

"You mean they were in the car with him, or—"

"No. Horace and his mom were in the trailer. Asleep, I think—I knocked, a few minutes before, and Horace didn't answer. When the white man came and got in the car, I tried to ask what he was doing, and he called me a really bad name. Then he just drove off with them."

"This white man. What did he look like?"

"Like a train engineer," the girl said. "But without the hat."

In her mind's eye, Letitia saw Angus Rutherford standing out front of his shop in his overalls, watching Hippolyta carry her teleporter to the car. "Was he short, with glasses? White hair?"

"That's him." The girl nodded. "He knows you?"

"Not yet," Letitia said.

ON THE BEACH

At first, her pupils contracting in the glare, Hippolyta feared the teleporter had failed and left them stranded in the desert of Armageddon. But Horace's arms remained solid around her, and as her panic subsided, she heard the sound of surf over her own quickened breath; she smelled salt air, and felt the give of the sand beneath her feet.

Her previous visit to Terra Hiram had been at night. Now the planet's sun was up. It hung low in the sky above the ocean in front of her, its bright light reflecting off the water and the white sand of the beach.

"Mom," Horace gasped, "I got to breathe."

"Sorry," Hippolyta said, loosening her embrace. "It's OK. We're—"

Out of the corner of her eye, she spied a moving dark shape amidst the brightness. Jolted instantly back into panic, Hippolyta tried to run and pull Horace with her, but succeeded only in throwing them both off balance.

They sprawled in the sand. Urgently Hippolyta disentangled herself—Horace grunting as she stiff-armed him in the gut—and rolled clear, then sat up shouting and waving her arms, trying to make herself the target of the attack she knew was coming.

No attack came. The lumpen black shape remained where it was.

Horace sat up more slowly, shading his eyes. "Is that—"

"Scylla," Hippolyta said. The fearsome monster, a giant black ball filled with tentacles, capable of swallowing men whole, as she had seen firsthand on her previous visit here—but deflated now, collapsed in on itself in the sand, its sun-cured hide peeling away in long strips, tattered pennants that fluttered in the breeze off the ocean.

"What happened to it?" Horace said.

"I don't know. But we need to get off this beach."

They stood up, Hippolyta keeping a wary eye on Scylla's corpse while Horace looked around in amazement. "So this is Mr. Winthrop's planet," he said. "For real. And you got your own teleport device . . ." He stooped and picked up the transport unit, which Hippolyta had dropped. "Is this what you went into town for yesterday?"

"We'll talk about it later." Hippolyta took the transport unit from him, then seized him by the wrist as you would a small child in a department store and led him away.

The beach ran beneath a line of cliffs. A short distance away, a narrow promontory extended out over the water. A domed observatory perched at its tip, while a flat-roofed cottage was set back nearer to the main cliff line. Between the two structures, a zigzag staircase enclosed in a metal cage was fixed to the promontory's side.

Hippolyta scanned the top of the promontory as they approached, but she could see no sign of Ida. "She could be sleeping," Horace speculated. He nodded at the observatory. "If that's all I had for entertainment, I'd sleep in the day too. And I know *you* would."

"I hope you're right," Hippolyta said, still thinking of Scylla. The monster's demise ought to have been a source of relief, but instead it struck her as a bad omen.

They reached the stairs. Hippolyta opened the gate at the bottom of the enclosure and paused, listening.

"What?" Horace said.

"There was an alarm, last time."

"Maybe she forgot to set it."

"I doubt it. I don't like this."

She made Horace go onto the stairs first, but kept a hand on his shoulder so he wouldn't run ahead. As soon as the gate was shut behind her, she stepped past him and took the lead.

"Ida has my old thirty-eight," she said as they climbed, keeping her voice low. "Now, I don't believe she'd shoot me without giving me a chance to talk first, but I don't want to risk spooking her. So you're going to wait out of sight on the stairs with your mouth shut until I give you the all clear, understood?"

"What if she does shoot you?" Horace asked.

"She won't."

"What if she does?"

"Damn it, Horace," Hippolyta said, her voice rising dangerously. "Would you just *mind* me for once?"

She left him on the final landing before the top and mounted the last flight of stairs alone.

To exit the staircase it was necessary to pass through a separate enclosure, a square cage with inner and outer gates. As Hippolyta had learned the hard way, this cage was booby-trapped with a set of electrified coils that could be used to stun the occupant. Before stepping inside, she looked around carefully. As far as she could see, the promontory was deserted, and the doors to both the observatory and the cottage were shut. Facing the latter, she announced herself in a loud voice: "Ida? It's Hippolyta Berry. I know you didn't want to see me again, but I didn't have much choice in the matter. Could you please come outside so we can talk?" When this got no response, she turned towards the observatory and repeated herself, but Ida didn't show.

"OK!" Hippolyta called. "I'm coming inside!" She entered the cage. As the gate swung closed behind her, she looked up at the coils, waiting to see if they'd spark. They didn't. Hands trembling, Hippolyta turned her attention to the second gate and managed to fumble the latch open. She emerged onto the promontory.

Still no sign of Ida. Continuing to call out, Hippolyta went over to the cottage, entering through the kitchen, which was unoccupied. She searched the other rooms, looking not just for Ida but the gun as well. She found neither.

When she returned to the kitchen, Horace was standing in the open doorway.

Hippolyta was furious. "*What* did I tell you?"

Ignoring her anger, Horace pointed at a boxlike object on the counter beside the sink. "Is that the food maker?" The device, which resembled a miniature oven, was capable of conjuring a wide assortment of meals through a combination of magic and physics. Or had been capable: looking at it now, Hippolyta saw that it had been partially disassembled, the swing-down door detached, panels pried off within and without, various internal components laid out on the countertop. "I didn't touch it," Horace said, reading the accusation in her eyes.

"Don't touch *any*thing," Hippolyta said. "Come on."

They went back outside. Grabbing Horace by the wrist again, Hippolyta circled around to the far side of the cottage.

A high double fence separated the promontory from the alien jungle on the cliffs. In between this barrier and the back of the cottage was a large cairn of stones topped with a makeshift cross, and three more crosses driven into the rocky ground.

Hippolyta focused her attention on the fences. "They electrified?" Horace asked, following her gaze.

"Something like that." The fences' staggered gates were closed, and a red light on a control box just inside the barrier indicated that the defenses, whatever they were, were active. Hippolyta looked for a matching control box or some other means of switching the fences on and off from outside, but there didn't seem to be one, which meant that Ida hadn't gone out this way.

There was only one other place she could be.

At the observatory door, Hippolyta knocked and called Ida's name repeatedly but got no answer. Finally she gripped the doorknob, then turned to look at Horace. "I'd like you to wait out here," she told him. Speaking in as reasonable a tone of voice as she could muster, since anger clearly wasn't working. "Just until I have a chance to see what's what."

"Mom—"

"Please, Horace. Please let me do this."

Something in her expression convinced him to relent. "OK," he said. Then: "Just don't get shot."

"I won't," she promised.

The shutters in the observatory dome were open, making it almost as bright inside as out. Hippolyta's eyes went immediately to the telescope, a sleek and gleaming silver tube that was as much a work of art as a scientific instrument. The observer's chair, rather than resting on the floor, was mounted like a pilot's seat at the back end of the scope.

Someone was sitting in it. From her position by the door, Hippolyta couldn't see the occupant's face, but they had long gray woolly hair that spilled down over the back of the chair.

"Ida?" Hippolyta said. "Ida, it's me . . ." Her voice echoed beneath the dome, but the figure in the chair remained silent and unmoving.

She walked towards the telescope, approaching not in a straight line but a broad arc, this orbit bringing the chair's occupant slowly into profile. It was Ida, all right. That she was dead was no surprise at this point, but her advanced state of emaciation came as a shock. She looked almost mummified: cheeks hollowed out, skin stretched tight over the bones of her face, teeth exposed in a rictus. Her eye sockets were dark pits. Below the neck, she was swaddled in blankets. A skeletal hand reached from under the covers to grip a control stick on the arm of the chair, and this, combined with her teeth and the slight backward tilt of her head, created an impression of flight, as if the tele-scope were a rocket on its way to the stratosphere.

"Oh Ida," Hippolyta said. "I should have come back sooner."

She heard a creak and looked over to see Horace peering around the side of the observatory door, which she'd left ajar.

"It's all right," she told him. "You can come in now if you want. But it's not a pretty sight."

Horace came over to stand beside her. His eyes widened at his first clear view of Ida, but he didn't look away.

Hippolyta put an arm around him. "You OK?"

Horace nodded, still not taking his eyes off Ida. "Does it hurt?" he asked, after a moment. "Starving to death?"

"I'm not sure. I think I read somewhere that the hunger pangs go away, once your body figures out you didn't just forget to eat. But it takes a long time—months, if you're healthy enough to start with—and I can't imagine those last weeks are pleasant." She sighed, and a shud-der went through her.

Horace tilted his head to one side. "What's that?"

"What?"

"That." He pointed to a blue rectangle on the floor beneath Ida's chair. A book. Before Hippolyta could stop him, he stepped forward and crouched down to grab it, taking care not to jostle Ida.

It was a large notebook, hardbound, its cover bearing Winthrop's monogram and the half-sun sign of the Order. Standing beside his mother again, Horace opened it to reveal a handwritten title page:

OBSERVATIONS

of the Terra Hiram system

property of

Hiram Winthrop

Winthrop's name had been crossed out, and a different hand had inscribed beneath it:

Ida C. Odette

Holding the book between them, Hippolyta and Horace skimmed the record of discoveries it contained. Before his death, Winthrop had identified four planets in addition to the one on which they stood. Ida had found two more, naming the first of these for herself, and the second for her lost daughter, Pearl, who'd run off with Winthrop's son.

Ida's last will and testament was tucked among the pages describing planet Pearl's discovery. It was written on two sheets of paper torn from the back of the notebook, and took the form of a letter.

"Hippolyta," it began.

It is vain of me to imagine you will ever read this, but as Mary liked to say, all things are possible through the Lord. At the very least, I pray that He protected you from the consequences of my weakness. I know you were suspicious of my "gift" and may have cast it away without opening it. I hope so.

I am sorry I tried to kill you. I told myself I was protecting my daughter. That was a lie, but even if it had been true, murder is still murder, and I cannot claim self-defense against someone who meant no harm to me or mine.

As you will know by now, I have been punished for my sin. Three days after I sent you back alone through the portal, the food maker stopped working. I have tried to repair it, but to no avail, and the manual is no help. I do still have water, so my final fast promises to be long.

Do not pity me. The knowledge of my coming death has freed me to admit what I fought so hard to deny: that Pearl is already dead. I have known it in my heart for years, just as my own mother knew, without being told, that my brother had been killed, but as long as I lacked proof, I could hope that it was not so. That is why I could not go back to Earth with you, and why I tried to insure that you could never return here or send another in your stead.

But I am beyond all false hope now. I know that Pearl has gone to where my brother is, and my mother and father too. Soon enough I will join them.

I am afraid I lost your gun. Knowing my days were numbered, I determined to kill Scylla, whom I have never forgiven for eating James Storm. I went down to the beach and waited for her, letting her get as close as I dared before I opened fire. The bullets seemed to have little effect beyond angering her; and though I had been careful not to stray far from the stairs, the race back to safety was close-run. By the time I dragged myself back up the cliff I was exhausted. I slept a full day and woke dizzy and weak, while Scylla appears as lively as ever. I know I hit her, though, and in time, if God wills it, her wounds may fester. But I expect to meet the Lord before she does.

I will not ask you to forgive me. But I do have a last request. Mary's body remains under the stones behind the cottage. She was always afraid to spend eternity here, so far from home. Her last name was Bell, and her people were from Savannah. She had a sister and two brothers there who might still be alive. I know it may be impossible to explain her long absence to them, but to return her to her native soil and allow them to mourn her properly would be a godly act.

The fate of my own bones is of far less concern. Scatter them beneath the sky or throw them in the sea, here or on Earth—I am not particular. I would tell you to just leave them where you find them, *but knowing how I plan to spend my last hours, that won't do. You will need the chair for yourself.*

The telescope is yours now. Find your own planet and name it.

Your fellow stargazer,
Ida Carstairs Odette

Hippolyta's tears splashed the paper as she finished reading.

"I'm sorry your friend died, Mom," Horace said.

"So am I," she replied. And letting the notebook and the letter slip from her grasp, she put both arms around him, buried her face in his shoulder, and wept.

THE CHILDREN OF ROANOKE

⧓

The winding nature of the path made it hard to judge distance, but they'd been walking for more than an hour and by now, Atticus reckoned, they should have encountered another railroad. This second line, the Norfolk and Western, had appeared on one of his father's more recent maps, cutting through the swamp just over a mile south of the highway.

It wasn't the only modern feature of the landscape to have gone AWOL. Since 1763, when a Virginia militiaman named George Washington had founded the Adventurers for Draining the Dismal Swamp, people had been digging canals to gain access to the swamp's timber and shrink the size of the wilderness. Though Washington's ultimate goal of converting the entire Great Dismal to farmland had not yet been realized, lumber companies continued to dig new drainage ditches right up to the present day; the swamp was riddled with them.

But they appeared to have left the present day behind with the traffic noise on U.S. 58. As they continued to follow the path beneath the trees, they saw and heard nothing that would have seemed out of place a century ago. No planes passed overhead; no chainsaws buzzed in the distance. The only sounds were nature sounds: birds; insects; unseen mammals creeping or crashing through the underbrush; and once, a rhythmic chopping like a hand ax, coming from a dense thicket where no man could have stood, which Atticus decided must be a woodpecker.

The flattened vegetation on which they trod was springy and uneven. They were constantly off-balance, and had to step carefully to
avoid tripping. But however much the muscles in their legs and ankles
complained, they could only feel sympathy for anyone who'd come this
way without a ready-made path. At one point, Atticus tried to take advantage of a gap in the undergrowth and rest his feet on solid ground
for a moment. His reward for this minor deviation from the route was a
long bloody scratch on his arm, delivered by a thorn vine that he hadn't
even seen. Now multiply that by ten thousand, he told himself, and
imagine instead of hiking boots, you're wearing whatever passed for
shoes on a slave plantation.

The terrain was getting wetter. Standing pools of water appeared,
stained brown by the organic matter in the soil. A guidebook that Atticus had skimmed before the trip referred to this as "peat tea" and said
that despite its unappetizing appearance, it was safe to drink, being too
acidic for disease-causing bacteria. Good to know: their canteens were
almost empty.

The path took another turn, and sunlight broke through the trees
up ahead. They were coming to the end of the forest. Atticus wondered
whether they'd reached the Norfolk and Western tracks at last, but
when they pushed through the reeds at the edge of the tree line, what
lay beyond was not a railbed but a wide-open marsh.

A marsh born of flame. The guidebook had talked about this as
well: how fires in the Great Dismal, started by lightning and doused
by rain, could feed on the carbon-rich peat soil, leaving scars in the
landscape that filled up with water. Looking across the marsh, Atticus
could see scorched remnants of old trees surrounded by new growth:
vines, reeds, grasses, and shrubs, and saplings eager to stake a claim
where their ecological predecessors had fallen. These islands of green-
ery were enveloped by a shallow brown sea, with bits of flotsam hinting
at an ankle-breaking tangle of dead wood beneath the surface.

The sun was higher and hotter now, and the smell of fresh sweat drew mosquitoes and other biting insects. Atticus bent his head to slap at the side of his neck, and his eye was drawn to a disturbance in the water: a cottonmouth snake nearly a yard long, swimming among the reeds.

He stepped back from the water's edge and turned to his father. "So people lived out here, huh?"

"I know what you're thinking," Montrose said, "but it wouldn't be much of a refuge if it were all safe and easy. People who knew the ways of the swamp could make a decent life here, though. Poor, but free. And if you open your eyes, you'll see there's beauty here, too." He pointed to the jagged crown of a dead tree trunk where an eagle with a catfish in its talons had just settled down to eat, while colorful smaller birds feasted on bugs in the reeds below. Atticus took his father's point, though he couldn't help noticing the pair of turkey vultures circling overhead in search of their own lunch.

But no matter. They had more walking to do: the path continued as a series of small hummocks, aligned to form a fractured causeway extending out into the marsh.

Montrose once more took the lead, and as they picked their way carefully over the snake-infested waters, he began telling a story about the first maroons to call this place home. It was a tale that Atticus had heard before, in bits and pieces throughout his childhood, but today Montrose spoke with new knowledge and authority, which made Atticus wonder who he'd been talking to in his dreams.

The lost colony of Roanoke," Montrose said. "Not the first or the second, but the third."

"The second was the famous one, right?" asked Atticus. August 1590, Governor John White returned to Roanoke Island with an overdue shipment of relief supplies and found that the colonists had vanished into thin air, the only clue to their fate the word "CROATOAN," which was carved into a tree at the edge of the settlement. Atticus had gotten the sober version of the history in grammar school, and a more fanciful retelling, complete with witches and werewolves, from the pages of *Weird Tales* magazine.

"Yeah, that's the one everybody talks about," Montrose said. "But a few years before that, the English set up another colony on the same island. That one didn't fare well, either. When Francis Drake stopped by to see how the settlers were doing, they begged him to take them home, which he did. But what most history books won't tell you is he also left people behind. In Drake's fleet, there were hundreds of ex-slaves who'd helped him fight the Spanish in the Caribbean, and he'd promised them a new life in North America in exchange for their service. So while the white folks went back to England, these Moors and West Africans and Carib Indians took over the settlement they'd abandoned. By the time John White came to set up the second colony, they'd all gone missing, too. But I don't believe they died. I think they stayed on Roanoke Island just long enough for the white folks to sail out of sight and then hotfooted it to the mainland.

"The third Roanoke, though. That's the *real* lost colony. The one no one talks about, because to even admit it existed would contradict everything people want to believe about this country's history.

"It was on the Carolina mainland, on a strip of land running south from the Great Dismal Swamp to the Albemarle Sound, east of the Chowan River. The official name for the settlement was Albemarle, and that's the name you'll find if you look it up in a history book, but the people who actually lived there called it Roanoke, after the Indian name for the Sound, which was the Sea of Roanoke.

"It was a hard place to get to. To reach it overland from Virginia, you'd have to pass through the Great Dismal, which was a lot bigger in those days. The water route had its own difficulties: the Sea of Roanoke was too shallow for big ships to navigate, so to come that way you'd have to sail a small boat down past the Outer Banks and pray that bad weather didn't catch you out in the open. If you did survive the journey, you might wonder why you'd bothered. Even outside the Great Dismal, Roanoke was as wet as it was dry, the land broken up by marshes and streams. To a rich man looking to set up a big plantation and ship cash crops back to England, it was worthless country.

"But if you were poor, or outcast? If all you wanted was a plot to raise a family on, out from under the heel of the Crown? Then Roanoke might seem like the promised land, worth risking everything to get to. And people did: mostly white folks, at first—indentured servants skipping out on their contracts, and fugitives from debtors' prison—and then, a little later, colored slaves, looking to live free."

"Out from under the heel of the Crown," Atticus said. "But the Crown got there eventually, right? It became an actual colony?"

"Eventually, yeah, though at first that was mostly on paper," said Montrose. "In 1663, King Charles II issued a new charter for the Province of Carolina, and the Lords Proprietors set out to establish an official government in Albemarle—but to get the people already living there to go along, they had to make all kinds of concessions to the Roanoke way of doing things. The colonists in Virginia were all about industry: they broke their backs, and their servants' backs, toiling from sunup to sundown. But the people of Roanoke didn't live to work, they worked to live. They did what they had to, to put a roof over their heads and food on the table, but once they had those basics covered, they got to kick back and enjoy their time on earth.

"Even the physical layout of the colony was different. Every other English settlement in the New World was organized around a fort or a stockade, so the colonists would have some place to fall back to when the Indians attacked. Roanoke had nothing like that. People lived spread out all over, partly because of how the land was broken up, but also because they weren't afraid. The Tuscarora, who were the real sovereign power in those parts, were their allies. And not just their allies, but their kin. It's like history took a left turn there for a while, to show what America could have been: black folk and white folk and red folk all living side by side, making families together, without regard for color, or creed. They had freedom of religion, too, real freedom, like not even the most radical Dissenters dreamed of back then. Most of the colonists were unchurched, not because they weren't spiritual, but because they didn't see a need for organized faith. They just believed what they wanted to believe, worshipped how they wanted to worship, and left each other in peace." Here Montrose paused, the utopian nature of what he was describing butting up against his own cynicism. "That's the *legend*, anyway," he continued, shrugging. "I'm sure the reality had its share of problems. Still . . . If I were going to be stranded in the past? As a colored man, with a mind of his own? I could think of worse places for my time machine to break down.

"Of course, that's what doomed them in the end. Even after they accepted the Crown's charter, they went right on welcoming fugitives, protecting them. The governor of Virginia would write to Roanoke saying, 'Hey, we got reports of runaway slaves headed your way, you seen 'em?' And Roanoke would write back, 'Oh, gosh, we did hear tell of some colored folks like the ones you're looking for, but word is they already passed through, headed towards Florida. You want 'em back, you'll have to take it up with the Spanish.'" Montrose grinned. "You can imagine how that went over. And what was even worse, some of the people in Roanoke started preaching abolition—preaching it from the heart, the way even white folks will when it's their own family's future on the line.

"Storm clouds started gathering around the turn of the century. Settlers on the south side of the Albemarle Sound had more orthodox notions about how a colony should be run, and their numbers were growing. They wanted plantations worked by slaves, new roads to get their goods onto ships, the Church of England as the state religion, and no more coddling of fugitives or poor people. Back in London, they had a new queen and friends in Parliament who saw things their way. But to seal the deal, they had to get rid of the old guard up in Roanoke.

"Now like I said, most of the Roanoke colonists were unchurched, but an exception to that was the Society of Friends. Quakers were welcome in Roanoke, and because of their organization and their political ties to England, they were seen as natural leaders. Quakers served in the North Carolina assembly and helped preserve and defend the Roanoke way of life. So to get them out of the way, the anti-Roanoke faction put in a new rule requiring members of the assembly to swear an oath of allegiance to the monarch."

"And Quakers can't swear oaths," Atticus said. "It's against their faith, right?"

"Exactly," said Montrose. "Now the way this hustle worked, Quakers were allowed to run for office, but if they won the election, they'd be asked to swear, and when they refused, they'd be disqualified, and the guy they just beat would take office instead."

"'Heads I win, tails you lose.'"

"That's how it was supposed to go," Montrose said. "In the election of 1708, the colony ended up with two competing governments. One, led by a former governor named Thomas Cary, consisted of Quakers and unchurched who'd won the popular vote, while the other, led by William Glover, claimed victory on the basis of the oath rule. But when Glover and his people tried to take power, Cary stepped up and said, 'Hold on, gents. Here in Roanoke, we don't abide by stolen elections. If you value your health, you should consider a change of climate.' Then Glover suddenly remembered a pressing engagement up in Williamsburg and ran off to hide in the Virginia governor's mansion.

"Cary's Rebellion, they called that. But really it was Roanoke's rebellion. For a long while it was an armed standoff, but the people of Roanoke knew a fight was inevitable now, and they did what they could to prepare. In 1710, England sent in a new governor, Edward Hyde, and when Roanoke wouldn't recognize his authority, either, that's when the shooting started.

"The old settlers gave a good account of themselves, at first. Roanoke even had its own navy, two shallow-draft boats manned by free Negro sailors, with cannon smuggled over from England. If Hyde and his local militia had been all they had to contend with, they might have won the day. But Governor Spotswood of Virginia saw this as a chance to settle old scores, and sent a force of Royal Marines to reinforce Hyde.

"That would have been the end of it, if the Tuscarora hadn't decided to intervene. They were still Roanoke's allies, and more to the point, they were smart enough to know that this change in government meant nothing good for them. So while Hyde and his people were still celebrating their victory over the rebels, the Indians attacked the new settlements south of the Albemarle Sound. They burned farms and homesteads, killed colonists, and tortured a government land surveyor to death.

"Hyde screamed for more backup, and this time South Carolina answered the call. Charleston sent an army: thirty white officers leading a force of about five hundred Yamasee and other Indians who'd been promised slaves and plunder in exchange for their help. But when they arrived, they found a surprise waiting for them. The Tuscarora had built forts in their villages. I'm not talking simple palisade enclosures, either. These were serious, European-style fortifications, built to withstand a heavy assault."

"They steal the blueprints for those?" Atticus asked.

"They had eyes," Montrose said. "The Tuscarora had been dealing with white folks long enough to know what their forts looked like. And they had outside help, too: an escaped slave, Harry the engineer, who worked as a sort of defense consultant for them.

"In the spring of 1712, the South Carolinians laid siege to the fort in the Tuscarora capital. They spent weeks trying to shoot, blast, and tunnel their way inside, but they couldn't crack it. Finally their ammunition started to run low, so they called for a truce and negotiated a 'peace treaty' with the Tuscarora.

"Of course the peace only lasted long enough for the white folks to retreat and regroup. The next year they were back with a bigger army, and this time they brought siege experts. The big weakness of the Tuscarora forts was that they used pine logs in the construction. Pine resin's flammable as hell—it's what they make turpentine out of. So in March of 1713, the South Carolinians attacked Fort Neoheroka and set it on fire. There were nearly a thousand men, women, and children inside, and of those, about four hundred were captured and enslaved. The rest died fighting or were burned alive.

"That was the turning point. The Tuscarora fought on for a couple more years, but after Neoheroka, the writing was on the wall for them—and for Roanoke. A lot of the surviving Indians left the area and went north to join their brothers in the Iroquois Confederacy. The old guard of Roanoke left too, but they didn't go as far. They'd started out as fugitives, after all—as maroons—and now in the crunch they fell back on that tradition. They went into the Great Dismal, to the heart of the swamp where not even Royal Marines dared follow, and built a new society there.

"North Carolina became a slave colony—and a little later, a slave state. The new powers that be did their best to erase the memory of Roanoke, and for the most part, they were successful. But the legend persisted among the slaves, passed on in whispers: there was a refuge in the swamp, and if a man was brave enough, and lucky enough, and got deep enough into the Great Dismal without dying, he'd find people there waiting to help, and a place to live free."

"So if Roanoke disappeared in the 1710s," Atticus said, "that'd be, what, a hundred forty years before Great-grandpa Turner made his escape? A century and a half? And you're saying that for all that time, there were people out here, a *society*, hidden away from the outside world . . ." He wasn't questioning his father's account. He was marveling at it. But Montrose took his tone as one of skepticism.

"You see any libraries around here?" Montrose said. "They didn't keep written records. The only people who did that were the white folks who lived along the edge of the swamp, and they couldn't admit the truth about what they were dealing with. When they talked about swamp dwellers raiding their farms and helping their slaves run off, they didn't use the word 'maroon.' It was 'outlaws,' or 'renegades.' But it wasn't renegades, it was Roanoke—the descendants of the lost colony. They were here, when our ancestor came. They gave him shelter. And a few years later, when the Civil War started and Nat Turner went out into the world to fight, the children of Roanoke went with him, to avenge their ancestors and correct the old injustice. To set the country back on a better path." He paused before adding, with another cynical shrug: "As best they could, anyway."

They'd reached the far side of the marsh and were back under the trees. The forest here was older, with more hardwoods, mostly red maple and black gum, and the undergrowth was sparser, allowing for freer movement, though they still had to be mindful of thorns and poison ivy.

The path had disappeared, but they no longer needed it. Whatever they'd been brought here to see was close now. They could sense it, just up ahead, some invisible radiation causing their skin to prickle. They picked their way forward through the trees, following a subtle rise in the terrain.

Sunlight marked a small clearing up ahead, but their view of it was blocked by the leaves and branches of a maple that had fallen over in the direction of their approach. They circled the downed tree, pushed through some scrub brush, and found themselves at the edge of a broad, shallow depression in the earth.

It wasn't just topsoil that burned in the swamp. Once ignited, peat fires could smolder beneath the surface for a very long time, leaving voids that slowly filled with water or formed sinkholes that could swallow men whole. This depression didn't look like a sinkhole, though. To Atticus's eye, it looked more like a small blast crater, with clods of earth thrown up all around the rim; across from where they stood, he could see the roots of two more trees that had been toppled outwards.

At the crater's center, still partially embedded in the soil, was a human skeleton. Atticus, who'd read stories of "bog mummies" discovered in Ireland, would have expected the peat to act as a preservative; but the exposed bones were bare, as if the force that had unearthed them had also scoured them of any lingering remnants of tissue.

There could be little doubt of whose bones these were. Beneath its broad hips, the skeleton's left leg was shorter than its right, and badly mangled: foot twisted out to the side, ankle fused into a solid lump, fibula and tibia warped by a mosaic of poorly healed fractures. It was painful just to look at, and Atticus was amazed that the woman had been able to walk at all, let alone travel for miles across country such as this.

Yet even as he pitied her, the dead woman seemed to wink at him, and he heard the cackling laugh from his dream. Another wink, and the butterfly that had stopped to rest in one of the skull's eye sockets flew up into the sunlight, wings glittering.

Montrose bowed his head.

"Hello, Miss Hecuba," he said.

NO HEAVEN AT ALL

⧏⧐

It started with Andrew Jackson, I guess," Horace said.

The alien sun had set, dissolving the horizon in fire and painting the sea in streaks of orange and red. They'd taken chairs from the cottage and now sat on the open promontory, watching the long light of dusk slowly fade over the water.

"It was in history class," Horace explained. "Mrs. Ellis was telling us about President Jackson's last words. He was on his deathbed, and his family and his slaves were gathered around him, and some of the slaves were crying. And he called them his children, and said he hoped to see them all again in heaven.

"And Mrs. Ellis, you know, she has this thing she does, when she's quoting something she thinks is ridiculous. She gets this *tone* in her voice."

"Scornful?" Hippolyta said.

"Smirky," said Horace. "Like, sure, Andrew Jackson, *you're* going to heaven . . . Everybody in class had a good laugh at that, and I laughed too, but I also thought about it. And what I thought was, from Andrew Jackson's point of view, it made a lot of sense to believe he was going to heaven. I mean yeah, he'd done awful things—killing all those Indians, owning all those slaves—but it's not like he ever got punished for it. He got rich. He got to be president. And even some of the people he owned were sad that he was dying. Why *wouldn't* he think he was going to heaven?

"So anyway," Horace continued, "it was a few weeks later that Celia got shot. And you remember, the day after it happened, we were over at the Winthrop House, and Celia's dad was sitting in the parlor, looking all . . . *crushed*. And Mrs. Wilkins, she was standing beside him, trying to console him, telling him that it was a terrible cross to bear, losing a child, but Celia was in a better place now. And when she said that, I started thinking about Andrew Jackson again.

"It's like, everybody believes God is on their side, and everybody thinks it's silly that other people believe God is on *their* side. And it's hard to think straight about it, because we've all got a stake one way or another, but when I do try to set my feelings aside, and look at it, you know, objectively? On the evidence? I got to say, what Mrs. Wilkins believes makes a lot less sense than what Andrew Jackson believed. I mean, all that business about 'the last shall be first'—if God loves colored people so much, why would He make them wait until they were dead to get justice? Why not help them out right now?"

"So what are you saying, Horace?" Hippolyta asked. "You think Andrew Jackson might have been right?"

"No!" He shook his head, firmly. "I mean, I considered that, but I couldn't make it go. Andrew Jackson was a monster. If God sided with him, that'd make God a monster too, and that, I just don't think that's true."

"OK. But then what are you thinking?"

"What I'm thinking is, Andrew Jackson being wrong doesn't make anybody else right. Maybe everybody's wrong. Maybe there's no . . . no heaven at all. Maybe this life, good or bad, is all there is. And if your life gets stolen, then it gets stolen, and there's no reckoning for it. Celia was *thirteen years old*. Thirteen years, that's like no time at all. But maybe that's all she got, and now it's used up and there's nothing more for her. Ever. And then the slaves? And the Indians? And all the other people in history who got cheated? Nothing more for them, either. Ever. And it scared me, to think that might be so. It scared me and it made me mad. I've been mad about it ever since."

He paused, breathing hard, as though winded from a long run, and Hippolyta laid a hand on the back of his neck to calm him. The muscles there were knotted tight, and the bump where he'd been stung stood out in sharp relief.

"What do *you* believe?" he said suddenly. He turned to her, eyes searching, desperate. "You really think Celia's with God now? You think there's someplace . . . someplace that's . . ."

"Do I believe there's an afterlife?" Hippolyta said. "Take a look around you, Horace. Think about where we are. Then remember how we got here."

But Horace shook his head. "This isn't heaven. It's amazing, all right, but it's not heaven. God didn't bring us here."

"No, God didn't bring us here," Hippolyta agreed. "A dead man did. Mr. Winthrop's *ghost*, Horace. We're here because I made a deal with a ghost."

"Mr. Winthrop's not in heaven, either. He's trapped in a house in Chicago. And that's amazing, too, but it's got nothing to do with God."

"That's what Mr. Winthrop would say. But—"

"And anyway," Horace went on, "Mr. Winthrop's another rich white man, just like Andrew Jackson. So what if he did find a way to buy some extra time for himself? That still doesn't help Celia. It doesn't . . . it doesn't help *me*."

He continued to stare at her, eyes pleading. Hippolyta was momentarily at a loss. She knew all the things you were supposed to say to a child who expressed doubts about the Lord, but Horace was too smart to be swayed by rote answers and would only resent being condescended to. She needed to speak in a way that he would hear. As she struggled to find words, her own eyes strayed skyward; and there, in her old friend the heavens, was the inspiration she sought.

"Horace," she said. "Look up."

Directly overhead, a spiral galaxy hung in the sky like some great ghostly pinwheel. The full brightness of Terra Hiram's day had rendered it invisible, but now in the fading dusklight it appeared, still tenuous but gaining definition as night drew on.

"Whoah," Horace said, his misery displaced by sudden wonder.

"The Drowning Octopus," Hippolyta told him. "That's what Winthrop called it."

"Octopus I get," he said. "But why drowning?" Then, remembering the watery horizon: "Oh, right . . ."

"Yeah, it makes perfect sense when you see it set. It looks real close, too, doesn't it? Almost like you could reach up and touch it. But it's not. It only seems that way because it's so big."

"How big?"

"To measure it would take a lot of time on Ida's telescope. But our own Milky Way is about a hundred thousand light-years across, and Andromeda, which is the biggest spiral galaxy we know of, spans almost twice that."

"A hundred thousand light-years. So if you were out on the edge of the Milky Way, and you turned on a big spotlight . . ."

"It'd take a hundred thousand years for the light to get to the other side," Hippolyta said. "A thousand centuries, at the speed of light. It's hard to wrap your head around that kind of distance, but the real mind-bender? On the scale of the universe as a whole, a hundred thousand light-years is *nothing*.

"So in your history class," she continued, "did you talk about Copernicus yet?"

"Yeah, sure. He's the guy who figured out the earth goes around the sun."

"The first one to get credit for it, anyway," Hippolyta said. "But you know, that's not the whole story. People remember Copernicus for the thing he got right, but they forget what he got wrong. His concept of the universe was still based on the old Ptolemaic model, which said there was one sun, one moon, and six planets. Out past Saturn, there was nothing but the sphere of fixed stars, which was an actual sphere, like a big crystal eggshell studded with lights, holding everything in."

Horace's face registered surprise. He wasn't familiar with Ptolemy, but he'd read something very much like this in a comic book once, and it was strange to think that real people—scientists—had actually believed it. "What was outside the sphere?"

"God," Hippolyta said. "Jesus. The angels, who were in charge of making sure the planets kept moving in their orbits. With a setup like that, you can see why people expected that Earth should be at the center of it all, and why it scared them when Copernicus put the sun there instead. But it wasn't *too* scary, because even with Earth in a different position, the universe was still small enough that it was easy to believe that human beings were the most important thing in it. That it was created *for* them.

"But astronomy didn't stop with Copernicus. People kept on looking up at the sky, discovering things, figuring things out. By the time Andrew Jackson said goodbye to his house slaves, there were *seven* planets, and Urbain Le Verrier was hot on the trail of Neptune."

"And then Pluto," Horace said smiling, knowing how important the search for that planet had been in Hippolyta's own history.

"Yeah," she said, "and by then, the universe had gotten huge. Copernicus had no idea. Not just one sun, or one galaxy. Billions of galaxies, each with billions of suns, and who knows how many planets and moons. And that's just the part of the universe we can see. Nobody knows how big it really is, or what all is in it. And that *is* scary. Against that infinitude, to go on believing that human beings are special—let alone a certain type of human being—that's hard. Not that folks don't still manage, but it's a struggle.

"And God's a struggle, too," she added. "I see people wrestle with it. Those university classes I've been taking? There's this one girl I met, a preacher's daughter named Candace Bates. She wants to be a doctor, and I think she'll be a good one, but some of what she's learning in the science courses has her hanging on to the catechism by her fingernails. She took the astronomy elective just to get a break from Darwin. Little did she know."

"So she's struggling with her faith," Horace said. "But what about you?"

"Well, remember, I grew up looking at the stars. I always knew there was more to the universe than what they let on in Sunday school. And just as important, my daddy taught me to think like a scientist, which means not only do I *not* know everything, I know I *can't* know everything. There's always going to be more to learn.

"It's the folks who think they have it all figured out who have the hardest time," she said. "When they find out what they believe isn't so, they panic; instead of changing the *way* they believe, they jump from one certainty to another—usually a negative one. So if the God they grew up believing in turns out to be too small for the universe they live in, that must mean there's no God at all. No reason to hope."

"But what about you?" Horace repeated. "Do you believe in God, or don't you?"

"I believe, in my way." She looked skyward again. "This all had to come from somewhere, after all. But if you're asking me, do I think God is an old man with a beard who's got nothing better to do than worry about my problems . . . Well, no. I think He has to be more than that. A lot more. The creator of an infinite universe would have to be infinite too, every bit as strange and hard to comprehend, and just as full of surprises."

"Yeah," Horace said, eyes narrowing, "or maybe He just doesn't exist."

"It's possible," Hippolyta conceded. "Maybe the universe . . . just happened. Science can't really help with that, because when you start talking about ultimate origins, you run into theories that can't be tested.

And you can't prove a negative. So the only way to know for sure would be to meet the Creator face-to-face. If we ever do."

"And you can live with that? Not knowing? Maybe *never* knowing?"

"I can. And I'll tell you something else: So can you."

"No." He shook his head. "I don't know if I can live with it. I think maybe I'm like those folks you were talking about, the ones who need to be certain."

"You're not," she said. "That much I do know: You can live with doubt. It's in your blood."

"What are you talking about?"

"I'm talking about the reason you're here at all. The universe might have just happened, but you didn't. You're alive because of choices other people made."

"What people?"

"Your ancestors, of course . . . You know, your uncle Montrose, he likes to go on about how the Turners had it harder than the Berrys, in slavery. I take his point, but I don't think it's right to say that any slave had it easy, even the ones who didn't end up hiding in a swamp. Even my own ancestors, the Greens, belonging to that Dutch family in upstate New York . . . I'd like to believe that Northern slavery was kinder than the Southern variety, but that's nonsense. The only thing kind about it was that it ended sooner. While it was going on, though? Talk about uncertainty: to be someone else's property. And you can bet that in the North, just like the South, the system was set up to punish anyone who stepped out of line. Punish them *hard*. So if they ever did truly despair, there was always a way out. One sure way.

"But they never took it. Not the Greens, or the Berrys, or the Turners. However many times they had to choose between a life of uncertainty and the surety of death, they always chose life. That's how we happened. Everything good in my life, and that includes you, and everything good in *your* life, all of that is only possible because of that choice.

"And now it's your turn," she said. "I'm sorry that Celia got killed. I wish I could tell you for sure that she's in a good place now, but you're right, it's not for me to say. But you, Horace—you're still alive, and that matters. I would hope that it matters to you, and that that's enough, but if it isn't, remember those people who came before you, who made it possible for you to even think about giving up—and remember the ones who'll come after, who'll only get to make their own choices if you *don't* give up.

"And if that's still not enough, then remember me. You know, I get so scared for you, especially now that you're not a cute little boy anymore but a young man, a man I know some people are going to hate or be afraid of. The world's better than it was, but there's still a million ways for a young colored man to step wrong, and if something were to happen to you—oh God, Horace, if something were—it would break my heart forever. Please, Horace, I'm begging you, don't do that. Don't . . . don't break my heart."

"Mom," Horace said, a hitch in his voice. "Mommy, come on, I would never—"

"It's OK," she told him. "It's OK to have doubts. We all do, and you'd be stupid not to. Because you can't know everything. But that uncertainty cuts both ways: if the things we don't know were all bad, you wouldn't even be here to worry about them. So when you feel yourself despairing, remember that just because you can't think of a reason to hope, doesn't mean there isn't one. And as for God, remember that even a universe where He didn't exist could still act, sometimes, like one where He does. When you least expect it, you'll find yourself in light. I believe that. I believe—"

A horrible cry rent the air. Startled, Hippolyta and Horace both looked towards the ocean. Far out on the water, near the still-bright line of the horizon, something had just breached the surface. Silhouetted against the twilight, it was hard to make out in detail, but it was enormous—much larger than any terrestrial whale—and the sound it made was enormous too: a combination of a high-pitched shriek and a rumbling bass roar whose subsonic notes resonated with the stone of the cliff face, so that the promontory itself seemed to shudder.

It was terrifying, or should have been. But what Hippolyta felt was not fear, but awe—as if the universe, and whatever gods there are, had chosen that moment to weigh in on the conversation. When Horace clutched her hand, she sensed his excitement, and knew that he felt as she did.

Together they stood up, squinting and shading their eyes for a better look. But by the time they were fully on their feet, the creature was already sinking back beneath the waves. They waited to see if it would rise again, but it seemed one glimpse was all they were to be granted. A minute passed, then five, then ten, and the sea remained smooth and unbroken.

When the last of the twilight had faded and Winthrop's Octopus shone bright and clear above them, Horace released his mother's hand and let out a long sigh of what sounded like relief. She touched the back of his neck again; the muscles were relaxed now, and his skin was cool, with a light sheen of perspiration like the residue of a fever that has broken. Hippolyta pulled him close, and they stood that way for another minute, staring at the dark horizon, and then Horace spoke.

"We got to bring Ida and Mary back to Earth," he said. "They need to go home."

"They do, and we will," Hippolyta promised. "But first we're going to get ourselves out of this fix we're in. And we're going to take back what's mine."

RETURN TO THE RED PAWN

❧

Letitia had the cab drop her off one street over from the Red Pawn. When she came around the corner, there was a limousine idling in front of the pawn shop and a white man in a chauffeur's uniform standing by the curb. She ducked into a doorway before he noticed her.

Angus Rutherford came out of the shop carrying a cardboard box. The chauffeur took the box and put it in the trunk of the limo. Then he handed Rutherford a small black case, much like the one Hippolyta had delivered yesterday, only this one wasn't locked. Rutherford opened it and looked at the contents and nodded his head. Then he went back inside the shop and the chauffeur got in the limo and drove away.

Letitia emerged from her hiding spot. As she approached the Red Pawn, the door opened again and Rutherford reappeared, without the case. "Mr. Rutherford?" she said.

He regarded her with a scowl. "You're in the wrong part of town. The nigger pawn shops are all—"

"—north of Bonanza," Letitia finished for him. She raised the pistol she'd bought half an hour ago and pointed it at his chest. "I know."

Letitia had purchased a pair of handcuffs along with the pistol. She sat Rutherford in a chair in the back room of his shop and made him shackle himself to an exposed pipe on the wall.

The Stygian urn that Hippolyta had picked up for Mr. Winthrop was sitting on a workbench in the middle of the room. The sight of it filled Letitia with foreboding, for while it confirmed that Rutherford had been the white man at the motel, if his goal had been robbery, he'd have had no reason to leave Horace and Hippolyta alive.

Rutherford for his part seemed unafraid, as if being held at gunpoint were a minor inconvenience. "I don't know what you think you're doing here," he told her. "But I can promise you'll be sorry."

"Don't play stupid," Letitia said. "You know why I'm here."

"You're with the other one, aren't you? I thought I saw someone else in the car, yesterday. But I assumed it was the boy."

"No, that was me in the car. The boy has nothing to do with this." Pointing the pistol again: "Where are they?"

Rutherford ignored the gun. "My God," he said. "Winthrop must be more desperate than I thought, if he's down to relying on—"

"Where *are* they?"

He shook his head. "You can't kill me."

"Oh yes I can," Letitia said. "I know you don't have immunity. If you did, you'd never have let me in here."

"Immunity." He seemed surprised that she would know that term, but his surprise turned quickly to smugness. "It's true, Winthrop never would share the secret of his invulnerability spell. But how do you suppose he managed to survive his own death, when that spell failed him?"

"You helped design the Winthrop House," Letitia said nodding. "Told him how to build it so it'd keep his spirit intact. And you've got a soul-catcher of your own, is that it?"

"Yes." Rutherford studied the liver spots mottling the back of his uncuffed hand. "This body has seen its best days. In a way, you'd be doing me a favor if you freed me from it. But of course I couldn't really let an insult like that pass. And unlike Winthrop, I've actually made plans for my resurrection, so I won't need to waste time improvising. I'll be back in a new body before this one turns cold, and then I will make it my mission to teach you the meaning of regret."

"Well, that's very scary," Letitia said. "But you're in my classroom at the moment, so I'll be the one handing out lessons today." She turned to the workbench. Sitting beside the urn was the case Hippolyta had delivered yesterday. It had been opened, and the contents laid out on a strip of clean white cloth. "I see you got your coins." She picked up the bronze medallion. "This must be the one from Minoa. Hippolyta told me it was the most valuable of the lot. I would have guessed the gold coins, but then I'm not a collector . . ." She flipped the medallion into the air, which made Rutherford jerk as if he'd touched a live wire; catching it with her other hand, Letitia juggled it back and forth a few times before dropping it back on the workbench. Then she turned to a tool rack on the wall, finger on her chin, and after a moment's deliberation selected a steel hatchet. "This'll cut through bronze, right?"

"Do it and I'll fucking kill you." Not a trace of smugness in his voice now.

Letitia smiled. "Let me tell you the first rule of threatening people. You need to come up with something you weren't planning to do anyway. I came here to find my friends, not to destroy your property. But I'll do what I have to do." She hefted the hatchet to test its weight, making a few practice chops in the air. "So the way this is going to work, you're going to tell me what you did with them, and answer any other questions I might have. The first time I even *think* you're lying, it's going to cost you that bronze. Second lie, you lose the gold *and* the silver coins, and whatever was in that other case the chauffeur gave you. After that, I go in the front of the shop and see what else looks expensive. I hope your insurance is paid up. Now, one more time: Where are they?"

The expression of hatred on his face was absolute. But she'd found his weak spot.

"In the desert," he said. "At the Nevada Proving Grounds."

"Proving Grounds? You mean the A-bomb test site?"

"Yes. I have a colleague who works there. A man of rank, who owes me favors."

"But why? Why would you—"

"Well first of all, I *wouldn't* have," Rutherford said, "if your friend had come today, like she was supposed to. But the timing worked out, so I decided to take the opportunity to send Winthrop a message. I assumed he'd be tracking his courier's progress in some way. I wanted to remind him how dangerous it would be, to try to retaliate against me. More than that, I wanted to let him know that I'm done doing business with him." He shook his head. "The man's been a ghost for twenty-two years, and he's still finding new ways to piss me off."

"Like sending a colored woman to your door? And for *that*, you murdered an innocent boy and his mother?"

"I didn't murder them," he said. "They were still alive when I turned them over to my colleague. Unconscious, but alive. Of course, they're probably dead by now, but—"

"*Probably* dead? What does that mean? You think your colleague might not have gone through with it?"

Rutherford hesitated before answering. "No," he said. "If I told you that, I'd be lying. My colleague called to confirm they'd been delivered to the test site. And I don't need to tell you that the bomb went off as scheduled."

"Then how could Horace and Hippolyta still be alive?"

"The transport unit," Rutherford said. "When I retrieved the teleportation device, the transport unit was missing. I assume it was hidden somewhere in the trailer, but I didn't have all night to search for it—my colleague was already on his way. And it didn't really matter. Most of the value of the device is in the base unit."

"What good's the transport unit without it?"

"That depends. If your friend had already programmed a destination into it, she could use it to escape the blast."

"If," Letitia said. "And if she woke up in time."

"Yes."

"No. You're lying to me."

"I'm not lying," Rutherford said. "I'm describing something that's theoretically possible. I'm not saying I believe it happened. I think your friend and the boy are dead. If you're smart, you'll accept that, and get the hell out of here. But if you insist on clinging to hope—"

"Say I want to cling. Then what?"

"If they teleported away and survived, a second activation of the transport unit would return them to the vicinity of the base unit."

"And where's that, now? In the limo?"

He nodded. "On its way to a client of mine."

She thought for a moment. "Your client's not going to be upset with you, for selling him a teleporter with no transport unit?"

"As it happened, I had a spare. I just needed time to finish synchronizing it with the base unit . . ."

"As it happened?" Letitia snorted. "You don't strike me as a man who does extra work for no reason." Then it came to her: "You were going to use the spare to steal the machine back. Give Hippolyta the teleporter, wait for her to drive away, let her guard down, then pop into the trailer in the middle of the night, probably murder us all in our sleep . . . Only she messed up your plan by coming a day early."

Rutherford bristled. "This wasn't about her, you stupid bitch. It was about Winthrop. I expected him to send a *real* courier—someone with power, someone I'd actually have to be wary of. If I'd known he was working with niggers, I wouldn't have bothered with finesse."

"Yeah," Letitia said, glancing at his cuffed hand. "Somebody misread the situation, clearly. But lucky for you, I'm a hopeful person, so I'm going to choose to believe Jesus was looking out for my friend. Where do I find your client?"

"He has an estate—a ranch—just outside the city. Uncuff me and I'll take you there."

She snorted again. "That's all right. I'll find my own way. You just give me the address. And then," she added, "you can forget I was ever here."

❀   ❀   ❀

She left him shackled to the pipe, slumped in the chair with his head lolling to one side. She took Winthrop's urn, and on impulse scooped up the coins as well.

As she was walking out through the front of the shop, a mechanical owl perched behind one of the counters turned its head and focused its camera-lens eyes on her. The *snick-snick-snick* as it captured her image was drowned out by the ticking of a pair of clocks on the same shelf. Letitia took no conscious notice of it, but at the door she paused and looked back in sudden doubt, thinking that she'd overlooked something.

The moment passed. She turned and went out and hurried down the block in search of another cab.

BONE LADDER

⚜

"Mind where you're stepping," Montrose said.

Atticus circled Hecuba's skeleton to get a closer look at another object he'd spied poking out of the soil. He bent down and came up holding a relic from his dreams: a cut crystal decanter. Grime had rendered it opaque, but when he held it to his ear and shook it, he heard the leaflike rustle of something inside.

The decanter's stopper was fused in place and wouldn't budge. Atticus gripped it as tightly as he could and tugged, and the body of the decanter suddenly broke in two, separating like the halves of a crystalline eggshell and disgorging a yolk of yellowed paper.

It was a sheet of stationery with **SEABOARD & ROANOKE RR** printed along the top edge. Hand-sketched beneath this was a tree with spreading bare branches and a slanting dark rectangle at its foot that read as an open grave. The letters *O* and *W* were scrawled beneath the grave site.

"Ow?" Atticus said.

"Oak Woods," Montrose replied. "That's your grandmother Lucy's burial plot, I think."

"What are you talking about? Grandma Lucy's buried in Riverside Cemetery, in Kalamazoo."

"Her *other* plot. The one she had before she went to live with your aunt Ophelia. She reserved herself a spot in Oak Woods Cemetery right after we came up to Chicago. After what happened with Daddy's body in Tulsa, she wanted to make sure we'd have a place to put her, if history repeated itself."

Montrose's father, Ulysses, had been murdered on the night of May 31, 1921, at the start of what became known as the Tulsa Race Riot: shot dead by a white man in a passing car as he carried seven-year-old Montrose away from the violence. Neighbors brought Ulysses's body home to where his wife and daughter had just finished packing their own car for an escape from the city. Grandma Lucy, making a decision she would regret for the rest of her life, had opted to leave Ulysses behind in the house rather than cram him in with the luggage. She had him placed in their marriage bed, laid a cross on his chest to ward off whatever evil might find him there, and pledged to come back for him as soon as the children were out of immediate danger.

She never saw him again. The next morning at dawn, thousands of armed white people came swarming across the train tracks below Archer Street and put the entire neighborhood of Greenwood to the torch. By the time Lucy was able to return, nothing remained of the house but a scorched foundation, and there was no trace of Ulysses at all, though she sifted the ashes for days. Either the fire had burned hot enough to incinerate him completely or his remains had been moved to an unmarked mass grave with other colored victims of the massacre. The uncertainty ate at her, and left her determined never to inflict it on anyone else.

"It didn't really make any sense," Montrose said. "Even if Daddy had a plot picked out for himself in Tulsa, it's not like they leave the grave open for emergencies, and there's no way we were going to take the time to dig a hole that night. But it gave her comfort, knowing she'd done what she could to prepare. She got a good deal on it, too. That tree? It's right over the grave site, like crowding into it. Most folks wouldn't go for that, but Mom saw it as a bonus feature. She used to say, 'Just toss me in without a box and let the roots pull my soul up into the branches. Then when the storm passes, you can come back and talk to me any time you like.'"

"We still own the plot?" Atticus said.

"Yeah, I think so," Montrose said. "Even after Mom moved to Michigan, she insisted on hanging on to it. She still wanted to be ready, just in case the apocalypse hit while she was visiting for Thanksgiving. After she passed, George talked about selling it off, but I'm going to take a wild guess that he never got around to it."

They both looked at Hecuba, her exposed bones waiting patiently at the heart of the crater.

Montrose patted the backpack on Atticus's shoulders. "Get this emptied out," he said. "We got our marching orders."

That's all of her," Montrose said.

It was afternoon, now. They'd gently extracted Hecuba's remains from the muck, moving with the slow deliberation of archaeologists. Montrose had taken particular care with the bones of Hecuba's twisted leg, as if fearing it might still cause her pain.

"I don't know," said Atticus, still scanning the soil of the crater. "I've been trying to keep a count, and it seems low. Aren't there supposed to be like two hundred bones in a human body?"

"Yeah, but you got to know how to count them. Your skull alone has got around two dozen pieces to it."

"Plus the teeth?"

"Teeth ain't bone, they're enamel. But don't worry, we got all of them, too. All the ones she had left."

"OK, Pop. If you say so."

"I do." Montrose shouldered the backpack and stood. "She brought us here. If we did miss something, she'll let us know before we get too far."

"So where to now? Back the way we came?"

"Yeah. If we follow those tracks west a few miles, they'll bring us into Suffolk, and we should be able to get a bus there." Montrose turned and stepped up to the lip of the crater—and paused there, frowning. "Shit."

"What?"

"Listen."

Atticus did so, at first hearing nothing beyond the background noise of the swamp. But then he climbed up beside his father and opened his mouth so he could hear better, and a new sound came through. It was back in the direction of the marsh, distant but getting closer.

Dogs.

They fled deeper into the swamp, the sound of barking growing louder behind them. As Atticus dodged among the trees and tried not to trip over vines and low shrubs, he looked in vain for a ready-made escape route like the path that had brought them here.

All he could do was follow his father. Montrose sprinted ahead, moving with a steady purpose that suggested he knew where he was going, the bone-laden backpack pounding him between the shoulder blades as though Hecuba were urging him on.

A swath of sunlight appeared up ahead. They broke through a thick stand of brush and emerged on the edge of a large pond; a broad shingle of bare soil sloped down into the tea-colored water. Looking to the left and right, they saw that the pond was too wide to go around. It wasn't that far across, but the opaqueness of the water made it impossible to judge depth.

Atticus noticed an oddly shaped log floating in the middle of the pond off to his right. The log appeared to have eyes, and he could have sworn he saw it blink. But even as he turned to focus on it, it sank below the surface, the dark water closing smoothly over it.

There were no alligators in the Great Dismal. The guidebook had been clear on that point: venomous snakes, yes; and lizards, toads, frogs, and salamanders. Also black bears, bobcats, gray and red foxes, marsh rats, weasels, several species of bat, and a host of stinging and biting insects.

But no alligators. Hard as it might be to believe, standing here perspiring on a summer's day, the swamp was too cold for them. There'd been reports of them back in colonial days—old wives' tales, the guidebook suggested, or the Indian equivalent, stories passed down from much further in the past, ancient times when the swamp had been bigger and the world warmer. Whatever shred of truth might have inspired these stories, the guidebook said, had long since evaporated into myth.

Sure, Atticus thought, but logs don't just sink.

While Atticus tried to convince himself that he hadn't seen what he'd seen, Montrose stepped to the edge of the shingle and put a cautious foot forward into the water. The sole of his boot had barely broken the surface when he encountered resistance—something hard and springy, in the nature of a tree root, but smoother and broader, like the rung of a stepladder. He tested his weight on it a moment, then put his other foot forward, finding another rung beyond the first. This one had a slight curvature in it; he put his arms out, for balance, and took another step, and another.

Five paces out, he stopped and looked back, Hecuba's ribs shifting in the backpack as he did so. "Pop?" Atticus said, the phantom alligator momentarily forgotten, displaced by this new wonder: his father, walking on water, borne up like Peter on the Sea of Galilee.

"Don't ask questions," Montrose counseled. "Don't think. *Trust*. And *move*, fast." The dogs were very close, now.

Atticus nodded, and taking a deep breath followed his father out onto the surface of the pond. The unseen ladder continued, bearing them forward, arms outstretched like unsteady Jesuses.

They were most of the way across when a pair of bloodhounds burst out of the brush onto the shingle. The dogs bounded forward,

barking furiously, but skidded to a stop at the water's edge. They snuf-
fled the air there, apparently not liking what they smelled, and then sat
back, baying.

Montrose reached the far bank and crashed through a tall stand
of reeds. Atticus, still on the water, made the mistake of glancing back
and nearly lost his footing. He pinwheeled his arms and caught himself. As he stepped onto land, a voice behind him called out, "There's
one of them!"

Atticus dove forward into the reeds, even as a shotgun boomed
across the water. He hit the ground, pellets rattling the foliage overhead, and rolled, flattening himself into a furrow in the dirt as the
shotgun fired another blast.

There was a pause. Atticus shifted position and carefully raised his
head to peer back through the reeds. Four men had joined the bloodhounds on the shingle. Two of them, one big and one small, were
dressed in Virginia state trooper uniforms; the big trooper was the one
with the shotgun, while the smaller man had a hunting rifle slung over
his shoulder. Beside them, in civilian clothes, was the North Carolina
prison guard who had been thrown from his horse yesterday morning.
He was holding his M1 rifle, and as he moved about the shingle Atticus
saw that he was limping.

Sheriff Eustace Hunt filled out the quartet. He'd replaced his rifle
from yesterday with a shorter-barreled weapon with a drum magazine:
a Thompson submachine gun. "What's the holdup?" he said, speaking
to the smaller trooper, who appeared to be the hounds' handler. "Get
those dogs to flush them out."

"Something's got 'em spooked," the trooper said. He grabbed one
of the bloodhounds by the collar and tried to shove it forward into the
water, but the dog resisted, digging in with its paws and finally turning
to snap at the man.

"Fuck it, I'll flush them out," the big trooper said. He entered the water at the same spot Montrose and Atticus had, and sank almost im-mediately up to his thighs. He kept going, holding the shotgun at the level of his chest to keep it dry.

He'd taken another half dozen steps, the pond lapping at his belly now, when a big green log with eyes came out of the water and took one of the dogs. The smaller trooper threw himself backwards to escape the snapping jaws and scrambled away on his elbows while the other bloodhound bolted back under the trees. Sheriff Hunt opened fire with the Thompson. The .45 slugs tore chunks of flesh from the alligator's back, but the gator didn't seem to feel it, as if it really were made of wood; it eased back casually into the pond, dragging the dead blood-hound with it.

The big trooper stood paralyzed with fear as the gator slid past. Then a jolt went through him; he dropped his shotgun in the water and, making a gesture like a bullfighter raising a cape, stared in horror at the cottonmouth hanging by its fangs from the meat of his forearm. "Shit! *OH SHIT—*"

"Jesus!" the smaller trooper cried. He was writhing on the ground, slapping frantically at his arms and chest. "Get 'em off me! Get 'em off—"

Something roared back under the trees, loud enough to be heard above the cries of the troopers. "Oh fuck," said the prison guard, turn-ing around. The roar came again and the guard shouldered his M1 and Sheriff Hunt raised the Thompson and they both began firing.

Montrose put a hand on Atticus's shoulder. "Come on," he whis-pered. "Let's get, while the getting is good." Atticus nodded and got up and followed his father away into the swamp, while behind them the screams and sounds of gunfire continued.

RETURN TO EARTH

❧❦

Embracing once more, Hippolyta and Horace took a last look up at the spiral galaxy, which had crept a few degrees closer to the ocean horizon. Then Hippolyta clicked the button on the transport unit and the night sky of Terra Hiram was replaced by an arched ceiling hung with globe lights.

They separated and looked around. They were in a large rectangular room whose longer walls were lined with bookshelves. The teleporter base unit sat on a polished wood table in front of them; though large enough to seat at least a dozen people, the table had only one chair. To their right, beyond the table's end, they could see a closed door. In the other direction, the room extended another forty feet past a collection of tall display cases.

There was no one else in the room with them. Relaxing slightly, Hippolyta turned her attention to the teleporter, eyes widening as she noticed the new transport unit. She removed it from the dock and compared it to the one she was already holding; they looked almost identical, but the new unit had a raised nub on the clicker button that the other lacked, which made it possible to tell them apart by feel. Useful.

"Now we can each have one," Horace suggested.

"Don't even think about it," Hippolyta replied. She nodded in the direction of the display cases. "Go see if you can find a box or something to carry the machine in. But don't touch anything else."

"Yeah, sure." In fact, Horace had already spotted a cardboard box right underneath the table, but rather than point this out he took the opportunity to go look around.

The display cases mostly contained more books, presumably ones that were rare or valuable, though in the nature of works created before the invention of the modern dust jacket, it could be hard to tell what they were even about, let alone what made them special. Horace wandered among them reading titles off display cards and pausing here and there to take a closer look at an unusual binding.

One of the few nonliterary artifacts was a plaster cast of a white man's face; the display card identified this as "Blackwood death mask." Horace knew what a death mask was—he'd researched them for a horror comic he'd done one Halloween—and he knew that, just like photographs of dead people's faces, they were always done with the eyes closed. But the Blackwood mask had been sculpted to show the eyelids open, and the blank stare of the exposed orbs gave Horace gooseflesh.

Beyond the display cases at the far end of the room, an alcove housed a chest-high marble pedestal topped with a velvet cushion. Hanging on the wall behind the pedestal was an oil painting that depicted a white woman in a see-through nightgown sprawled in sleep; above her head, the Renaissance equivalent of a thought balloon showed the image of her dream, in which she stood completely naked on a balcony overlooking a vast city of white towers. Horace stared at the painting for several moments, committing it to memory so that he could draw it later.

Then he lowered his eyes to the silver skeleton key that rested on the velvet cushion. Tilting his head to one side, he checked for signs of a pressure plate under the cushion. He couldn't see anything, but a magical booby-trap might not be visible. Better not, he cautioned himself. We're in enough trouble as it is.

Then he shrugged, and picked up the key. It was heavy and slightly warm to the touch. Holding it up towards the nearest light, he could see fine symbols etched along its length, letters from the mystical language of Adam.

He slipped the key into his pocket and returned to his mother.

Hippolyta had put the replacement transport unit back in the dock and had a hand on the side of the base unit. A single red crystal lit up on top of the machine, which seemed to please her. She pulled the side lever.

"What are you doing?"

"Improvising." Hippolyta nodded at the slanting face of the base unit. "This is the only other address I know."

Horace studied the number array. All of the little windows read 001, except for the one in the lower right corner, which was set to 002. "Where's it take you?"

"Outer space. You remember my story about using Mr. Winthrop's teleporter, the big one with the projector? And I saw that asteroid orbiting the twin stars?"

"What would you want to go there for?"

"I wouldn't," Hippolyta said. "At least, not without a space suit . . . But we've got no weapons, and somebody might try to stop us getting out of here. Anyone tries to lay a hand on you, I'm giving them a hug."

It took him a second to get what she was saying. "But you'd die too, then."

"Not if I'm quick. Long as I keep my head, I'll have plenty of time to blink myself back before I pass out. And unlike the person I'm tackling, I'll be ready for it."

"You should let me do it," Horace said. "I'm faster than—"

"No." Her face grew stern. "Absolutely not."

"Mom—"

"*No*, Horace. This is not a discussion. You're going to carry the machine. I'm running defense. End of story."

She took the transport unit and went over to the door. When she cracked it to peek out, a klaxon went off. She hurriedly pushed the door shut again, but the alarm continued to sound. "Grab the machine!" she told Horace. "We need to make a run for—"

Footsteps approached along the corridor she'd glimpsed outside, their tread heavy enough to be heard above the whoop of the klaxon.

"*Hide*," she said. Horace ducked under the table. Hippolyta flattened herself against the wall beside the doorway.

The footsteps reached the door. There was a pause, and the klaxon shut off.

The door flew open. A big white man in a suit came through it. Before Hippolyta could react, he fell to his knees and pitched forward onto his face. The gun he'd been carrying went skittering across the floor.

"Still works," Letitia said, appearing in the doorway like a fairy godmother with her wand held high. She smiled at Hippolyta, then bent down to wave at Horace. "You all ready to go home?"

HITCHING A RIDE

⊰⊱

About an hour before dusk, Atticus and Montrose emerged from the swamp onto a dirt road. Before they could decide which way to follow it, they heard a motor and looked to see a station wagon coming towards them. It was a red Woody wagon, the same model that George drove, and Atticus, exhausted from the long day's trek, wondered how his uncle had managed to find them here. But as the car drew nearer, he saw that the driver, while a Negro, had gray hair, and the boy sitting on the passenger side was too young to be Horace.

The old man eased the wagon to a stop beside them and leaned smiling out the driver's window. "Evening," he said. "You folks been out hiking in the swamp?"

"Started as a hike," Montrose replied. "But then we got ourselves good and lost, so the last few hours it's been more of a true-life adventure. We still in Virginia?"

The old man laughed. "That you are. You need a lift somewhere? Got a car around here?"

"No car," Montrose said. "But if you know a place we can catch a bus north, that'd be helpful."

"Where north?"

"Washington." This from Atticus, who'd noticed the District of Columbia plate on the wagon's front bumper.

"That's right," Montrose said. "Supposed to meet my brother there. Then we're all going up to my grandpop's place in Philadelphia."

"Well, I'm headed up to Washington right now," the old man said. He nodded at the boy, who, uninterested in the adults' conversation, was focused on a book in his lap. "I've got to get this young man back to his parents. You're welcome to climb in back if you want. We got our camping gear back there, and if you stretch out on the bedrolls it should be pretty comfortable." He grinned. "Long as you don't mind the smell of catfish."

"Don't mind it at all. And of course, we'd be happy to pay for your gas . . ."

But the old man dismissed the offer with a flick of his hand. He nodded at the boy again. "I live in the capital with my son's family now, but I grew up around here. This part of the world, we look out for strangers in need."

"So I've heard," said Montrose.

GET YOU HOME

⊰⊱

The white man at the airline ticket counter was adamant: "The flight is full."

"When I called half an hour ago I was told there were plenty of seats available," Hippolyta insisted. "I reserved three of them."

"You aren't on the list." He patted the sheet on the clipboard beside him; when Hippolyta tried to see for herself, he turned the clipboard over.

"What you're doing is illegal," she said. "You know that, right? You're an interstate carrier. The I.C.C. says you can't discriminate."

The ticket clerk leaned towards her, smiling amiably, like a friend who meant to share a secret. "There aren't any lawyers here," he told her. "You want to file a complaint, go right ahead, but you're not getting a seat on my airline tonight."

"I'll file a complaint, all right. Get your manager out here."

The clerk's smile widened, showing teeth now. "My manager's off today. But you see those guys over there?" He pointed to a pair of men in uniform chatting up a blond woman at another ticket counter a short distance away. "That's my cousin Pete and his friend Dave. Say the word, I'll have them haul you back to the security office, and you can try lecturing them about the law. How's that sound?"

Power is what matters, Hippolyta thought. She suppressed her anger, an all-too-familiar exhaustion rising to take its place. "I hope one day you learn just how awful you're being," she said. Then she turned and went back to the seats in the terminal where Letitia and Horace were waiting.

"Misplaced our reservation?" Letitia guessed.

"Yeah, apparently I just imagined making that phone call," Hippolyta said. She sighed. "I suppose we could wait for him to go on break, see if his relief is more helpful. Or try a different airline." But the two other airlines she'd called before coming here hadn't even let her make a reservation.

"What about taking the bus?" Horace said.

"Next one to Chicago leaves at four thirty in the morning," Hippolyta told him. "And if anyone's looking for us, that's how they'll expect us to travel. Worse comes to worst, I'd rather spend the night here and try to get a flight out tomorrow."

"I'm going to go make a phone call," Letitia said. "Wait here for me . . ." She stood up and headed off across the terminal.

Hippolyta sat down in the seat Letitia had vacated. "I'm really sorry about this, Horace."

"What have you got to be sorry about? You didn't do anything wrong."

"Yeah, I did. You wouldn't be in this mess if I hadn't brought you with me. And after all my talk about wanting to keep you safe—"

"Are you kidding me? I wouldn't have missed this for anything." He smiled at her, in a way he hadn't in what seemed like forever. "Another planet, Mom. You took me to another planet. Who else gets to do that on vacation?"

"I also nearly got you blown up by an atom bomb."

"Yeah, that too!" He laughed. "*And* we nearly got trapped in a wizard's house. Don't forget that."

"Oh, I wasn't about to forget that . . ." She shook her head, marveling at his attitude.

"And *now*, we're making a desperate getaway. The only bad part I can see is that no one back home is ever going to believe it."

"Yeah, well, about that, Horace—"

"I know," he said. "I can't tell anyone."

"I'd really prefer that you didn't." She hesitated. "And I don't just mean your friends."

He looked at her. "You're not going to tell Pop what happened?"

"I haven't decided," she said, meaning no. "It gets a little complicated, because this arrangement I've had, doing errands for Mr. Winthrop? Your father doesn't know anything about that."

"Why not? You worried he'd try to make you stop doing it?"

"Worried about him worrying about it, let's say. This might be hard for you to understand, but the thing about being married, sometimes . . . It's not so much you keep secrets from each other, but sometimes you just don't mention certain things, if doing that would only cause trouble. Maybe your marriage will be different," she added, seeing Horace's evident skepticism. "I hope so."

Horace thought it over. "All right," he said. "I won't tell Pop . . . if you promise to take me planet-hopping again."

"We'll talk about it," Hippolyta said.

Letitia was gone a long time. Just as they were starting to get worried she returned, accompanied by a good-looking Negro man. "Hippolyta, Horace," she said, "this is Anthony Starling. We made friends at the poker table last night."

"*I* was being friendly," Starling clarified, grinning. "And Miss Dandridge took full advantage."

"Anthony's a pilot," Letitia said. "Got his own plane and everything."

"Really?" said Hippolyta. "You wouldn't be flying to Chicago by any chance, would you?"

"I wasn't planning on it," Starling told her, "but Letitia claims she knows about a card game up there where I might be able to win back some of the money she took off me." He nodded at the two cardboard boxes stacked on the seat at Hippolyta's side. "Is that all you've got for luggage?"

"We're traveling light."

"Well that's good, actually. My plane's parked in a hangar at the far end of the field, so it's a bit of a walk." Holding up the suitcase in his hand, he added: "This isn't too heavy, if you'd rather I carry those for you."

"That's all right," Hippolyta replied. "You just lead the way. We got this covered." She put one arm around Horace, and with the other hugged the box containing her teleporter. Thinking, Let's get you home.

PART II

THE BODY SNATCHERS

RUBY'S GLASS SLIPPER

❧❧

Miss Lightbridge kissed Ruby just as Ruby was about to turn back into a colored girl.

It was the night of Missy Mitchell's bridal shower. The founding principle of the Lightbridge Employment Agency was that women should have the right to pursue whatever career they wished, which technically included the right to become a housewife. But Missy had an undergraduate degree and until a few weeks ago had been talking about medical school; to see her marry a bank manager from Evanston instead had to be a bitter pill to swallow. And while Miss Lightbridge was too professional to let her disappointment show publicly, in private she was less restrained with her feelings, especially when she got a few drinks in her. Ruby didn't see this twist coming, though.

The whole day started off wrong, Ruby stepping off the elevator on the agency's floor and colliding with a colored woman who was in the process of storming out. "Excuse *me*," Ruby said, but the woman plowed right past her, boarded the elevator, spun around, stabbed at the lobby button, and stood staring daggers back through the glass curtain wall at Missy Mitchell in reception. The woman's face contorted as she fought to maintain the last of her composure, but then, maybe deciding there was no point, she shouted "*Fuck* you!," which turned Missy's mouth into a shocked O. "Fuck you, too," the woman said, focusing her ire on Ruby now. "Fuck *all* of you."

This was followed by an awkward ten seconds during which the elevator doors failed to close. "Fuck," the woman said, to herself this time, and hammered at the lobby button. Ruby felt her heart pulled in two directions at once. She was angry at the woman for cursing her, but she was also mortified on her behalf. Bad enough to have your grand exit fizzle out, but like all embarrassments, to have it happen in front of white people, as if reality were conspiring against you for their amusement, was a hundred times worse.

Finally the doors slid shut. Ruby went inside to reception. "What was that about?"

"She wanted a job," Missy said. Making it sound ridiculous, as if the woman had asked her for a parrot.

"We are still an employment agency, right?"

"An *accounting* job," Missy clarified. "When I told her we didn't have anything for her, she blew up at me."

"Did you check the want sheets?" Ruby said. "Because I could swear I saw two accounting jobs on there just yesterday."

"There were, but one of them has been filled already, and the other is for the Carroll brothers." The Carrolls, Al and Sal, owned a string of women's hat shops. They only hired good-looking white girls, even for back-room positions that didn't involve dealing with customers. For accounting, Ruby supposed the brothers might stretch their definition of white to include Jewish girls, but there was no way a Negro was getting that job.

Still, though. "Did you at least ask her to fill out a contact form, so we could let her know if something came available?"

"The conversation never got that far. I told you, she blew up at me."

"Well, what exactly did you say to her?"

"I don't remember *exactly*," Missy said. "But it was *honest* . . . Look, Hillary, I know we're not supposed to turn anyone away, but it's my last day here, and I didn't see the point in wasting my time, or her time, pretending a job might come available when I know that it won't. Is that so wrong?"

Yes, Ruby thought, but the invocation of her work name stopped her from pressing the matter. To Missy and her other coworkers at the agency, she was Hillary Hyde, a redheaded white girl from Bloomington who'd been hired as Miss Lightbridge's secretary after she approached Miss Lightbridge to ask for career advice. Ruby sometimes wondered what would have happened if she'd come to Miss Lightbridge as her true self—as Ruby Dandridge, a colored girl more dark-skinned than the one who'd just left here—but she didn't wonder very hard. Miss Lightbridge would have *spoken* to a colored girl, if she wasn't in a hurry. But would she have invited her to lunch? Or made a spontaneous job offer over dessert? Ruby didn't think so. More to the point, it didn't matter, because as her true self, she would never have approached Miss Lightbridge in the first place. She would have assumed it was a waste of time.

"I see what you mean," she said to Missy. Then: "Enjoy your last day."

The first time she'd taken the potion that transformed her into a white girl, Ruby had fantasized about becoming a high-powered secretary in a skyscraper somewhere. The building that housed the Lightbridge Agency was only six floors, and the extent of her power was debatable, but Ruby still loved her job. It paid better than any other work she'd ever done, it was genuinely interesting, and the fact that she got to sit down did not grow old.

This morning she bypassed her desk and knocked on Joanna Lightbridge's door. "How did it go?" Miss Lightbridge asked as she came in. "Everything squared away for tonight?"

Ruby nodded. "The whole thing was just a big mix-up. They had your check, and the reservation. I'm sorry it took half the morning."

"No, that's fine. So long as the bar doesn't run dry tonight." Miss Lightbridge paused, looking at Ruby in that perceptive way she had. "Is there something else?"

"There is, actually . . ." Ruby closed the door and told her the story of what had just happened with the colored woman. Miss Lightbridge listened attentively, but Ruby, who was quite perceptive in her own right, sensed that this was mostly politeness.

"That's unfortunate," Miss Lightbridge said when she'd finished. "I do wish Missy had handled that differently."

"I'm not happy with Missy, but that's not the reason I'm telling you about this. I—"

"I know," Miss Lightbridge said. "But we've talked about this before, Hillary. I want to help as many women as I can, but ultimately I'm at the mercy of the clients. I can't force them to hire employees they don't want."

"That's not really true, though, is it?" Ruby said. "A lot of your clients didn't want to hire women at all, at first. Or pay them what they're worth. I've seen you go to bat on that, twisting people's arms . . ."

"Yes, I twist arms, and I charm, and now and then I even bribe, but there are always limits. I can only push so far, so fast, before the clients go elsewhere."

Ruby knew she could only push so far herself here, but for the sake of the woman in the elevator, she said: "Maybe you need to find different clients."

Miss Lightbridge cocked her head at this, in a way that made Ruby think she'd overstepped, but then she said: "You have someone in mind, Hillary?"

"Not a specific someone. But I *was* thinking we could—"

The phone rang. Not the one on Miss Lightbridge's desk that Ruby routed calls to, but the phone on the shelf behind her, the direct line that only one person ever called on. "Hello, Sydney," Miss Lightbridge said, answering on the second ring. "Can you hold on a moment?" Cupping her hand over the speaker, she dismissed Ruby: "Close the door on your way out?"

Sitting at her own desk a moment later, Ruby stared at the framed photo next to the blotter. It showed a handsome white boy in uniform. This was Tommy Benson, her imaginary long-distance boyfriend; she'd gotten his picture from a men's magazine and his job description from a *Life* article about the Communist threat in Indochina. Tommy was a Marine Security Guard, stationed at the American embassy in Saigon, in South Vietnam. Ruby—or rather, Hillary—hadn't seen him in person in nearly a year, but they spoke on the phone regularly. Tommy always called in the early evening (early morning, his time), which was why Hillary always needed to go straight home after work. The other girls at the agency sometimes teased her about this, but so far as Ruby could tell, none of them questioned Tommy's existence.

The only person who might have suspected was Miss Lightbridge, who had her own big secret. Most people assumed that Sydney Broadstreet was a man's name, but Ruby, who'd heard Sydney's voice the handful of times she'd called on the office phone, knew she was very much a woman. And because Miss Lightbridge's office wasn't as soundproof as it was supposed to be, Ruby also knew that she and Sydney often fought, passionately, like a married couple who loved and hated each other in equal measure.

Which wasn't Ruby's concern. Her concern, today, was figuring out how to get Miss Lightbridge to listen—really listen—to the idea that had just occurred to her.

What sort of clients would have no objection to hiring Negroes? Other Negroes, of course. The solution was obvious, if not without its problems—starting with the fact that Miss Lightbridge, like most white Chicagoans, regarded the South Side as no less foreign than Vietnam. And because of that, Ruby expected many South Side business owners would be hesitant to work with a white-run employment agency.

George Berry could probably help. She could drop by the Safe Negro Travel Company, see if he had any advice on which businesses to approach, and how. Though of course George would want to know why Ruby was asking, and what her connection to the Lightbridge Agency was. Visiting him as Hillary posed other challenges. Ruby would have to be clever, get her two selves working in tandem to bridge the race gap; she'd done it before.

But first she had to have a real talk with Miss Lightbridge. And judging by the muffled shouting she could hear from behind the closed office door, that conversation wasn't going to happen this morning.

Miss Lightbridge emerged from her office a few minutes later. To anyone else, she would have appeared lightly flustered, but Ruby understood immediately that today's fight with Sydney had been an especially bad one. "I have to go out," Miss Lightbridge said. "If anyone calls for me, tell them it's a family emergency."

"Do you know when you'll be back?"

"This afternoon, I hope."

"Don't forget Missy's party tonight."

"No danger of that," Miss Lightbridge said. And whether that was true or not, Ruby could tell that she had already forgotten what they'd talked about earlier.

This was going to take some work.

By five o'clock, Miss Lightbridge still hadn't returned to the office, so Ruby saw to locking up and got the girls organized and into cabs for the ride over to Smith's Tavern in Streeterville, where Miss Lightbridge had reserved a back room with a buffet and private bar.

There had been no problem with the reservation. Ruby had just made that up as an excuse to come in late this morning. Between that and the extra-full dose of potion she'd taken, she hoped to avoid having to run out of the party at an embarrassingly early hour—though unlike Cinderella, she knew she wasn't going to last until midnight.

It was almost nine by the time Miss Lightbridge appeared. By then, the bridal party had long since moved out into the main room of the tavern, the girls, Missy included, dancing with the other customers. When Miss Lightbridge came in, they all gathered around her, concerned about the "family emergency," but Miss Lightbridge raised her hands and assured them that everything was fine, just fine, she was sorry to be so late. Then she called for a glass of champagne and gave a long toast to Missy and her upcoming marriage that no one other than Ruby could have doubted was heartfelt. Everyone applauded when she was done. Miss Lightbridge gave Missy a big hug, and as the jukebox started up again, raised her hands once more, saying, no, no, she was *not* a dancer. Instead, she grabbed another drink from the bar—a double shot of vodka this time—and headed for the back booth where Ruby was sitting quietly with a glass of soda water.

"Not a fan of the jukebox selections?" Miss Lightbridge said, sliding in beside her.

"Not really," Ruby said. She studied Miss Lightbridge's face, which was as flushed as if she had been dancing. "You all right?"

"Not at all." Smiling cheerfully in Missy's direction, she knocked back the vodka in one throw, then added, still smiling: "What a waste."

"I don't know," Ruby said. "She seems happy enough. And she could still be a doctor. Medical school tuition shouldn't be a problem, with a banker for a husband."

"I'm more likely to become a doctor now than she is. He's forty-three years old, did you know that?"

"Her fiancé? Really?"

"Bob McDougal," Miss Lightbridge said, pronouncing it like the name of a disease. "A man who pursues a woman that much younger than he is has no interest in supporting her career ambitions. Trust me on that."

It sounded like there was a story there, and it occurred to Ruby that, in her current state, Miss Lightbridge might even be willing to share it. Not that she'd dream of asking. But thinking about that made her think of the first time she and Miss Lightbridge had shared a table, at lunch on that day when Hillary had come asking for advice. Ruby had been on guard there as well, choosing her questions with care, but still, up until dessert, the conversation had been freer and more open than any she and Miss Lightbridge had had since.

It was the job offer that had changed things, of course. Ruby had had many bosses who pretended to be her friend, and some of them might even have believed it, but to her that was self-evident nonsense, because how could you be friends with someone who could take away your livelihood on a whim?

And yet she did sometimes wonder what it might have been like if that lunch had gone differently, and Miss Lightbridge really had become her friend, the kind of friend she could ask any question, no matter how personal: About her past. About her relationship with Sydney Broadstreet and what that meant. About how it felt to be white all the time, to just take that for granted.

Put this foolishness out of your head, she admonished herself. You want to be someone's friend? Be a friend to that woman in the elevator today. Go home, get a good night's sleep, and spend the weekend figuring out how you and Hillary are going to convince Miss Lightbridge to start helping colored women find careers too.

She stole a glance at the watch on her wrist. Miss Lightbridge, perceptive as always even flushed with alcohol, noticed.

"Do you want to get out of here?" she said.

Ten minutes later, having slipped out of the tavern through the back door, they were walking west along a quiet avenue. Miss Lightbridge seemed to have a destination in mind, but Ruby, who sensed she had very little time left, was looking for a way to say goodnight and part company. The easiest thing would be to flag down a cab, but the ones she'd seen were all occupied.

"Miss Lightbridge," she finally said, "where are we going?"

"It's all right, Hillary," Miss Lightbridge replied. "You can call me Joanna. We're not at work."

You can still fire me off the clock, Ruby thought. "Joanna, where are we going?"

"To this little club I know. It's not far. Do you like jazz?"

"I'm fine with it. But Miss Lightbridge, Joanna, I can't go to a club tonight."

"Of course you can. It's Friday."

"I know that, but I've got to be up early tomorrow. I'm expecting—"

"A phone call from your boyfriend?" Miss Lightbridge stopped walking and turned to her, eyes brimming with secret knowledge. "Doesn't he usually ring you in the evening?" Her tone was playful, but the smile on her face added an edge to it, as if Ruby must be some kind of fool to think that Miss Lightbridge couldn't see through her.

"I can't go to a club tonight," Ruby repeated, unable to think of what else to say. "I'm sorry, but I can't."

And that was when Miss Lightbridge kissed her, full on the mouth. Miss Lightbridge was taller than she was, and the combination of surprise and momentum as she swooped in threw Ruby off balance, so that she had to put an arm around Miss Lightbridge to steady herself. Miss Lightbridge seemed to take that as a go signal; she wrapped both her arms around Ruby and tipped her back, the way a leading man in a movie might do.

Ruby just went with it at first, her thoughts a confused mix of What on earth? and Now what?, while her wide-open eyes looked past Miss Lightbridge's shoulder and scanned the street for witnesses. But they were on a dark stretch of sidewalk, between streetlamps, and there didn't seem to be anyone else around. Which probably wasn't a coincidence.

She felt a familiar tingle in her fingertips. Still looking over Miss Lightbridge's shoulder, she raised her right hand until she could see the blood welling up from under her fingernails. The change was starting.

She broke free of Miss Lightbridge's embrace then, the passion-
ate intensity of the clinch requiring her to use more force than she
intended. She ended up shoving Miss Lightbridge away, propelling her
backwards towards the curb, where she caught herself, on the brink of
falling, and looked at Ruby in shock, as if Ruby had slapped her without provocation. "I'm sorry," Ruby said, shocked as well. "I have to *go*."

And then she was running, down the street in the direction they'd
already been headed. She had gone no more than a dozen paces when
a telltale pulse and flex in her feet made her stop to take her shoes off.
She slipped off the right one without difficulty, but as she tugged off
the left her grip slipped and she ended up pitching the shoe backwards
at an angle, sending it clattering into the gutter near where Miss
Lightbridge still stood gaping at her.

No time to go back for it. Still holding the right shoe, Ruby took off
again. As she picked up speed, feet slapping the pavement, she raised
her left hand to the front of her dress. Her bra, which she'd bought
from a mail-order catalog, was a special kind that hooked in front, and
she'd practiced unhooking it on the move, pinching the clasp through
the fabric of her dress. She got it undone, and then, as her breasts
swelled and her torso began to thicken, she tugged sharply on the dress
itself, popping the threads on a pair of hidden pleats in the sides, giving
herself more breathing room. All of this without breaking stride.

She reached the corner of the block and turned right, hearing
Miss Lightbridge calling after her. Her hair had begun to coarsen and
curl, like a hot-comb job frizzing on a wet day. She didn't look in the
windows she ran past, but she knew what she'd see if she did: Hillary's
fair skin melting away like greasepaint, exposing Ruby's own much
darker hue.

Headed north now, she could see a brightly lit restaurant up ahead,
with occupied tables out on the sidewalk. But closer to hand, an alleyway beckoned; Ruby put on a final burst of speed and darted into it,
even as Miss Lightbridge rounded the corner behind her.

The alley dead-ended in a brick wall. But about halfway down on the left-hand side was a steel door that probably led into the restaurant kitchen, and lined up opposite it were a series of big dumpster bins. Stepping carefully around shards of broken bottle glass, Ruby made her way to the dumpsters and crouched in a narrow gap between two of them, trying to make herself as small as possible.

Footsteps echoed at the mouth of the alley. "Hillary?" Miss Lightbridge called. Ruby felt a tickle in her nose, and bit her lower lip to stop from sneezing. "Hillary?" Miss Lightbridge repeated. Then: "Damn it."

More footsteps, receding. Ruby stayed where she was until long after the sound had faded.

A QUESTION FOR THE REVEREND

⊰⊱

Cancer," Reverend Oxbow said.

"In my bone marrow," George told him. "At least that's where it started . . . I've been feeling run down for a while now, and then like a month ago I started getting these night sweats, and aching in my joints, and I found this weird bump on my shin bone." His left hand slipped beneath the table as he spoke and he rubbed at the protrusion below his knee, which felt like a pea-sized bit of gravel stuck to his skeleton. "So finally I went to see Doctor Blaylock. He ran some tests and gave me the bad news. I got six, eight months on the outside."

"And there's nothing they can do?"

"The short answer's no," George said. "The cancer's in my blood now, so they can't cut it out. They could try to poison it, with chemicals, and Doc says that might give me a few extra months, but I'd be sick as a dog, and I'd be giving up the month or two of relative good health I got left."

"I'm sorry, George," the reverend said. "You told Hippolyta yet?"

"No. You're the only person other than Doc Blaylock who knows. I'd like to keep it that way."

The reverend nodded. "I wondered why you wanted to meet me all the way down here." The diner they sat in was in Riverdale, some ten miles south of the Washington Park neighborhood where George and the reverend both lived and worked. "The way you sounded on the phone, I was worried you were going to confess to a crime."

"Well, don't quit worrying yet," George said. "I'm not done talking." He continued: "I don't consider myself a particularly courageous person. I like to think I'm a realist, though. I know I've got to die someday, and I've always known, being a colored man, it was going to take more than a little luck to get my full three score and ten. I was twelve years old the first time someone pointed a gun at my head, and there have been plenty of times since I've come close to getting killed. But this, this is different."

He paused. His hand went down to his shin bone, and then, coming back up, stopped to take his wallet from his pocket. He extracted a photograph from the billfold and carefully uncreased it before laying it on the table. It showed a young, light-skinned Negro woman standing on a boardwalk. A strong wind tugged at the hem of her skirt and whipped up whitecaps on the water behind her, and she was laughing, holding on to her hat with both hands to keep it from flying away.

"Viola Cobb," George said. "My fiancée, back in the day. This was years before I met Hippolyta," he explained. "Viola and I knew each other as kids in Tulsa. After the '21 massacre, both our families came up to Chicago, ended up living on the same block. We were boyfriend and girlfriend through most of high school, and she promised to wait for me while I went away to Howard." He looked down at the photo and smiled, sadly. "She was a beautiful girl. And smart. Not as smart as Hippolyta, but sharp. Ambitious, too, and with a real head for business—we'd have made a hell of a team if we'd got the chance.

"She lived just long enough for me to graduate college and propose. A week after I put the engagement ring on her finger, she got diagnosed. Cervical cancer." George shook his head. "I didn't even know what a cervix *was*." Beneath the table, his hand found the bump on his shin bone again. "It was a bad cancer, though, and it was fast. It killed her in just three months. But first it turned her into a different person. I don't know if it was the pain, or the drugs they gave her at the hospital, or if the cancer just got in her brain, but it's like all of her sweetness just curdled, and her intelligence, it turned into a weapon for cutting at people. And you couldn't hold it against her, you know—she was half out of her head, suffering so bad—but she'd *say* things, awful things, and I don't just mean to me. To her parents. To her sisters. To all our friends.

"After she passed, I mourned her a good long time—years, really. And while I did come to terms with losing her, I can't say I ever got past the memory of what the cancer did to her. That part of it still haunts me. And so like I say, I know we're all dust in the end, and my turn is bound to come, but I don't think I can face dying the way Viola did. Not like *that*."

"No?"

George tucked Viola's picture away and put the wallet back in his pocket. "Don't worry, Rev. I'm not planning to kill myself."

"OK." The reverend did not sound convinced. "What are you planning, then?"

"Well what I'd like," George said, "is to not die at all. To not have cancer."

"You want to pray for a miracle?"

"No, I already tried that. It's like my mother always said, what's the first two words that come to mind whenever you get bad news? 'Oh God.' And if He does see fit to send me a miracle, I won't refuse it, but respectfully, I'm not going to hold my breath on that."

"So what, then? If the doctors can't help you—"

"The doctors can't," George said, "but I know someone else who probably can."

"Who?"

"I'd rather not say his name. As for *what* he is, I got to ask you to indulge me here, because it's going to sound crazy. And I don't mind if you think that to yourself, but what I want, what I need, is your best moral counsel, based on the premise that it's *not* crazy."

The reverend looked perplexed, but he nodded. "I'm listening."

"The man I have in mind, he's a kind of magician."

"You talking about a faith healer?"

"He'd describe himself as the exact opposite of that, I imagine. A man of reason, not faith."

"A man of reason who does magic?"

"Like a scientist," George said. "They perform miracles, don't they? Or what seem like miracles."

"Sure, OK. But if a scientist said he could cure cancer, I wouldn't necessarily think that was crazy. And I don't know why you'd need moral counsel about it."

"Because the man I'm talking about isn't a good man," George said. "And I doubt he's going to help me for free."

"Now it sounds like you're talking about a faith healer again," the reverend observed. "The kind who cheats you out of your life savings."

"I'm not worried about being cheated. I got money to spare, but I don't think he'll want that. He is—he was—a rich man, and in his current circumstances, I can't see him having much use for cash. If he agrees to strike a bargain with me, I think he's going to want me to do something. Perform some service."

"Some service like what?"

"Well, that's my question to you," George said. "I haven't always been a good man either, but I try to be. I want to be. But I really don't want to die like this. So what am I allowed to do? What, what acts can I commit, to save myself?"

"What sins, you mean," the reverend said. "That's what we're talking about, right? You want to know what commandments you can break?"

"That's what I'm asking, yeah."

"All right," said the reverend. "Let me answer this way. I have a friend, Reverend La Farge, who's a chaplain at the university hospital in Hyde Park. A few years back, he and his wife took a holiday in the Holy Land, and he asked me to fill in for him while they were away.

"It was the afternoon and evening shift. I was the Protestant on call, and there was a priest, Father Donovan, who handled the Catholics— though sometimes we'd swap if we had a patient who cared more about complexion than theology, if you know what I'm saying. There was a rabbi, too, a Polish fellow named Janowski. The three of us would meet up in the cafeteria at the end of the shift. The first night, Donovan brought a bottle of wine, and after that, we took turns. It was nice, like our own little ecumenical after-hours club.

"Father Donovan was a great storyteller, especially after he had a couple drinks in him. The rabbi was a little more reserved, but friendly enough—he looked me in the eye when he spoke, so, you know, no problem. The one weird thing about him, though, is he wouldn't eat meat. At first I thought that was about keeping kosher, and I felt kind of bad for him, because we're talking hospital food, right? And I mean, even the meat's not that great, usually, but the rest of it—you got those nasty mashed potatoes from a box, canned fruits and vegetables, and maybe some scary Jell-O surprise for dessert.

"So one night we were drinking a little harder than usual—I'd brought bourbon instead of wine—and then Donovan gets up to use the restroom, so it's just me and the rabbi at the table. And I see he's only got mashed potatoes and boiled cabbage on his plate, which is a real shame, because that night they were serving these short ribs that weren't half bad. So I say to him, 'You know, Rabbi, these ribs are beef, not pork. I wouldn't want you to miss out.' And he looks at me and says, 'I appreciate your concern, but it's not what you're thinking. I just can't eat meat. Not since the war.'

"There was something in his eyes, when he said that—if I'd been sober, I'd have taken the hint and changed the subject. Instead I put my foot in it. 'What happened in the war?' I say. 'You get sick?' 'No, not sick,' he says. 'Hungry.' And he leans forward and pulls up his sleeve, and shows me the number tattooed on his arm. Which, of course— Jewish guy from Poland, right? What was I even thinking?

"And then, before I can back off and apologize, he tells me this story about how he was in a concentration camp. It was towards the end of the war. He'd spent most of the occupation hiding out, but someone he trusted betrayed him, a few months before the Russians showed up. The Germans knew they were losing by then, and they were determined to finish the job—they were gassing prisoners night and day, but their other big weapon was starvation. 'They didn't feed us,' the rabbi said. 'They didn't feed us, but it was a death camp. There is always food in a death camp, if a man is desperate enough.'"

"Jesus," George said.

"Yeah, I was kind of at a loss for words," Reverend Oxbow said. "You know, what's the etiquette when someone confesses to cannibalism? They didn't teach us that in seminary."

"So what did you say?"

"Nothing. I just sat there with my jaw flapping open while the rabbi went on talking. Only now it was more like he was reciting a catechism. 'It was a horrible thing,' he said, 'but it was necessary. God's law is clear: Life is the highest value. Any act that preserves life is not only permitted, but required. Only murder is forbidden. I did what was required. I survived. But I will never eat meat again.'

"And that was it. Father Donovan came back then, and two minutes later we were talking about football. I did wonder, after, why the rabbi had told me that story, but it wasn't too hard to figure out. He wasn't just telling me, he was telling himself, reminding himself why he'd done what he'd done. Which I imagine a man would have to, having gone through that. And that got me thinking about my own ancestors, in slavery, in the Middle Passage—God knows what they had to resort to, to get by. To make my life possible.

"So to get back to your question, I'd have to say I agree with the rabbi's catechism. God gave us the Commandments to live by, not to die by. If it's a matter of survival, you can break any and all of them, save one. So you tell me, George: You think this magician of yours is going to want you to kill somebody?"

"I don't know what he's going to want," George said. "But I won't agree to do that."

"I'm not just talking about murder one," the reverend said. "I think we should take manslaughter off the table, too. The thing about bad people, bad things tend to happen around them, and not just the ones they intend. So when you're deciding whether to perform this service, whatever it is, you want to give some thought to the ways it might go wrong, and who might get hurt if it does."

"Oh, I will. Believe me."

"You want to think about your family, too. Say you make a deal with this guy, and you end up disappointing him. What if he decides to take it out on Hippolyta, or Horace? Or what if they get dragged into it some other way?"

"Well," George said, "if he can cure my cancer, I got every incentive to not disappoint him. As for my family, the truth is, they're already involved. We've had dealings with this guy before. A couple years ago, he helped us out when my nephew Atticus got in trouble with this other magician."

"I'd love to hear that story."

"It's a long one. And it would *really* sound crazy. But the upshot is, while I got no illusions about this man's character, I trust him to deliver. Assuming I've got something he wants."

"OK," said the reverend. "It sounds like you know what you're getting into. Sounds like you've made up your mind, too. Like, maybe before I even got here."

"Maybe," George acknowledged. "Sorry if I brought you all this way for nothing."

"All part of the service. And I can still pray for you, you know. Never hurts."

"I'd appreciate that," George said.

OVER THE RAINBOW

It took Ruby a long time to get home. No cabs would stop for her. Bus drivers were less particular, thank goodness, but her disheveled appearance earned her some dirty looks from the other passengers. And she had to walk the last quarter mile, her bare feet aching every step of the way.

Home was a two-story townhouse in Hyde Park. The neighborhood was racially integrated by Chicago standards, but Ruby still felt more comfortable coming and going as Hillary after dark. She moved swiftly past the streetlamps, hoping none of her white neighbors were looking out.

When she came in sight of the townhouse, there was a man sitting on her front stoop. The stoop light was on, but the man had his head down, and the brim of his hat cast his face entirely in shadow. Ruby could think of only one person who would be waiting for her at this hour, though—and of course he would show up on a night when she was too tired to run anymore.

She came and stood outside the gate at the end of her front walk. "So you found a way back into the city," she said. "I wondered if you would."

Then the man looked up and raised a big brown hand to his head. He took off the hat, revealing the face, not of Caleb Braithwhite, but of Ruby's brother, Marvin, who lived in Massachusetts.

"Hey, Ruby," Marvin said. He smiled, and she saw that he was sporting a big bruise on his cheek. "Can I come inside?"

Marvin had contracted polio as a boy, and the disease had rendered his left arm permanently withered and weak. He could still be self-conscious about it in public, but with Ruby, who'd used to defend him against other children's teasing, he was able to relax. Once inside the house, he took off his suit jacket, unbuttoned his shirt, and rested his arm on the kitchen table while he used his good hand to smoke.

He was pretty banged up. Besides the facial bruise, Ruby could see blood spotting the front of his undershirt, and gauze wrapped tight around his ribs. "Cops," Marvin said, when she asked who'd done this to him, adding that there'd been trouble over the rainbow, which to anyone who didn't know him well would have sounded like evidence of a concussion.

"Over the Rainbow," Ruby said. "That's that club you go to?"

Marvin nodded. "Dorothy and all her friends are there. It's in this old brick building in an industrial part of town. Place used to be a foundry, I think. There's no sign on the door, but a few of the bricks on the street side are painted yellow, so newcomers can find it."

"Follow the yellow brick road?"

"Yeah. Vice squad knows it's there, of course, but they're supposed to be taken care of. Only this week, I guess, someone didn't get their bribe, or maybe they're trying to negotiate a higher rate. They raided the place just before midnight." He touched the bruise on his cheek. "Came in swinging."

"They arrest you?"

He nodded again. "Usually they give you the option, you know, pay a 'fine' on the spot to avoid getting booked. Trouble was, one of the cops recognized me as a reporter. The *Afro-American*'s been running this series about police brutality, and you can guess how much they love that . . . They took my stay-out-of-jail money and locked me up anyway. Beat on me some more for good measure. Then around three in the morning, they called the paper's publisher at home, told him where I was, and why."

"And he *fired* you?" Ruby said. Not surprised, but outraged.

"It's a family newspaper." Marvin shrugged, wincing as he did so. "Anyway, by the time I got myself bailed out, my landlord had heard, too. Came home to find an eviction notice on my door."

"I'm so sorry, Marvin." Remembering how hard it had been for him, passing up a job offer at the *Chicago Defender* and moving out east instead, mostly to put some distance between himself and Momma and her endless attempts to set him up with "the right girl," a good Christian woman who would fix him.

"It's not all bad news," Marvin said. "I still got some people in my corner—my editor, for one. He can't rehire me, but he thinks he can help find me a job at another paper."

"Where at?"

"California, most likely. If it does work out, it might not be right away, though, so would it be OK with you if I—"

"Stay here? Sure, as long as you like. There's plenty of room."

"I can see that." Marvin grinned. "I was going to ask how you were doing, but I guess I don't have to, if you can afford a place like this. That place you've been working at, what's it called, the Lighthouse Agency?"

"Light*bridge*."

"They must pay you pretty well."

"They do. Or at least they did, until tonight."

"What happened tonight?"

"You'll love this," Ruby said. "My boss? Miss Lightbridge? She kissed me."

"Yeah?" His expression turned sly. "You kiss her back?"

"I ran away."

"You know that's not uncommon, the first time."

"Well, there's not going to be a second time."

"That's not uncommon either, to tell yourself that. But—"

"I'm not just saying it," Ruby insisted. "Miss Lightbridge and me getting together, there's no way on earth that could work out well. Which means I'm probably going to get fired on Monday."

"You got money socked away, if that happens?" Marvin asked, concerned now. "The rent on this place must be huge."

"I've got plenty of savings, don't worry about that. As for rent, I don't pay any."

"You're telling me you *own* this place? Has this got anything to do with whatever scheme got Letitia that house that she's living in? And if so, is there still a chance for *me* to get in on it?"

"You wouldn't want to get involved. Believe me."

"Well, I'd like to hear the details, at least," Marvin said. "Just to judge for myself."

"It's complicated." Ruby hesitated, considering how much of the truth she could share with him, some part of her thinking, All of it, and recognizing, in that thought, how lonely she'd become. "You know it's funny, you showing up at my door like this," she said. "There's this secret I've been keeping, a big secret, the kind that makes you feel cut off from everyone who doesn't know it, which in my case is everyone. And I've been dying to let someone in on it, just so I can talk it over, you know? But most folks wouldn't believe me if I told them, and the ones who would—like Letitia—wouldn't understand."

Marvin nodded. "I'm familiar with that type of situation. But your secret—it's not the thing with Miss Lightbridge."

"No," Ruby said. "But it's one of the reasons Miss Lightbridge and me aren't happening. She'd *never* understand. But I think maybe you might."

"I'm all ears."

"You remember three summers ago, Letitia, Atticus, and George Berry came out to Massachusetts, and they stopped by your place?"

"Sure, I remember," Marvin said. "They were headed for this weird little village, Ardham, in the woods up near the New Hampshire border. Atticus's father had disappeared up there, and they were going to get him back. Which they did, but when they stopped by again on their way home, they wouldn't say a word about what had happened. Whatever they'd been through, I could tell they felt lucky to have gotten out alive."

"They were lucky," Ruby said. "But it wasn't over. Ardham belongs to this family, the Braithwhites—rich white folks, the kind whose ancestors came over on the *Mayflower*. The heir to the family fortune, Caleb Braithwhite, followed Atticus and the others back to Chicago."

"What for?"

"The Braithwhites are part of this secret society, with chapters all over the country. Ordinarily the different chapters don't get along, but Caleb had this master plan to bring them all together, under his rule. Thing was, the head of the Chicago chapter, a guy named Lancaster, thought *he* should be the man in charge. So Braithwhite pretended to back him, with the idea that he'd double-cross him when the time came."

"And how do you come into this?"

"Lancaster was a police captain, among other things," Ruby explained. "He had eyes all over the city, and he was smart enough not to trust Braithwhite. So Braithwhite needed a confederate, someone Lancaster didn't know about, and who he might not think to suspect even if he did."

"The help," Marvin guessed. "What were you, Braithwhite's maid?"

"Not his maid, no. So far as anyone else knew, there was no connection between us at all. But *a* maid, yeah, that was one of my disguises."

"What were the others?"

"We'll come to that," Ruby said. "My deal with Braithwhite was, I'd help him for as long as it took to topple Lancaster—six months, maybe a year. Once Braithwhite had his crown, he'd sign over this house to me."

Marvin let out a low whistle. "Generous."

"You wouldn't say that if you'd met Lancaster or his people. It was danger pay, and I earned every penny of it."

"So what happened?"

"Braithwhite's double-cross came off as planned. Pretty much. Lancaster and his whole chapter ended up dead." One of them by my hand, she didn't say, seeing Hillary standing in the snow with a gun. "But by then I'd realized, I couldn't let Braithwhite win, either. So after he double-crossed Lancaster, we double-crossed him."

"We?"

Ruby nodded. "We had our own little secret society going, at the end. There was me; Atticus and his father, Montrose; George and Hippolyta and their son, Horace; some Masons from Montrose and George's lodge; and—"

"Letitia?"

"Yeah, 'Titia too. It's a long story, and even now, I'm the only one who knows all of it. I never told the others the whole truth about my relationship with Braithwhite. I was too ashamed." Ruby paused. "And too selfish. We didn't kill Braithwhite," she continued. "There's times I wish we had, but we didn't. We *banished* him, ran him out of Chicago in such a way that he could never return. So I was free of him, but because I'd broken our deal, I never got title to this house."

"But you're still here," Marvin said.

"Yeah, I am . . . The first time I came back, after that night I betrayed him, it was just to collect my things, take a last look around. But then a few days later, I came back again, and then again the day after that . . ."

"Why?"

"I'm coming to it," she said. "Every time I *did* come back, I expected to find the locks changed. Braithwhite might be banished, but he's still got his money, and lawyers. No reason he couldn't keep me out if he wanted to. But a whole year went by, and nothing changed—my key still worked, and nobody else moved in. Eventually I got tired of wasting money on cab fare and decided to move back in myself. Even then, I hung on to my old apartment awhile, just in case."

"But nothing happened."

"Not yet, no. It's two and a half years now that Mr. Braithwhite's been gone. There's days I almost forget, and think this house really is mine."

"Maybe he forgot, too," Marvin suggested. "Decided to let bygones be bygones."

"Yeah, I tried to convince myself of that," Ruby said. "You know how in stories sometimes, there's a villain who's so smooth and likable you almost don't notice how bad they are, except now and then when they let the mask slip? That's Mr. Braithwhite: evil, but nice about it. So I tried telling myself that maybe he wasn't mad, maybe he even *admired* me for being clever enough to put one over on him. And maybe, because of that, he decided to hold up his end of the bargain after all, and just let the rest go." She shook her head. "But in my heart I don't believe it. Mr. Braithwhite isn't the type to let things go. And he doesn't forget." She looked up at the ceiling light. "Rent's not the only thing I don't pay here. I've never seen a power or water or phone bill, either."

"That could still be lawyers, acting on autopilot. You think a rich man pays his own bills?"

"It's not lawyers. It's Braithwhite. He knew that if he left the house open, I'd come back here. Which means he wants me here, which means he's not done with me. Not done with any of it, maybe."

Marvin frowned. "Then why stay? If he's as evil as you say—"

"This part's easier if I show you," Ruby said, making a decision. "We need to go downstairs."

"To the basement? What for?"

"It's not a what," Ruby told him. "It's a who."

THE WINTHROP HOUSE

⌘

The ghost who answered the door at the Winthrop House wasn't the one George had come to see.

"Evening, Mr. Fox," George said. "I hope it's not too late."

Celia's father made no response, his red-rimmed eyes looking through George rather than at him. He had a shaving cut under his chin that had crusted over and left a line of dried blood down to the hollow of his throat. His sweat-stained shirt was misbuttoned. He reeked of alcohol, the smell of gin not only on his breath but exuding from his pores.

"Mr. Fox?" George prompted, gently.

The red eyes struggled to focus. "I know you?" Mr. Fox said, his voice a low rasp.

"It's George Berry, Mr. Fox. We've met. I'm a friend of Letitia's."

"'Titia's not here. Nobody is." Seeming to include himself in the latter statement.

"I know 'Titia's away," George said. "I spoke to her on the telephone earlier tonight, and she asked me to come over and take care of something for her." He had a more detailed cover story prepared, but guessed now he wouldn't need it. By the time he finished speaking, Mr. Fox's eyes had glazed over again. The man turned and walked off without another word, leaving the door ajar.

George came inside and stood in the Winthrop House's central atrium, a two-story space roofed with a skylight. Archways to the left and right opened into the dining room and a large parlor. Mr. Fox had retreated to the former, taking a seat in front of a chessboard that was set up at one end of the dining table. A quart bottle of gin rested beside the chessboard; George recognized the label, having grown familiar with that particular brand during his mourning of Viola Cobb. As awful as that loss had been, he could only imagine how much worse the death of a child would be. He thought of Horace out west with his mother and prayed they were both safe; but the face that appeared in his mind's eye wasn't his son's, but that of Viola in the torment of her last days.

He turned his attention to the atrium's centerpiece: a large marble fountain featuring a bronze statue of Hecate, three-faced goddess of the moon. This was a tribute to Hiram Winthrop's late wife, a literal witch who had aided him in his research. Letitia, who found it hideous, had at first wanted to tear the whole fountain out and reclaim the floor space, but as part of her détente with Winthrop's ghost, she had agreed to leave it be, only clothing Hecate's nakedness to avoid offending her tenants' sensibilities. A house tradition had evolved where the statue's costume changed with the holidays. For Halloween, Hecate wore black and a traditional pointy hat; in December, she became a three-faced Santa; for Valentine's, she put on pink satin and showed a hint of cleavage. Tonight, in a nod to the Fourth of July, she was dressed as Lady Liberty, in a mint-green gown and cardboard crown. An American flag hung from one of the torches she held in her hands, while the other torch stood free, a beacon to the huddled masses.

According to Letitia, Winthrop had no problem with this dress-up game, no matter how undignified the costumes became. His only rule was that the statue's three pairs of eyes must always remain uncovered. George felt the forward-facing pair observing him now, with far more attention than Mr. Fox had mustered, and he knew this wasn't just his imagination. Winthrop's spirit had full run of the house, but the source of his remaining power was buried somewhere below it, and by projecting his soul up through the base of the statue he could focus that power, to monitor comings and goings on the property—and, if necessary, defend it. "Better than any guard dog," Letitia had said.

George approached the marble ring of the fountain with his hands clasped in front of him. "Evening, Mr. Winthrop," he said. The words came out louder than he'd intended, and he threw a quick glance towards the dining room, but Mr. Fox, busy pouring, showed no sign of having heard him. He turned back to the statue and continued in a lower voice: "I'm George Berry, Mr. Winthrop. I'm sure you've seen me around the house before. I have a special request I'd like to make of you, if you'd be kind enough to grant me an audience." He paused, nervous, not sure how this was supposed to work. The absurd thought struck him that perhaps he should toss a coin or some other offering into the fountain.

But before he could do that or anything else, he heard the rattle of an iron gate beneath the gallery that ran along the back of the atrium. Sidestepping, George looked past the fountain at the Winthrop House elevator, the car waiting like an open maw to receive him.

THE WOMAN IN
THE BASEMENT

⊰⊱

I never pictured Snow White as a redhead," Marvin said.

They were in the basement, standing before a glass coffin. Equal parts casket and cold case, it rested atop a gray metal pedestal whose exposed piping was coated with ice; fingers of frost extended up the metal latticework of the coffin, but the glass panels remained free of condensation and offered a clear view of the woman inside. She lay with her eyes closed, head on a red satin pillow, red satin sheets drawn up over her body, leaving only her right arm exposed.

"Her name's Delilah," said Ruby. "She worked for the Braithwhites, in Ardham."

"How'd she end up in this?"

"Mr. Braithwhite said she got hit in the head. He didn't say how, but I think it must have happened when Letitia and the others were trying to escape."

"So is this like her punishment? For messing up?"

"He said he did it to save her. She was in a coma, slipping away, and he didn't know the right spells to heal her. So he put her on ice."

"Well, if she looks this good after three years in a box, I guess he did something right." Marvin glanced at the thick cable that snaked from the pedestal to a junction box on the wall. "Might be another reason he kept the power on." He turned his attention to the silver cuff around Delilah's right forearm; a coiling glass tube with a red thread at its center connected it to a spigot on the side of the coffin. "Is that . . ."

"Her blood." Ruby nodded, and a look of disgust crossed her face.

"Is that an ingredient? In the potion?"

"That's what he said. I try not to think about it."

"And you *really* turn into her?"

"You don't believe it."

"I trust you," Marvin said. "But if you weren't keeping a white lady in your basement, I'd be a *little* skeptical. And I'd still like to see it for myself."

"I'll show you," Ruby promised. "But not tonight. I got to conserve." She went over to an industrial refrigerator in another corner of the basement and opened the door. The space inside was mostly empty, but towards the bottom were a few glass shelves holding small vials of red elixir. "This was full, when Braithwhite went away. I had more than a thousand doses. Down to just a hundred forty-seven, now. I *should* still have closer to four hundred, but . . ." She nodded at the empty space.

"What happened?"

"It was maybe a month ago. I'd just come down and got my daily dose, and I don't know if I slammed the door too hard, or what, but one of the empty shelves up top came loose. It knocked loose the one under it, which knocked loose the one under that, and then it was like, elevator going down. Full shelves near the bottom broke the fall, but I lost more than half my supply." She shook her head, grimacing. "Neighbors a block away must have heard me screaming.

"I mopped up as much of the spill as I could," she continued, "and strained the broken glass out of it. But God knows if it's still good. I got it in a jug in the refrigerator upstairs, for when I get desperate."

Marvin squatted down for a closer look at the vials, and Ruby tensed, worried he'd pick one up and drop it. But he seemed to sense her apprehension and kept his hands to himself. "Each of these little bottles is a dose?" he asked.

"Yeah."

"How long does it last, when you take it?"

"A full dose is good for ten hours, usually. Sometimes twelve."

"Ten to twelve? It varies that much?"

"Some of the bottles are a little fuller than others," Ruby said. "It seems like it lasts longer on an empty stomach, too, so days I think I might run late, I don't eat lunch. The girls at the office think I'm dieting to preserve my figure, which in a way is true."

"What if you take less than a full dose?" Marvin asked. "You tried that?"

"Yeah, sure. There's like four teaspoons in a bottle. I need to take at least one teaspoon to get any effect at all—that's good for maybe an hour, hour and a half. Two teaspoons, that's four hours, maybe five."

"Enough for a half day."

"Well, but remember, I got to get to and from the office, too. I can't just change on the street." At least I try not to, she thought. "If I'm *sure* I'm working a half day, sometimes I'll take three teaspoons, save what's left. But that makes me nervous, because then I got to mix leftovers from different bottles, and I'm not sure if I'm supposed to do that."

"And you don't know how to make more? Braithwhite never taught you the formula?"

"No," Ruby said. "I don't know if he ever planned to, but we never got that far." She gestured for Marvin to get up then, and shut the refrigerator door.

"So what's it like?" Marvin asked, looking back at the coffin. "Being her?"

Ruby barked laughter. She felt like she could talk all night and not come close to conveying the experience of being Hillary. But she had thought about it. She said: "Do you still read the *Defender*?"

Marvin nodded. "Still got my weekly subscription."

"So you know Langston Hughes's column? Those stories he tells, about his friend Simple?"

Another nod. "One of my favorite parts of the paper."

"Mine too," Ruby said. "So there was this one story from a while ago, the punchline really stuck with me. Langston says something like, 'If I were white, no matter how much I loved Negroes, I don't think I'd volunteer to be discriminated against just to prove that I loved them.' And Simple says, 'If I were white, I wouldn't do that either.' And Langston says, 'Well, you wouldn't be a very good person, then.' And Simple says, 'Yeah—but at least I'd be white.'

"That's what it's like," Ruby told him, looking at the coffin too now. "I know it's wrong, to keep her in there. If I could let her out without killing her, I'd do it. At least I hope I would. But if I did, or if Mr. Braithwhite ever found a way to heal her, this would all be over. No more new potion doses, and even the ones I already had probably wouldn't work anymore. So this, what I've been doing, it was never really meant to last forever. To even wish that it could is a sin. And every time I take a dose, that's a sin too, because it *does* make me wish that.

"But when I'm out in the world as her, walking down the street, or in a store, and white people smile at me? Or better yet, when they don't notice me at all, because I'm just, normal? It's worth it. I'm not a good person, I'm a sinner, but at least I get to be white."

"We're all sinners," Marvin countered. "And you're a good person in my book. You always looked out for me."

"That was before," Ruby said. "I'm a damn monster, now. A blood-drinking vampire."

"You're *human*, Ruby." He put his good arm around her, and the feel of that contact, *human* contact with someone who might actually be capable of understanding her, nearly made her swoon. "You know," her brother continued, "you're not the first person to walk a crooked path to seem normal in the eyes of the world. Though I'll grant that your method is unorthodox."

"Yeah, well," Ruby said, swiping water from her eyes. "With a hundred forty-seven doses, I won't be doing it much longer."

"Unless you figure out how to make more." Marvin craned his head around. "What's in those filing cabinets over there?"

"Those? Those are Mr. Braithwhite's files. Research for his master plan . . . There's information about the Winthrop House, Lancaster and his people, and the other chapters of the Order."

"Nothing about the potion?"

"No. Nothing about magic at all. I checked."

"You mind if I take a look?"

"You're welcome to," Ruby said, "but you won't find anything."

"We'll see about that," said Marvin.

PARLEY WITH A DEAD MAN

⊰⊱

As George approached the elevator, he saw a flickering red light shining up through the gap between the elevator shaft and the car.

Under other circumstances, this might have given him pause. His brother and his nephew had never shared the details of their own parley with Winthrop's ghost, though even tight-lipped Montrose would probably have mentioned a lake of fire. But if it turned out he did have to swim through flames to avoid sharing Viola's fate, George was ready to do that. Or so he told himself.

As soon as he stepped inside, the iron gate slid shut and the elevator car began to descend. George turned and watched the atrium vanish from view. A moment later the car passed the basement—a dark, musty space where servants had once lived—without stopping. The red light, no longer flickering, grew brighter.

When the car came to a halt, George found himself staring into a broad cube with walls of concrete. The source of the red light turned out to be a large square of glass set into the floor, and a matching square in the ceiling above. The glass was frosted, which both diffused the light and concealed the exact nature of its origin, but the setup reminded George of an old science-fiction story in which the villain—was it Ming the Merciless?—had made petitioners to the throne state their case while standing in a disintegration chamber. He wondered what would happen if Mr. Winthrop decided his time was being wasted.

Better to die fast than slow, George thought. He stepped boldly from the elevator, only flinching a little when the gate rattled shut behind him, trapping him in the cube.

Set flush into the wall to his left was a metal rectangle the size and shape of a door, but with no handle or visible hinges. A smaller rectangle in the right-hand wall suggested a dumbwaiter hatch. Hanging on the wall directly opposite the elevator was a painted portrait of Hiram Winthrop. He was standing in a bookshelf-lined study, the deft use of perspective giving both the room and Winthrop himself a distinctly three-dimensional appearance. Beneath the painting was a metal cabinet with a keyboard on its front that George recognized as a teletype machine. So that's how we communicate, he thought.

But when he stepped up to the keyboard, he was surprised to discover that the keys were blank: unmarked black circles. George knew how to touch type, but he wondered how this was supposed to work with people, like Montrose, who didn't. Setting the question aside with a shrug, he raised his hands. But before his fingers could find the home row, the keys began to depress on their own. With a chugging sound, a sheet of printout paper emerged from a slot at the top of the cabinet, bearing the message:

STATE YOUR BUSINESS

George took a step back and raised his eyes to the figure in the painting. "Hello, Mr. Winthrop," he said. "As I told you upstairs, I'm George Berry. My brother is Montrose Turner, and he and his son, Atticus, struck a bargain with you a couple years back, regarding Caleb Braithwhite. I'm sure you remember—"

The clatter of the teletype interrupted him. He looked down to see the same message repeated, more emphatically:

STATE. YOUR. BUSINESS.

Straight to the point, George thought. Which was fine with him. Dropping the solicitous tone, he said: "I have cancer. Without a cure, I'll be dead in less than a year. My doctor can't help me. But I think you can. Am I right about that?"

A short burst of keystrokes, George unsure whether he heard three or just two. But the ink on the page read:

YES

Suddenly light-headed, George gripped the cabinet with both hands to steady himself. Thank God, he thought. Oh thank God.

As he regained his composure, the teletype added a postscript:

I AM NOT A CHARITY

"I understand," George said nodding. "I didn't expect you'd save my life for free. What do you want in exchange?"

The teletype chattered for more than a minute this time. As line after line appeared on the paper without pause or hesitation, George realized that Mr. Winthrop had been waiting a long while for someone desperate enough to ask him that question.

LIKE PRINCE CHARMING

⚜

When Ruby looked out her bedroom window the next morning, Miss Lightbridge was standing on the sidewalk in front of the house like Prince Charming, holding Hillary's lost shoe in her hand. For a confused moment Ruby wondered how the woman had tracked her here, but then she remembered the employment forms on file at the agency; she'd listed the townhouse as her home address even before she'd moved back in, figuring it might raise questions to have Hillary living in her old neighborhood.

There was no sign of a cab on the street, and Ruby realized that Miss Lightbridge must have been standing there for a while, trying to get up the courage to ring the bell. She considered waiting to see if Miss Lightbridge would lose her nerve and walk away, but that didn't seem likely, and anyway she needed to deal with this. Deal with it as who, was the real question.

Not going to waste a potion on my day off, she decided, somewhat impulsively. She dressed quickly, from her Ruby wardrobe, and hustled downstairs. She came out the front door just as Miss Lightbridge was letting herself through the gate.

"Can I help you?" Ruby said. She came down the walk the way Hillary would, confident, a woman on her own property, secure in her right to be here. She stopped just inside the half-open gate and looked Joanna Lightbridge in the eye.

"I'm sorry," Miss Lightbridge said, glancing up at the house. "I think I may have the wrong address."

"You looking for Hillary Hyde?"

"Yes. Is she . . ."

"Still sleeping."

"Ah," Miss Lightbridge said, clearly at a loss. When you saw a colored person come out of a white person's house, the natural first assumption was that they were the help, but Ruby wasn't acting like a maid. "And you are . . . ?"

"Hillary's friend. Ruby Dandridge."

"Her friend," Miss Lightbridge said.

"Yes. We're very close." Imagining herself as Hillary when she said this—imagining it strongly, as if she could enact the transformation through will alone. You know me, Ruby thought. I've worked for you for more than two years. And no, we're not friends, but if you recognize me now, maybe we still could be.

But the recognition taking shape in Miss Lightbridge's head was of a different nature. "You . . . live here with her."

"Yes, I do. We've always lived together."

"I see." Breaking eye contact, Miss Lightbridge glanced at the shoe in her hand, as if wondering how she'd come to be holding it. "Hillary dropped this on her way out of the party last night," she said after a moment.

"Well it's very nice of you to return it," Ruby said, plucking the shoe from Miss Lightbridge's grasp. "I'll make sure she gets it."

Miss Lightbridge looked up at the house again. Hoping, perhaps, to glimpse Hillary's face in one of the windows.

"Is there something else?" Ruby asked.

"No," Miss Lightbridge said. "But please tell Hillary . . . Tell her I hope to see her on Monday."

She walked away swiftly. Ruby watched her go, then shut the gate and went back up the walk, trying to decide how she felt about what had just happened.

Back inside the house, she heard her brother moving around upstairs. She went up and dropped off the shoe in her room, then went to the back bedroom where Marvin had been sleeping. He was in the attached bathroom with the door closed. She called his name, but he must not have heard her over the sound of running water in the sink.

She looked around the bedroom aimlessly, her mind still on the encounter with Miss Lightbridge. Marvin had made up his bed already. An accordion file folder rested on the coverlet. Ruby's gaze drifted to the wastebasket beside the bed and paused there, caught by a splash of red. She stepped closer. There was a jumble of gauze in the basket, and sitting on top of it was a thick gauze pad that was soaked with blood. "Good Lord, Marvin," Ruby said. "You getting a monthly?"

She picked up the basket and went over and knocked on the bathroom door. "Marvin?" No answer. She tried the knob, but the door was locked. She knocked again. "Marvin!"

The water in the sink shut off. Marvin opened the door. "Easy, Ruby," he said, stifling a yawn. "I'm still waking up, here."

"What is this?" she said, holding up the wastebasket. "Did someone cut you?"

"Road rash," Marvin said. "Or cell block rash, I guess. I fell down with my hands cuffed, going into the lockup, and got dragged up these cement steps. Scraped off a bunch of skin."

"Let me see." She reached for his top shirt button, but he shoved her hand away, saying, "Leave it be, I just got it wrapped up again."

"We should get you to a doctor."

"I don't need a doctor. It's not that bad."

"Yeah, that's why you got your ribs all bound up like a mummy, because it's not that bad."

"I'll be fine, Ruby."

She stared at him, lips pursed. After a moment, she said: "At least your face looks better this morning. I can hardly see the bruise at all." She reached up again, meaning to tilt his face towards the light, but he moved past her and went over to the bed.

"I found something last night, after you turned in," he said, opening the flap on the folder.

"That was in the filing cabinets?"

"Behind them."

"Behind them?"

"Yeah," Marvin said, "I had some other folders stacked on top of the cabinets to sort through, and one slipped down the back. When I went to get it I saw this was back there too." He extracted a sheet of paper from the folder and offered it to her. "I thought this was interesting. Look familiar?"

A diagram on the paper showed top-down and side views of a human figure lying on an altar-like platform. There was a small wound on the figure's right arm, and the side view showed a thin line of blood running down a grooved channel and dripping into a chalice. The margins around the diagram were filled with notations in a mix of what looked like French and another, more exotic language. "I don't recognize this other alphabet," Marvin commented.

"I do," Ruby said. "It's called the language of Adam. Sorcerers like Mr. Braithwhite use it in their spells. What else is in the folder?"

"Letters." Marvin showed her a sheaf of onionskin pages. "These are copies of a correspondence between your Mr. Braithwhite and someone named Alice Mandragora in the rare books archive of the Sorbonne Library. I think they're talking about your potion."

Ruby looked at the top sheet of onionskin. The letter was typewritten, in French. "You understand French?"

"*Un peu,*" Marvin said, holding his thumb and forefinger a hairsbreadth apart. "Last year, my editor was talking about sending someone to Paris to do a profile on Josephine Baker and some other Negro expats. I wanted the gig, and figured I'd have a better shot if I could at least fake knowing the language."

"You never told me about this."

"There was nothing to tell. Publisher killed the idea as soon as he found out how much the trip was going to cost. But I'd already bought a Berlitz book and some records by then, so . . . Anyway, I'll need a French-English dictionary to puzzle this out, but I recognize the words for 'blood,' and 'metamorphosis.' And they talk a lot about *le livre des noms*—'the book of names.' Does that ring any bells?"

"Yeah," Ruby said. "It's the title of a magic book, written in the language of Adam. Mr. Braithwhite and his friends got their hands on the oldest known copy."

"Where is it now?" Marvin asked.

"Destroyed. We took it from Mr. Braithwhite, right before we banished him. And Abdullah Muhammad—you know, Percy Jones, from high school, the one who converted to Islam?—he took the book and burned it."

"That's too bad," said Marvin. "I'd like to have seen that." Then, turning his attention back to the letters: "So can I borrow your library card after breakfast?"

AN APPEAL TO THE LODGE

George spent the early morning on the phone, reaching out to a few of the brothers in his Prince Hall Freemasons lodge and reserving an hour at the Masonic temple for a special meeting. This venue wasn't strictly necessary—George could have just invited them over to the apartment—but he felt that the sanctum might add extra weight to his appeal.

They gathered at noon. George stood beside the temple altar, facing an audience of three: "Pirate" Joe Bartholomew, the one-eyed lodgemaster; Abdullah Muhammad, aka Percy Jones, the lodge secretary; and Mortimer Dupree, who held no special office but who, like Joe and Abdullah, had been involved in some of George's previous adventures and had helped banish Caleb Braithwhite from Chicago. George thought that Mortimer would be the easiest of the trio to enlist in his cause, while he expected the greatest resistance from Abdullah. But it was Joe's response that he judged most crucial: the lodgemaster commanded enough respect to bring the other two along, but he was also the only one among them who stood any chance of changing George's mind.

George began by thanking them for coming on short notice and then launched into his appeal. He'd spent the balance of the morning rehearsing what he would say, but things started going off the rails almost immediately, for as soon as he shared the news of his cancer, the brothers interrupted to offer condolences and pledge their support.

"If this is about medical bills, George," Pirate Joe said, "you know the whole lodge will help out with that." Mortimer nodded fervently in agreement, and Abdullah added: "You don't need to worry about your family, either. Whatever happens, we'll look out for Hippolyta and Horace."

George hadn't anticipated this reaction and was genuinely moved by it, but even as he blinked back tears, another part of him was anxious to stay on track. "Brothers," he said, holding up his hands. "Brothers, I'm grateful, from my heart I'm grateful, but it's not a matter of money. It's more complicated than that." They fell silent and George thought to himself, State your business. "I had a parley with Hiram Winthrop's ghost last night. He told me he can save my life. But I need to do something for him in return, and that, that's what I called you here for."

He paused, eyeing Abdullah. But it was Mortimer who spoke up first: "There's a cure for cancer?"

George nodded. "Some kind of spell. He didn't tell me exactly what—"

"My grandma Estelle has cancer," Mortimer said. "In her pancreas. Do you think Mr. Winthrop would cure her too?"

And George just stood there, mouth open, not having anticipated this either.

Now Abdullah chimed in: "Men like Mr. Winthrop don't do two-for-one deals. Isn't that right, George?"

"I . . . don't know," George said. "Mortimer, I'm real sorry about your grandma, but I went to Mr. Winthrop to get help for me. I didn't even think to ask about anyone else."

"What does he want, in exchange for your cure?" Pirate Joe asked. "It must be something big, if you need our help."

State your business, George thought. Straight to the point.

"A body," he said. "He wants me to steal him a body." He removed the sheet of printout from his back pocket and unfolded it. It was a shopping list of sorts, but with only one item on it, described in exacting detail. "'An adult Caucasian male, deceased no more than seventy-two hours, with all limbs and extremities intact. No gross deformities. Skin of the torso unblemished by cuts, scars, burns, large birthmarks, or tattoos of any kind. Uncircumcised . . .' There's more, about the permissible causes of death, but the short version is, it needs to be something obvious that didn't require an autopsy and left the internal organs more or less in the right place."

He refolded the paper and once more eyed Abdullah.

"I know you're expecting me to raise a religious objection to body snatching," Abdullah said, reading his mind. "But I'm going to have to disappoint you."

"You saying you don't have a problem with this?" George asked.

"I've got all kinds of problems with it. It's sinful and obscene. Illegal, too—and if the cops catch us? Stealing a white man's body? They're going to beat us all bloody and put our pictures in the paper." Abdullah shrugged. "But weighed against saving a human life, none of that matters. Not in the eyes of Allah.

"But what does matter," he continued, "is what happens after. Let's say we do this, and Winthrop delivers on your cure. Then what? I mean, from the description, it's not hard to guess what he wants the body for."

"No, it isn't," George agreed. "He wants to resurrect himself. And before, not after. He says he needs to be corporeal, to cast the spell that'll cure me."

"So, payment up front. And if your cure doesn't work, tough luck."

"I'm not so worried about that part," George said. "The man did survive his own murder, after all. So if he says he can cure cancer, I'm inclined to believe it. But as for what he's going to do with a new life of his own—that I can't speak to."

"Oh yes you can," Abdullah said. "You know what kind of man he is, George. We all do."

"How is this resurrection supposed to work, exactly?" Pirate Joe interrupted. "We bring the body to the Winthrop House?"

"Packingtown," George said. "There's a warehouse there, near the stock yards, that Winthrop used as a workshop for some of his experiments. Place is still in his name, and it's got wards on it to keep out burglars. I'm supposed to bring the body there, and then there's this whole other sheet of instructions for what happens next. But you don't have to be a part of that."

"We are a part of it, though," Abdullah said. "We help you turn this guy loose on the world, we're accountable for anything he does. And," he repeated, "you know what kind of man he is."

"I do," George acknowledged. "I was up all last night, wrestling with that. Coming up with every argument I could think of, for why it might be OK. Like, he gets on with Letitia all right. And he did help us get rid of Caleb Braithwhite."

"He didn't help us out of the goodness of his heart. He did it for revenge, because Braithwhite's father was the one who killed him. And he did it because Montrose gave him back his stolen notebooks. As for Letitia, sure, he's civil enough with her right now, but what if once he's got a body, he decides he wants his old house back? Or speaking of books, what if he wants *The Book of Names*?"

George stared at him. "He can't have that. You burned it. Right?"

"It's gone," Abdullah said. "But you think he'll just believe that if you tell him? And if he does, you think he'll say thank you?"

"I hear you. Believe me, I hear you. But this cancer . . . I'm scared, brother. I'm goddamned terrified, like I can't even describe. And I know my head's not straight on this, but the one argument I came up with that I think might hold water is that unlike me, Winthrop's not on a clock. If all he needs is a body, sooner or later he's going to find a way to get one. I can pass on this deal, and maybe he'll have to wait another twenty years, or another century, but he's going to get out in the world again. The only difference is I won't be there to stand up to him, if he does turn to evil."

"You think you can stand up to him, George? Really?" Abdullah shook his head sadly. "I don't question your courage, but you're right, your head's not straight on this. I'd be willing to bet that Winthrop at full strength is more powerful than Braithwhite was, and we only beat Braithwhite with Winthrop's help. So who do we get to help us with Winthrop? And that's when, not if, he turns to evil."

George knew then that his appeal had failed. It wasn't just Abdullah's words, but the real regret with which he uttered them, as if he'd like nothing better than to take George's side in this. If only he could.

Then Pirate Joe said: "It's interesting, that part about the body's torso being unmarked . . . Winthrop had immunity, right? Like Braithwhite?"

George, already sliding into despair, took a moment to process the question. "Yeah, I believe so . . . Obviously it didn't help against whatever Braithwhite's father did to him, but he would have been invulnerable to most forms of harm."

"And it stands to reason he got his immunity the same way Braithwhite did." Joe pressed a hand to his breastbone. "A blood tattoo on his chest."

George nodded, seeing it now. "Yeah, of course," he said. "That's how he knew how to change Braithwhite's tattoo, to take away his power."

"So with this body, Winthrop wants a blank canvas," Joe said, "so he can give himself a new immunity tattoo. Which means when we first bring him back, he *won't* be invulnerable . . ."

Abdullah was frowning now. "Where's this going, Joe? You want to kill him again once we get George's cure? We talking murder, now?"

"Talking about saving lives," Pirate Joe said, "and the different attitudes people have on that subject. Some folks see a drowning man, they just turn their heads and keep walking." He touched a finger to his eye patch. "Like those white ambulance drivers who left me and my mom in that car wreck when I was a boy. With just a little effort, they could have stopped her bleeding to death—saved my eye too, maybe—but even the tiniest bit of help was too much to ask.

"Now, Winthrop, on the other hand, he will save you from drowning, *if* you're willing to strike a bargain—and he'll stand there haggling over terms even as you fight to keep your head above water. And you're right," he added, "guys like that don't do two-for-one deals. He'll keep his word to save George, but to save Mortimer's grandma, he's going to want another service in return.

"But the way I see it, a human life is a sacred thing. It's not a good to be bargained for, or held hostage. If Mr. Winthrop wants to come back into the world, OK, that's fair—his life is sacred too. And if he needs our help, we should give it to him, free and clear. But the same rule applies to him: if he can save lives, he should do it, not for personal gain, but because it's the right thing to do. He should save George, and Mortimer's grandma, and when he gets done with them, he should take a tour of the local hospitals, starting with the kids' wards. And if that's too much work for one wizard to handle, no problem, we'll find some volunteers to help carry the load."

"The spell," George said. "You want Winthrop to teach it to us."

"I want Winthrop to embrace decency and human kindness," Joe replied. "But if that's too tall an order, I'll settle for the spell, and Mr. Winthrop can go enjoy his new lease on life in some other part of the world. That sound good to you, George?"

"Sounds fine, if we can actually come up with a plan to make it happen. But Joe"—and here George hesitated, realizing he was about to undercut his own case—"Abdullah is right. Winthrop's at least as dangerous as Braithwhite was. Try to put the squeeze on him and we'll be lucky if he just laughs at us."

"Yeah, we'll need to be smart about it," Pirate Joe said. "And lucky. I'd argue it was worth the gamble even to save one life. But to cure cancer? For everyone?"

"All right," George said. "I'm on board if you are."

"How about you, Mortimer?" Pirate Joe asked.

"Oh sure!" said Mortimer. "I love my grandma Estelle."

"And what do you say, Abdullah?"

"I say we're going to get ourselves killed," Abdullah replied. "So it's a good thing I'm going to paradise when I die."

"OK," George said. "Now we just need a plan. And a body."

"I might be able to help with the second part," said Abdullah. "You remember my cousin Bradley? The one who got us into the museum when we were looking for *The Book of Names*? Guess where he's working now."

WHAT YOU DON'T FORGET

⊰⧓⊱

Hippolyta had once told Ruby about a Hungarian physicist, Leo something-or-other, who'd come up with the idea of the nuclear chain reaction—the process that made atom bombs explode—while waiting for a streetlight to change. Ruby's own flash of insight didn't have the same historical import, but it was no less dramatic for that.

She'd gone out to buy food. On the corner of the same block as the grocer's was an empty shop that had until recently housed a used bookstore. Now, as she waited at the red light, she glanced at the sign in the shop window:

**PALIMPSEST BOOKS HAS MOVED. COME
VISIT US AT OUR NEW LOCATION!**

In that same moment, a white woman who was also waiting for the light said to the little girl beside her, "When we get home, I'll need you to watch your brother."

Ruby looked at the woman, then back at the sign. The light changed. The woman and the little girl crossed the street. Ruby stayed put, transfixed by the chain reaction taking place inside her own head, a cascade formed not of subatomic particles, but questions.

Question number one: How had Marvin known where to find her last night? Other than the Lightbridge Agency and the Internal Revenue Service, she hadn't given her new address to anyone; most people didn't even know that she'd moved. With Marvin she'd been a bit more open, it was true: she'd told him about her new job, and might even have mentioned that she was living in Hyde Park now. But she hadn't got more specific than that, she was sure. It would have been different if she and Marvin were in the habit of writing letters to one another, but Marvin—ironically, given his job—had never been much for correspondence. He preferred to talk on the phone. Maybe that was the answer: he *did* have her new phone number, and maybe, as a reporter, he knew some way of getting the phone company to connect a number with a physical address. Maybe.

Question number two: Why hadn't she thought to ask question number one last night? But that was easy: after what had happened with Miss Lightbridge, she hadn't been thinking straight to begin with, and between her relief at finding someone she could talk to about it and her anger over the way Marvin had been treated, the question of how he'd come to be there simply hadn't occurred to her. On almost any other night, though, it would have been one of the first things out of her mouth. And so if for some reason Marvin hadn't *wanted* her to ask that question, he'd picked the perfect time to show up.

Which led to question number three: Who else did she know with an almost magical sense of timing, an intuitive knack for being in the right place at just the right moment? Like that other street corner where they'd met, seemingly by chance, on New Year's Eve two and a half years ago . . . And yes, Caleb Braithwhite had been banished from this city, barred from reentry by alterations to the enchanted tattoo on his chest. But he was determined and resourceful, and Ruby had little doubt that if he wanted back in badly enough, it was a matter of when, not if, he'd find a way. Hadn't she been expecting him all along?

The streetlight had turned red again. It cycled twice more while Ruby wrestled with question number four: What was she going to do now?

A final flash of inspiration set her into motion. She headed back to the grocer's, to pick up one more item.

When she got home, Marvin was sitting at the kitchen table with the onionskin pages and a notepad and the French-English dictionary he'd picked up at the library that morning. He had his back to the hall, and Ruby paused in the kitchen doorway to study him, examining the back of his head and the set of his shoulders for some hint of falsehood, anything at all that might indicate he wasn't who he appeared to be. But there was nothing; in any other context, she would have recognized him immediately and unquestioningly as her brother.

"Hey," Marvin said, turning his head to smile at her. "Everything all right?"

"I'm fine," Ruby replied. "Just a little tired from yesterday." She crossed to the sink and set the grocery bags on the counter. "Long lines at the store, too." She took the big jar of peanut butter out of one of the bags and set it to one side, in clear view of the table, but Marvin, scribbling on the notepad, took no notice of it. Ruby set about putting the rest of the groceries away.

"So I may have discovered something," Marvin said after a moment.

"Yeah?"

"Yeah," he said. "How sure are you that Percy—that Abdullah—actually burned *The Book of Names*?"

Ruby looked at him quizzically. "I didn't see him do it, if that's what you're asking."

"You were there that night though, right? The night 'Titia and the others turned the tables on Braithwhite and grabbed the book?"

"Yes and no," Ruby said. "It gets a little complicated, because yeah, I was part of the team, but *that* night, I was there as Hillary, pretending to be a white girl who worked for Braithwhite. My job was to sneak onto the grounds of Lancaster's meeting lodge with Hippolyta, take over this utility building, and cut the power to the main house. Which we did. After that, I took off through the woods . . ." After I shot the police detective who was going to kill Hippolyta. "So I was there, kind of, but I missed the main show in the lodge. But I heard all about it later from George and Letitia. I know they got the book, and I know they gave it to Abdullah. And I can't imagine that he wouldn't have burned it. He *wanted* to, I know that. He thought it was evil . . . So why are you asking?"

"In one of her letters, Madame Mandragora mentions another book, the *Codex Phantasmagoria*, which as far as I can tell is some sort of treatise on illusion. She thinks it would be helpful to the project she and Braithwhite are discussing. She also says that she owned two different versions of the *Codex*, but they both burned up in a fire. And then she adds, in a parenthetical, that if Braithwhite gets his hands on *The Book of Names*, he's going to want to be extra careful with it. So then Braithwhite writes back, saying he's real sorry to hear about the fire, but there's no need to worry about *The Book of Names*, because Winthrop's copy of the book has been"—Marvin put a finger on his notes—"*immunisé*. Immunisé, that literally means 'immunized,' or 'immune,' but it can also be used more generally to mean 'protected.'"

"Like, by an enchantment?" Ruby said. "The book is indestructible?"

"Sounds like it could be," Marvin replied. "At the very least, Braithwhite's not worried about fire. So maybe Abdullah tried to burn the book, but couldn't."

"Well if that's true, I never heard about it," Ruby said. "Not that I necessarily would. It's not like Abdullah and I are close or anything. But I assume he'd tell George, or Montrose."

"Maybe. Unless . . ."

"Unless what?"

"You said he thought the book was evil," Marvin pointed out. "If that's true, and if he couldn't destroy it, then maybe he'd just hide it somewhere and tell everyone it was destroyed, to keep the secret."

"Maybe," Ruby allowed. "Don't see how that matters to me either way, though."

"It might not," Marvin said. "I need to keep translating. But from what I've read so far, it sounds like in order to finish the project he's working on—which I definitely think is your potion—Braithwhite needs something from *The Book of Names*."

"Well, that's still no use to me. Even if the book still exists, and even if Abdullah was willing to lend it to me—which, why would he?—I can't read it. I told you, it's written in the language of Adam, and last I checked, Berlitz doesn't offer courses in that."

"No, I know you're right. And my hope is it won't matter. It could be all the information we need is in these letters. I'll keep plugging away at it."

"Let me know if there's something I can do to help."

Marvin smiled. "It's OK. I got this."

The groceries were all put away now. Ruby picked up the peanut butter jar, opened it, scooped out a dollop with her finger, and popped it in her mouth. "Hmm."

"What?" said Marvin.

"This isn't my usual brand," Ruby said. "I bought it because it was on sale, but it's sweeter than I'm used to, like they put honey in it." She stepped over to the table and held out the jar. "Here, tell me what you think."

For a moment it seemed as though he might decline, but then he stuck a finger in the jar and hooked a big glob of peanut butter into his mouth. "Tastes fine to me," he said, smacking his lips. "You're right that it's sweet, but not too much."

"Yeah? You want a sandwich?"

Marvin shrugged. "Sure. You got jelly?"

"Grape OK?"

"Grape's fine."

Ruby returned to the counter by the sink and stood there with her back to him, pretending to look out the window into the court-yard behind the house while she silently counted to five. Then she said: "You really think Abdullah might be hiding *The Book of Names* somewhere?"

"It's just a guess. But if he couldn't burn it, what else could he do?"

"Even if it's true, he'd never tell me. Maybe if George asked him . . ."

"That part I wouldn't be so sure about," Marvin said. "One thing I've learned as a reporter, sometimes folks with secrets are more will-ing to confess to people they aren't close to, especially if they aren't expecting the question."

"So what do I do, then? Walk up to Abdullah on the street and say, 'Hey, where's *The Book of Names*?'"

"You probably want to use a little more subtlety than that," Marvin suggested. "We can talk . . ."

He trailed off in midsentence. Ruby did another five-count before she turned around. When she did, Marvin had a funny look on his face and he was working his jaw side to side. "Something wrong?"

"Yeah," said Marvin. "I got this weird tacky sensation in my mouth . . ." He raised his right hand and touched the front of his throat. "Can you pour me a glass of water?"

"Sure." There was a glass in the drying rack beside the sink. She reached for it, but pulled back at the last second and said, "Oh, by the way, there's something else I meant to talk to you about."

"OK," Marvin said, his fingers massaging the front of his throat now. "But first, can you—"

"Yeah," Ruby continued, "on my way back from the grocer's just now, I was wracking my brain, trying to remember when I told you the address of this house. I know I must have, since you're here, but I couldn't for the life of me recall when."

"Ruby . . . water . . ."

"That's real funny, isn't it, how things like that just slip your mind? Yeah." She nodded, answering her own question. "But you know what you don't forget? Like, ever?" She cocked a thumb at the peanut butter jar on the counter. "Things you're deathly allergic to."

Marvin's eyes had gone wide and his right hand was locked around his throat. As he shoved his chair back from the table, his mouth gaped and let out a whoop as he struggled to draw air into his lungs. Ruby reached for the drying rack again; instead of picking up the glass, she grabbed a long-bladed knife.

"The real Marvin wouldn't be in the same *room* with an open jar of peanut butter," she said. "And he's no fan of grape jelly, either."

Brandishing the knife, she took two steps forward. Marvin raised his withered arm and extended it, palm outward. There were still several feet of open space between them, but Ruby felt a physical shove and stumbled back against the counter. The shove seemed to unbalance Marvin, too; he slid sideways out of his chair, and as he hit the floor, his right hand slipped from his throat and caught on the front of his shirt, popping buttons. Still gasping for air, he backpedaled, pistoning with his legs until he fetched up against the far wall. Then his gasps suddenly ceased, as if through some extraordinary act of concentration he had suppressed the need to breathe. He blinked, and blinked, and blinked again. On the third blink, his eyes changed abruptly from brown to blue. By then the flesh of his face and neck was crawling, the muscles seeming to move independently, while the color of his skin faded to reveal a paler, thinner visage—one that Ruby recognized.

The change continued, moving down the length of his body. With a loud crack of bone, Marvin's chest contracted, losing a full three inches of circumference. His withered arm was restored, atrophied muscles plumping up, regaining their vitality, while the skin whitened. By then, the anaphylactic crisis had passed, and he began to breathe once more, drawing in big lungfuls of air. The motion of his ribs caused the already loosened gauze bandages to slip down farther, and Ruby saw, to her horror, that a diamond-shaped patch of skin at the center of his chest had been not just scraped off, but *flayed*, leaving nothing but a thin transparent membrane to cover the underlying muscles and breastbone. As his chest continued to heave, drops of blood appeared on the membrane like red beads of sweat.

"Oh my God," Ruby said. Swallowing her disgust, she looked into the face of Caleb Braithwhite. "*You*," she said. "What have you done with Marvin?"

"Ruby," he replied, still weak and short of breath. "Calm down. Let's—"

"*What have you done with my brother?*" She started towards him again, and he once more extended his arm. The shove was stronger this time, knocking her back on her heels; she hit the counter with bruising force, and her arm was flung out to the side, jolting the knife from her grasp. She recovered quickly, more angered than hurt, and stooped to grab the knife again. But before she could reach it, it flipped up, balanced for an instant on the tip of its blade, and flew across the kitchen, its handle slapping neatly into Braithwhite's palm.

"Ruby—"

She threw the peanut butter jar at him. He flicked his left hand and the jar changed course in midflight, smashing against the front of the refrigerator. Next she went for the empty glass, but even as she touched it, it shattered. The whole drying rack did a somersault into the sink, and she ducked back to avoid the fragments of an exploding plate.

Her courage broke and she lunged for the back door. "Ruby, *wait!*" Braithwhite said, but the impression of a phantom hand tugging at the hem of her blouse threw her into a panic. She flung open the door and took off running.

THE FOURTH MAN

⚜

"Light's green, George," Pirate Joe said, a note of apprehension in his voice.

"I know," George replied. "But bear with me, here."

They were riding in Woody, George's wood-paneled Packard station wagon, passing through Canaryville, an Irish working-class neighborhood whose nervous proximity to Bronzeville made it an ill-advised place for Negroes to linger. But driving west on Forty-Seventh Street, George had noticed the white pedestrians exhibiting a curious lack of interest in the two colored men in the big red car. He thought he knew the reason, and had decided to put it to the test at this intersection.

On the corner to his left stood a uniformed beat cop. By now, the cop should have been on high alert, wondering what George and Joe were doing on his turf, but seconds ticked by and he didn't even glance their way, just went on jawing with another white man who also didn't look at them.

The light turned red. George touched his foot lightly to the gas pedal and eased Woody forward into the crosswalk. A white woman who'd just stepped off the curb detoured around them without complaint. She called out smiling to the cop, who finally turned his head, his eyes skating past the station wagon as if it weren't there. Throwing caution to the wind, George put a hand up to the window with his middle finger raised. The cop ignored the gesture, turning to introduce the woman to the other man he'd been talking to.

"What the hell?" Pirate Joe said. "They blind?"

"Something like that," George said. Then he stepped on the gas and drove through the still-red light.

No one cared.

It's a spell?"

George nodded. "Some kind of protective enchantment on the car. Braithwhite did it when we were in Ardham, that first time we met him. It was his way of making up for the trouble he'd caused us— though he forgot to mention that the trouble wasn't over."

"Must be nice," Joe said. "Like having diplomatic plates."

"I don't miss getting pulled over," George allowed. "But I never fully trusted the magic, and I've been extra careful since we gave Braithwhite the boot, in case what we did to him broke the spell somehow. Anyway, I'm sorry I sprung that on you back there, but if we're going to be trans- porting a stolen body, I thought it'd be good to know if it still worked."

After the meeting at the temple, Abdullah and Mortimer had gone home. Abdullah said he needed to double-check his cousin's work schedule, but he was pretty sure that Bradley would be on shift to- morrow night. It was Joe who'd suggested that he and George make a practice run to Winthrop's secret workshop.

They drove past the Union Stock Yards with the windows rolled up against the stench of manure. George turned north, balancing a map on the steering wheel as he navigated among the meatpacking plants and fertilizer factories.

Winthrop's warehouse was one of eight nearly identical brick struc- tures that lined a private alleyway. The building they wanted was des- ignated 106, but even without a number it would have been easy to distinguish from its fellows. All eight warehouses had rows of windows running just below the roofline, and in every case but one, these win- dows had been vandalized. The windows on building 106 were pristine:

not just unbroken, but free of dirt and grime, as if they'd been freshly washed. Nor was there any graffiti. Even the red color of the brick seemed more vivid than that on the surrounding warehouses.

A set of wooden double doors, large enough to admit a small truck, faced the alley. Black-painted metal stairs ran up one side of the building to a landing halfway between the ground and the roof; there was another door up there, and a ladder that continued to the rooftop.

George parked in front of the double doors and he and Joe got out. The lock in the center door stile had a star-shaped depression in lieu of a standard keyhole; the key, which had been delivered via the dumbwaiter hatch in Winthrop's cube, was in George's pocket. As he inserted the star-shaped plug into the hole, glowing Adamite letters appeared in a circle around it. He turned the key and the letters flared and went out, and a barely perceptible ripple in the air expanded outward from the lock, traveling up and around the exterior of the building. "Force field deactivated," George muttered. He pocketed the key again and they opened the doors and went in.

Inside, to the right of the entrance, stairs led up to a raised platform that connected to the door on the side of the building. Boxes, crates, barrels, and other containers were stacked on and below this platform. To the left, racks of industrial shelves held lab equipment, tools, glass jars filled with powders and other substances, and sundry other items. The aisle between the shelves and the platform led to an open space at the rear of the warehouse; there, beneath a skylight, they could see a large table draped with a white sheet.

"That's where we bring the body," George said, walking forward. "Winthrop's instructions said to look for a big table with a marble top."

There was something under the sheet at the center of the table. "I hope that's not a body already on it," Joe said.

"Can't be," George said. "After twenty-two years? That cloth would be stained through." But he slowed his pace, approaching the table warily.

The shape under the sheet did indeed suggest a corpse, albeit one too small for an adult human being. They could see what appeared to be a head at one end, and four short limbs arranged symmetrically. "Please God don't let this be a child," said Pirate Joe.

"Can't be," George repeated. He grabbed a fold of the sheet, braced himself, and then yanked it away with one quick motion.

It wasn't a child. It was a pig—a young sow, weighing perhaps a hundred pounds. The animal had been laid on its back and split open from its sternum down the length of its belly, exposing its viscera as if for dissection. George and Joe both recoiled, covering their mouths and noses instinctively. But there was no sign or smell of rot; the exposed organs were bright and suffused with color, as if the animal had only just been slaughtered.

George removed his hand from his face and leaned forward carefully, wondering whether the sow had been embalmed somehow, but there was no stink of formaldehyde either. No odor whatsoever. And it looked *fresh*. "Must be magic."

"The wards, you think?" Joe said. "Maybe time stops in here when the doors are locked."

"If that's true, then maybe you should just lock me inside until there's a nonmagical cure for cancer." George took a step back. "Look," he said pointing. Chiseled along the side of the marble slab were more of the Adamite letters. "It's the table. It keeps things from spoiling."

Joe stretched out a hand, holding it an inch above the marble surface. He was expecting it to radiate cold, but there was no noticeable change in temperature. Then he touched the slab directly, and his fingers and his palm went instantly numb. Quickly he withdrew his hand, flexing it until the feeling returned. "That is unnatural."

"We're going to have to move the pig," George said. He looked around and spotted a wheeled bin against the wall. He rolled it over to the side of the table. Meanwhile Joe searched the shelves, finding a pair of leather work gloves for himself and some asbestos mitts for George.

With their hands safely covered, they took a moment to consider how to lift the animal without spilling its guts out. Joe suggested it would be best to use the sow's legs as handles. George nodded agreement and took hold of the sow's forelimbs while Joe grabbed the legs in back. "Lift on three," George said.

The sow's body was stiff when they took hold of it. The rigidity of the leg muscles made it feel, through the gloves, as if they were gripping carved lengths of wood. But that changed once they started lifting. Almost as soon as the sow lost contact with the marble slab, the rigor went out of its body. Its muscles became first pliable and then soft, while its organs darkened and began to decompose, and black patches of rot spread across its skin. As quickly as this happened, it wasn't quite quick enough, for by the time George and Joe realized what was occurring, they had already hoisted the sow beyond the edge of the table. It was too late to put it back.

They got it over the bin just in time. With an awful ripping sound, the sow's skin split wide open, releasing a shower of rancid back fat. This was followed by much of its skeleton and its deliquescing organs. George didn't so much drop the sow's forelegs as fling them, and his memory was scarred forever by the sight of the sow's head with its eyes fallen in, bouncing off the bin's rim before tumbling inside.

Now there was a smell. It came boiling up out of the bin, accompanied by a thick bubbling sound. George jammed his face into the crook of his arm and stepped back with his eyes watering. "Jesus!" Pirate Joe cried. "Cover it!" Together they stooped and picked up the sheet and stuffed it into the bin on top of the mass of corruption that had once been a living thing. They rolled the bin outside and gave it a good hard shove to propel it away down the alley. Then they stood there, gulping in fresh air, the scent of manure from the stock yards now seeming like perfume by comparison.

When he'd recovered, George turned to Joe with a look of stark sobriety. "This is crazy," he said. "What the hell are we even doing here?"

"Saving your life," Joe replied. "Whatever it takes." He took off his gloves and put a hand on George's shoulder. "Come on, George. We need to make a plan. So let's go back inside, and you walk me through how this resurrection is supposed to work. And we'll figure something out."

"OK," George said. "OK."

They returned to the marble slab. George unfolded a sheet of drafting paper that Winthrop had given him along with the warehouse key. It contained a diagram of a constellation of chalk circles, ringed by incantations in the language of Adam, that they were to draw on the floor in preparation for the ritual. The largest circle would surround the table; a rectangle with a human figure inside showed the proper orientation of the body. Three smaller circles were arranged at the table's foot; these were joined to the large circle, and to each other, by a series of double lines. "I stand there," George said, pointing to the center circle of the trio, "and I need two volunteers to take the other spots. Once the ritual gets started, everybody's got to stay in their circles, and there can't be anyone else in the building."

"Is that for safety's sake?"

George shrugged. "Could be. Could be extra bodies screw up the magic somehow. Or maybe Winthrop just doesn't want any surprises. That last would be my guess."

"What goes there?" Joe asked, pointing at a fifth circle, smaller than all the others, that was connected to the large circle just above the corpse's head.

"Something Winthrop doesn't have yet," George said. "Some artifact, I guess. Whatever it is, he's expecting delivery within a week. Sooner rather than later, I hope," he added. "I'd like to get this over with before Hippolyta and Horace get back from their trip."

"OK." Joe nodded. "So we get all the pieces in place, and then what?"

"The ritual's a two-parter," George explained. "Part one, I blow on this horn, and me and my two assistants recite an incantation, and there's this bit with tuning forks . . . We do all that right, Winthrop's soul goes into the body, and he sits up on the slab. Then for the encore, we say another incantation, but this time Winthrop joins in the chorus."

"And what does that do? Lock his soul in place?"

"Maybe." George shrugged again. "All I know is, the ritual's not over until the dead guy sings, too."

"Sounds like that's our moment, then," Joe said. "During intermission, right after he gets his voice back. That's when we put it to him: if he wants that final chorus, he's got to renegotiate the deal."

"Yeah, right. And that's when he laughs at us."

"I don't think he'll laugh. If he doesn't want to bargain, I think he's going to get mad, *real* mad, and try to scare us into backing down."

"I'm already scared," George said. The look of sobriety returned, and with it a sense of despair. "There's no way this ends well. It's madness to even try."

Joe looked at him with calm determination. "You believe in God, George?"

"You know I do," George said. "But if that belief means anything, maybe it means taking whatever cup He decides to pass me. If He wants me to die the way Viola did, then maybe that's just what happens. Maybe it's a test."

"Maybe it is," Joe replied. "But maybe the test is for all of us, to see if we'll keep fighting for what's right even when the situation looks hopeless. And by the way, I don't think it is hopeless." He gestured at the diagram. "Your ritual's a three-man job, but we got four guys. I think we can use the fourth man to give ourselves an advantage, something Winthrop doesn't know about, so the three men facing him down can have a little extra courage when the moment comes. I know you're scared, and I am too, but so is Mr. Winthrop. It must drive him crazy, being trapped in that house while the world goes by without him. And the thought of being stuck there forever? I'll bet that terrifies him even more than dying. He's desperate to get out—he wouldn't be dealing with us at all if he wasn't. So if he does get angry, remember that's where the anger is coming from, from desperation. If we don't blink, I believe he will."

"And if he doesn't? If he decides to just kill us all?"

"The fourth man," Pirate Joe said. "Let's assume it's true we can't have him inside the building. So we put him on the roof." He looked up at the skylight. "Take out one of those panes of glass so he can hear what's going on—and so he's got a clear line of sight. And if worse comes to worst . . ." Miming a gun with his thumb and forefinger, Joe took aim at the slab.

"You volunteering to be the gunman?" George asked.

"I'd love to," Joe said. "But that's exactly why it can't be me. I start thinking about my mom at the wrong moment, I might pull the trigger out of spite. And it can't be Mortimer, either—I love the brother, but he's skittish."

"Abdullah?" George was surprised. "You really think he'd shoot Winthrop?"

"Only if it was right to. But if it's right to, he'll do it. And his hand won't tremble."

RETURN FLIGHT

꧁꧂

They waited in line for takeoff behind a DC-6 passenger plane, the same kind of aircraft that Hippolyta had initially hoped to be traveling on. The DC-6, with its four big propellers, could fly nonstop from Las Vegas to Chicago in just five and a half hours. Anthony Starling's little Cessna 170A couldn't hope to match that. With a cruising speed of 120 miles per hour, it was more like a fast car with wings—one that had to stop for gas every five hundred miles or so.

Anthony and Letitia sat in separate seats up front, while Horace and Hippolyta shared an upholstered bench seat that was just like the back seat in her late lamented Roadmaster. The dashboard was different than a Roadmaster's, sporting twin control yokes rather than a single steering wheel, but there were familiar touches as well, like the built-in cigarette lighter, and the glove compartment where Anthony stored the Dexedrine tablets he used to stay awake on long trips. And because the Cessna wasn't pressurized, the front side windows could actually be opened in flight if they decided they wanted fresh air.

The tower granted them permission for takeoff. When they'd cleared the runway, Anthony climbed to two thousand feet and did a slow circle around the city, pointing out landmarks. Horace spotted the blue oval of the Desert Ocean's pool, while Letitia eyeballed the wizard's ranch and Hippolyta looked northwest towards Indian Springs, blinking at the nuclear fireball of the setting sun.

They flew east over Lake Mead and the Hoover Dam, following the

Colorado River into Arizona. As they cruised above the Grand Canyon, the sun dropped below the horizon behind them, but a nearly full moon rose in its stead, lighting the way forward. At the canyon's far end they turned southeast, crossing open desert to intercept Route 66 near Winslow. The highway became their new guideline; Anthony took the Cessna down to five hundred feet, racing the headlights of the vehicles below.

They made their first refueling stop in New Mexico. They'd just passed over Gallup when Anthony put on headphones, took the radio microphone from its hook on the dashboard, and began speaking rapid-fire Spanish to someone named Sancho. Lights came on in the desert up ahead, illuminating a gravel airstrip that ran beside the highway. Anthony brought them in for a bumpy landing.

Nestled between the airstrip and the road was a small adobe house, with two wooden picnic tables set up outside next to the kitchen. A billboard facing the highway showed a Fokker Triplane flying nose to nose with a Sopwith Camel. The Fokker's Iron Cross had been swapped out for a Mexican coat of arms, while the British roundel on the Sopwith had been replaced by a feathered serpent with wings. SANCHO & THE DOÑA, DAREDEVILS! the billboard proclaimed, adding, in smaller letters: SIGHTSEEING $5 FOR 15 MIN. / FULL AIRSHOW $25 / FLIGHT LESSONS INQUIRE.

Sancho, aka Lieutenant Norbert Sanchez, turned out to be a fellow serviceman who'd flown with Anthony in Korea. He embraced Anthony warmly, then introduced his wife, Sally, who despite the name was as brown as he was, and their two daughters, Lula and Xoco.

The planes from the billboard were parked across the airstrip. Horace went over to take a closer look, accompanied by Anthony and Sancho, Sancho explaining that these were actually modern replicas, easier and safer to fly than the aircraft on which they were modeled— though they'd both been in poor shape when he'd found them, and he and Sally had put a lot of effort into making them flightworthy.

While the men discussed the ins and outs of plane restoration,

Sally sent her daughters into the house to prepare food for the guests, then sat with Hippolyta and Letitia at one of the picnic tables.

"Are you the Doña?" Hippolyta asked her.

"I am," Sally said. "It started as a joke. Sally's short for Quetzalli, which if you're an ignorant Spaniard sounds kind of like Quixote."

"Hey!" Sancho called. "I heard that!"

Sally ignored him. "So which of you is with Tony?"

Hippolyta looked at Letitia, who blushed. "Now, now," Letitia said. "We just met, and we're just friends . . ."

"You got to watch it, with these flyboys," Sally said. "Sancho and I were just friends too, back in grade school. But now here I am"—she spread her hands—"queen of the desert."

The meal was a mix of Mexican dishes and the blander tourist fare that Sancho derided as "German food"—hamburgers and frankfurters—though Sally seemed to prefer it. After everyone had eaten their fill, Sally had the girls pack the leftovers and some additional provisions in a basket, while Anthony and Sancho saw to refueling the Cessna. When Anthony tried to pay for the gas and food, Sancho refused to take his money. Anthony had anticipated this, though, so while he and Sancho argued good-naturedly, Letitia, acting as his confederate, slipped some cash to Sally, who accepted it with a wink. "Remember what I told you," Sally said.

They said their goodbyes and took off again, continuing to follow the highway. Hippolyta took one of the pillows Anthony had produced from the cargo space and rested her head against the window, looking out at the moon, which, as she drifted off to sleep, unfolded spiral arms and revealed itself to be Winthrop's Octopus in disguise. Other celestial wonders came out to join it and she wandered among them, while Horace lay his snoring head on her shoulder.

Deep in the night she woke to find Letitia flying the plane, with Anthony's encouragement. "That's it," he was saying. "Just pull back on the yoke and keep one eye on your airspeed."

"What do the foot pedals do?" Letitia asked.

"That's your tail rudder control. Tail rudder moves the plane's nose from side to side."

"I thought you use the yoke to steer."

"You do—turning the yoke rolls the wings. But you need to use the rudder, too, to keep the nose pointed in the same direction you're moving." He coached her through a series of right and left turns, the first of which made Hippolyta's stomach lurch. But as Letitia got the knack of using the yoke and pedals in tandem, the Cessna's motion smoothed out and became a gentle back-and-forth sway. "That's it," Anthony said. "You're a natural."

"It feels like dancing," Letitia said.

"If that's how you dance, I'm taking you to a ballroom when we get to Chicago."

Letitia laughed and said something else, but Hippolyta had drifted back to sleep by then and didn't hear it.

The next time she woke, the sun had risen and they were on the ground at an airfield in eastern Colorado. The place was like a truck stop for small planes, with a drive-up fuel island and a maintenance and repair garage at the edge of the tarmac.

They all got out to stretch their legs. As Anthony was gassing up the Cessna, a white mechanic in stained overalls approached, addressed him as "Sir," and asked whether he'd be needing hangar space for today. When Anthony said no, the man went on to list other amenities that the airfield offered. Hippolyta watched this exchange with a sense of mild astonishment, particularly the part where the mechanic pointed out the location of the restrooms—information that she had never in her life seen a white stranger volunteer.

"Did you fly us into an alternate dimension?" she asked, after the mechanic had moved on.

Anthony laughed at the question. "It's about economics," he explained. "After World War II, there was supposed to be this big boom in civil aviation. The dream was, everyone in the suburbs would have a plane parked next to the car in their garage. But reality fell short, so now places like this, if they're smart, they welcome every customer they can get. Jim Crow won't help keep the lights on. Not to be uncharitable," he added, watching the mechanic speak to another pilot who was the same shade as Sancho. "I know there are white folks who are as sick of the color line as we are. But it's a lot easier to do what your heart says is right when your wallet agrees. Who knows, maybe we are flying into a new world."

The old world was waiting for them in Iowa. They landed at another small airfield just minutes before a monster thunderstorm shut down the sky. As Anthony taxied towards the hangar, a white man came running out to meet the plane, but unlike the mechanic in Colorado, he wasn't friendly. Heedless of the danger from the propeller, he physically blocked the Cessna's path and gestured furiously back towards the runway.

Anthony killed the engine and got out. He had a heated discussion with the man, the others watching tensely from inside the plane, which was rocked by gusts of wind from the oncoming storm. A second white man joined the first, at which point violence seemed unavoidable, but Anthony offered them twenty dollars—ten times the normal hangar fee—and after conferring, they grudgingly stepped aside.

As Anthony got back in the plane, the first raindrops began to fall. "While I get this parked, you should all head over there," he said, pointing to a nearby terminal building. "See if they've got a storm shelter. This is tornado weather."

"You're coming too, right?" Hippolyta said.

"I'll be along if I see a funnel cloud coming. Until then, I'm staying out here." He eyed the two white men. "God can break my airplane if He wants to, but anyone else has got to go through me first."

"I'll stay with you," Letitia said.

"I appreciate it," Anthony told her, "but I can handle this."

"I know you can," Letitia said. "But I wouldn't want you to get lonely out here—and if we work together, maybe we can win your money back." She nodded at the white men, who'd resumed their seats at a folding table stacked with plastic poker chips.

Anthony laughed. "Winning it back is the easy part," he said. "The trick is walking away with it, after."

"I got some thoughts on a getaway strategy," Letitia said. She picked up her purse. "But you'll have to trust me."

"You sure this is a good idea?" Hippolyta said.

"We'll be fine," Letitia assured her. "You and Horace go look for that storm shelter. And if we don't all get blown away to Oz, see if you can bring us back some coffee when the weather clears."

The terminal housed a small waiting area for a regional airline that didn't fly on weekends. There was no restaurant or café, but a stand minded by a bored-looking white woman offered premade sandwiches and drinks. The woman, who appeared to be the terminal's sole occupant, was no happier to see them coming than the men in the hangar had been. "I only sell to people with planes," she said.

"We have a plane," Horace told her. "How do you think we got here?"

"God doesn't like liars," the woman replied, as lightning flashed outside. Then she picked up the magazine she'd been reading and turned her back.

The terminal had no tornado shelter, but stairs beside the restrooms led to an enclosed rooftop observation deck where they could watch for approaching funnel clouds. A pair of vending machines sold cigarettes and candy bars; Horace looked wistfully at the latter, but when Hippolyta offered him a nickel he shook his head. "I'm not giving this place a red cent." He took her hand and they sat together in silence, watching the rain lash the windows.

The storm lasted for two hours. No tornadoes formed. By midafternoon, the lightning and the rain had passed on to the west and patches of clear sky were breaking through the cloud cover.

When Horace and Hippolyta returned to the hangar, they were greeted by the sound of raised voices. As expected, most of the poker chips had ended up in front of Letitia and Anthony. But Letitia's getaway plan had been foiled by the arrival of three more white men, who'd showed up in the hangar just as she was raking in a last big pot. When the inevitable accusations of cheating started, two of the newcomers stepped up to support the two already at the table. But it was the third newcomer who was the real spoiler: he had a gun on his hip, and the presence of mind to stand back as the argument escalated. Even if Letitia had gotten her wand out and swatted the other four men, all she'd have earned for her trouble was a bullet.

Anthony didn't know about the wand, but he'd grasped the implications of the gun immediately and understood that their winnings had just evaporated. Now he was trying to deal with their other problem, which was that the Cessna's tanks were almost dry. "Listen here," he said, speaking to the man who'd first blocked their way on the tarmac, "you want to tell yourself it's cheating that three of a kind beats a bad bluff, I'm not going to fight with you. But we were already up plenty off hands that *you* dealt, and I know you didn't cheat yourself. So why don't you just give us a fill-up on gas and we'll call it even and get out of your hair."

"I'm not giving you *shit*," the man said. "You want to get out of here alive, you'd better start thinking about *walking* home."

"No," Anthony said, his voice going dangerously flat. "That's not happening. You're not taking my plane."

Hippolyta, who'd already grabbed Horace's wrist to stop him from entering the hangar, began to pull him away. Letitia slipped a hand into her purse. Then, just as matters were about to pass the point of no return, the man with the gun weighed in: "Give him the fuel."

The other white men all turned to look at him. "John, come on!" the man up in Anthony's face said. "You're not going to let them—"

"Give him the goddamned fuel, Davis," the man with the gun said. "I want them out of here. Now."

Of course it wasn't that simple. The Cessna's tanks could hold forty-two gallons; but Davis, who insisted on handling the refueling himself, only put in five gallons before shutting the pump off. "That's enough to get you in the air," he said when Anthony objected. "You want more, you can fucking well pay for it." Anthony turned to John, the gunman, who'd followed them out to the fuel island and now stood there like a referee. But John only yawned and looked away.

"Goddamn," Anthony said. The posted price was forty cents per gallon—six cents a gallon more than he'd paid in Colorado—which only added to the sense of being robbed, again. But the alternative was trying to find and land at another airfield with less than an hour's fuel—and at this point in the journey, it wasn't just the plane that was running on fumes. "Fine," he relented. "Pump another thirty." Once the fuel was on board, he took care to pay with exact change. Davis walked away smirking with his money.

"I'm sorry," Letitia said, as they taxied to the end of the runway. "That wasn't how I planned it."

"It's not on you," Anthony replied. "I wanted to sit down at that table as bad as you did—and it was worth it, to see the look on his face when you made that last call. We just got unlucky." The smile he gave her then was genuine, but Hippolyta, watching from the rear seat, could also see the tension at the back of his neck, the same tension she'd felt in Horace's neck on Terra Hiram.

But for Anthony Starling, the antidote was close at hand: he pushed the throttle all the way in, guided his plane down the runway, and pulled back on the yoke. As the world and its troubles fell away beneath him, he let out a long exhale and waggled the Cessna's wings. Shaking it off.

❈ ❈ ❈

There's Harlem," Anthony said.

Hippolyta, who'd been dozing again, opened her eyes and sat up, wondering if they'd somehow overshot Illinois and traveled all the way to the East Coast. But the evening skyline up ahead was Chicago's.

"Harlem Airport," Anthony clarified, banking the plane and pointing down at a grassy field crisscrossed with runways. "Corner of Eighty-Seventh and Harlem Avenue. They had one of the first colored flying schools in the country."

"Is that where we're landing?" Horace asked.

"I wish," said Anthony. "But they lost their lease on the property last year. Owner wants to put up a shopping center." Banking the plane again, he gave the field a little salute. Then, steering for the lakefront, he reached for the radio mike. "Meigs Field tower, this is November seven-three-three-five-three, requesting clearance to land . . ."

He's not coming with us?" Hippolyta said.

Letitia shook her head. "After he finishes getting his plane squared away, he's going to get a hotel room. I offered to put him up at the Winthrop House, but he wants a real bed, not the couch in my parlor."

Hippolyta smiled slyly at her. "Real bed's not on the menu?"

"Not tonight. But he's taking me out to dinner tomorrow."

"Queen of the desert, here I come."

"Now, now," Letitia said. "Let's get a cab. If you like, I can drop you and Horace straight home, and deliver that urn to Mr. Winthrop for you."

Hippolyta thought about it. Home meant George, who, she'd belatedly realized, was going to have to be told *something* about what had happened in Las Vegas. She couldn't just forget to mention what had become of Mr. Tunstall's trailer. Or her car.

"That's all right," she told Letitia. "We'll go to the Winthrop House first."

When they came in the front door, Mr. Fox was lying on the foot of the atrium staircase—literally *on* it, like he'd mistaken the bottom steps for his bed. He was curled up on his side, stair treads jammed against his ribs, his folded hands forming a pillow for his cheek. Snoring.

"Oh," Hippolyta sighed, seeing him there, and Horace put down the box he was carrying and went over to help. Letitia threw an accusing glance at Hecate, like, You just stood there and let this happen? But it was pointless: Mr. Fox wasn't on the short list of things Mr. Winthrop cared about, and right now, his full attention would be focused on the urn in Hippolyta's arms.

"Come on, Mr. Fox," Horace said, gently nudging him awake. "Let's get you up to bed." Mr. Fox opened his eyes, uncomprehending at first, but with some encouragement Horace got him on his feet and put an arm around him and led him, stumbling, to the elevator.

"Poor man," Hippolyta said. "Was he like this before we left?"

"Not this bad, no," Letitia said, eyeing the empty gin bottle on the dining-room table. "I probably shouldn't have left him in the house alone"—another angry glance at Hecate, here—"but I'm his landlady, not his mother."

"The other tenants are all away?"

Letitia nodded. "Atticus is off with Montrose, of course, and Charlie Boyd is on vacation. And Mrs. Wilkins is visiting her grandson in Detroit. She invited Mr. Fox to go with her, but her grandson's got twin girls about Celia's age, and I guess Mr. Fox thought that'd be like torture."

Horace and Mr. Fox were up on the gallery, now. The elevator returned to the ground floor on its own, the gate slamming open impatiently.

"Maybe you should take that urn home with you tonight," Letitia suggested. "Bring it back tomorrow, or the next day."

"No, it's OK," Hippolyta said. "Mr. Winthrop kept his end of the bargain . . . I'll be back up shortly."

As the elevator began its descent to the subbasement, the telephone rang. Letitia walked over to the little phone stand and picked up. "Hello? . . . Ruby? Where . . . I'm sorry, where have *I* been? Out of town, which you'd know if you . . . What? No . . . *No*, Ruby. I just got in the door, I'm tired, and I am not calling another cab tonight. You want to talk, you can come here . . . I don't *care* how important . . . Ruby . . . *Ruby* . . . All right, all *right* . . ." Holding the receiver between her ear and her shoulder, she reached for the pen and pad beside the phone and scribbled down an address. "Lake Street under the L tracks . . . Yeah, I got it, but I'm warning you right now, you haul me all the way downtown at this hour, it better be about the Second Coming . . . All right. Just give me a little time to catch my breath. I'll be there in an hour."

CASH UP FRONT

Are you," Abdullah's cousin Bradley said, "out of your damn minds?"

He'd agreed to meet Abdullah during his meal break, at a late-night takeout joint across from the university hospital complex. But when Bradley saw the other Freemasons waiting with his cousin, he very nearly bolted; Abdullah had to physically drag him over to the group. And learning what they wanted from him didn't improve matters.

"The *morgue*? You want me to sneak you into the goddamn morgue?"

"You don't need to come inside with us," George told him. "We just need you to get us past security."

"I *am* security," Bradley said, slapping the front of his uniform. "And you know how hard it was for me to *get* this job, after you got me fired from the museum?" He shook his head. "No sir. No way, no how." He turned to go, only to stop and pivot back as George held up a folded wad of cash. "What's that?"

George unfolded the bills and peeled off two hundreds. "Abdullah was telling us that even with this job, you're a little behind on your debts."

"More than a little," Bradley said. George peeled off three more hundreds. Bradley stared frowning at the money, clearly tempted but exasperated too, to be put on the spot like this. To stall for time while he thought it over, he turned to his cousin. "You OK with this, Percy?"

"With bribing you to get us in? Not really," Abdullah said. "I think family should do for family without expecting to get paid—which is why I'm going to pretend that George is just being charitable. But as for what we're planning to do tonight, yeah, I'm OK with it. And coming from me, that should mean something."

Bradley didn't seem as reassured by this as Abdullah might have hoped. "Here's the problem," he said, looking at the money again. "I know you probably think you're all smart, coming here on a Sunday night, but people don't stop dying just because it's the weekend. There's an attendant on duty in the morgue round the clock, to take deliveries. I don't know the guy who's working tonight, which means I can't tell you when he goes on break, or even if he goes on break. Which brings us to problem number two, which is that the morgue is on the ground floor, right down the hall from the emergency room, so there's doctors and nurses going by all the time. The four of you hang around outside, waiting for the morgue guy to leave, and somebody's going to ask what you're doing there."

"We understand," George said. "But it's not the main morgue we want to get into. We want the other one."

"What other one?"

"The one down by the steam tunnels," said Abdullah. "The one you said they use to prep cadavers for the medical school."

"Oh, man," Bradley said. "I told you about that? And you want to go down there?"

"Is there an attendant?"

"No. It's locked up tight, but there shouldn't be anyone there this late. It's creepy as all get-out, though."

"Creepy we can handle," George said. "Do we have a deal?"

"Two things," Bradley said. "First, I want that five hundred dollars, *plus* the rest of the cash in that wad."

"No problem," said George, who'd expected this.

"Second, I can't take you in right now. I'm picking up food for two other guys besides me, and after that I got some other things to take care of. So what you're going to have to do is go around to this fire door on the far side of the building and wait for me to come get you."

"How long?"

"An hour, maybe an hour and a half. Depends . . . That's the best I can do."

"All right," George said nodding.

"I got a few other conditions," Bradley continued. "Once I get you down there, you're on your own. You get caught, I don't know you. And whatever happens, this is the last time you ask me to sneak you in anywhere. I don't care if the world's ending, next time you leave me out of it. And last but not least . . ." He held out his hand. "It's cash up front."

CONFESSION TIME

⁙

The diner on Lake Street was open all night, and its layout was such that Ruby could stand in the shadows across the street and see everyone inside through the big plate-glass window. At this hour the only customers were an elderly white couple finishing up a meal at a window table and a colored man perched on a stool at the counter. Ruby focused on the colored man, who'd arrived just minutes after she had. She studied his body language, alert for any tic or gesture that seemed familiar. He was a southpaw, which should have been reassuring—Caleb Braithwhite was right-handed—but thinking about that made Ruby realize how little she still understood about the transformation. Marvin's peanut allergy had affected Braithwhite while he wore Marvin's shape; did handedness work the same way? Hillary was right-handed, as Ruby was, but then most people were.

Ruby was still dressed in the clothes she'd been wearing when she fled the townhouse. She'd spent last night at a cheap hotel and had used most of her remaining cash to buy a gun, a little .22 semiautomatic. Its effectiveness as a weapon was debatable, but it was easily concealed, and in her current circumstance, stealth counted for more than stopping power; if Braithwhite even suspected she was armed, she'd never get a shot off. Really, the gun was just a talisman, a rabbit's foot to give her courage. She needed help, and she knew it, which meant it was time to confess her sins.

The old couple had just paid their check and left when the cab arrived. Ruby watched Letitia get out, frowning in suspicion when she saw that Hippolyta was with her. She checked that the .22's safety was off and started across the street.

Hippolyta saw Ruby coming and nudged Letitia, who was looking in the diner window. Letitia turned around and her sister addressed her coldly: "What's *she* doing here? I told you to come alone."

"You're lucky I came at all," Letitia said. "Now what—"

"In second grade," Ruby interrupted, standing on the curb now with her right hand cupped at her side, "what was the name of that boy who put the big wad of gum in your hair?"

Letitia was thrown by the question at first, but then she said: "It was third grade. And it wasn't a boy, it was Tanya Robinson."

"How'd you get her back?"

"That little pink sweater she loved so much," Letitia said. "She left it hanging on the back of her chair while she went to use the girls' room, and I took a pair of scissors to it."

Ruby shifted her gaze to Hippolyta. "Where'd you and George meet?"

"At the Smithsonian natural history museum," Hippolyta said. "It was the summer of '41, and he and Montrose had brought Atticus to D.C. to see the sights. George and I were in the rotunda, both looking up at the dome, and we crashed right into each other."

"OK." Ruby nodded, relaxing slightly.

"OK?" said Letitia. "What the hell is going on, Ruby?"

"Caleb Braithwhite," Ruby said. "He's back in town."

They took a booth at the rear of the diner, Ruby sitting with her back to the wall so that she could watch the front entrance and the man at the counter. The waitress came and they all ordered coffee, Hippolyta asking for a sandwich and a slice of pie as well. But by the time the food arrived, Ruby had begun to speak, and the story she told made Hippolyta forget that she was hungry.

"A *magic potion*?" Letitia said. "That turns you into a *white girl*?"

"Keep your voice down," Ruby cautioned.

"This white girl," Hippolyta said. "Is she—"

"A redhead." Ruby nodded, guessing what she was thinking. "You met her once."

"Met her where?" Letitia said.

"Outside Lancaster's lodge, the night we ran Braithwhite out of town," Hippolyta said. "You remember, I went to meet that white lady who worked for Braithwhite, and we snuck onto the grounds together. I was supposed to leave her handcuffed in that building with the guards, but she outsmarted me. And then she saved my life . . ." She looked at Ruby. "That was you?"

"That was me," Ruby said nodding. She told them about the town-house, the glass coffin in the basement, the devil's bargain she'd struck with Braithwhite, and the secret life she'd been leading since his exile.

"And that's why no one sees you anymore?" Letitia said. "That's what you've been doing? *Passing*?"

"I guess so," Ruby replied, and despite her shame, she smiled. She looked down at her hands, which were notably darker than her sister's. "You never would have guessed I could pull that off, would you?" Turning serious again, she gave them an edited version of the events of Friday night, omitting the part about Miss Lightbridge kissing her, saying only that she'd come home late to find the Marvin-who-wasn't-really-Marvin sitting on her stoop. "He said . . . he said he got fired from his job, and needed a place to stay, so of course I took him in. But yesterday I got suspicious that his story didn't add up, and I figured out a way to trick him into showing who he really was."

"But how could it be Braithwhite?" Letitia said. "How could he be back here, doing magic again, after what we did? His tattoo—"

"He got it removed, along with half the skin on his chest. I caught a glimpse when I was fighting with him. It's like this open wound. I think he keeps it bandaged all the time, because of the bleeding, and it looked painful . . ."

"Good," Letitia said. "I hope he is suffering. If he did anything to Marvin—if he's got him locked up in a basement somewhere—"

"Yeah, I thought that too, at first," Ruby said. "But then last night when I was hiding out, I had another thought, and I decided to try Marvin's number in Springfield, just to see. And he answered. It was really him," she added. "I made sure of that, first thing, and then I asked him how he was. He said fine. He hasn't been fired, hasn't had any other trouble, either."

"Well, that's some good news, at least . . . isn't it?"

"Marvin being OK, sure. But as to what it means . . . That cold case Mr. Braithwhite put Delilah in, I know that's meant to keep her alive, but I always thought it was part of the transformation ritual, too, like the potion wouldn't work if she were awake and walking around. But if that's not so—if Braithwhite can turn into Marvin *without* Marvin being in a coma . . . Well, don't you see? He could be anyone, then. He could be one of us."

Letitia and Hippolyta exchanged glances. "OK," Letitia said after a moment. "But we know he's not one of *us* . . . Hippolyta and I both passed your quiz outside, and if you weren't Ruby, you wouldn't have known the right answers either."

"What about George and Horace?" Ruby asked.

"We haven't seen George yet, since we got back," Hippolyta told her, "but I shouldn't have any trouble knowing if he's real. And Horace was with us all day."

"Where's he now?"

"At the Winthrop House," Letitia said. "Braithwhite wouldn't dare bother him there, not with Mr. Winthrop on guard . . . We should all go back there. See if Mr. Winthrop can help with this."

Ruby shook her head. "No."

"Ruby."

"I got one too many warlocks in my life already," Ruby said, adamant. "I don't need another. And I don't want to make any more deals or owe any more favors. I just want what I already paid for."

"You mean your townhouse?"

"I mean a life," Ruby said. "A normal life, where I don't have to work twice as hard for half as much, and the world just lets me *be*." Here she paused, struck again by the difficulty of communicating what it was like to be Hillary and what that meant to her. "It's like, last December? Miss Lightbridge shut down the agency from Christmas Eve to New Year's, gave everybody a week off. She was going out west with this friend of hers, to go skiing, and she asked what I was doing on my vacation, like she expected me to actually *do* something, fly to the Bahamas or whatever . . . So I told her I was going to see my family down in Bloomington—"

"Bloomington?" Letitia said.

"—and Miss Lightbridge was like, 'Oh, Hillary, it's lovely that you're seeing your family, but I hope you don't spend your whole week there. You're young, you should have an *adventure* . . . Well," Ruby said. "At first I thought, right, that's *just* what I need, more adventure in my life. But the idea was in my head then, and after a while I thought, you know, why not? And then I saw an ad for this winter carnival a couple hours away up in Wisconsin. It reminded me of that Christmas village Momma and Daddy took us to that time, you remember that, 'Titia? So I thought, OK, I'll have an adventure. A day trip, but as Hillary.

"So I got up early the day after Christmas, got changed, and took the bus up there. It was a cute little town, like the kind you'd see in a snow globe. And the festival was all right—they had these ice sculptures that were something to see. But what I really loved? From the moment I got off the bus? Was just walking around. Walking around this little town that I'd never been to before, that I knew nothing about, and that I hadn't bothered to look up in any guidebook. And I just walked, and if I saw a shop that looked interesting I went inside; when I got hungry, I picked a restaurant; if I got tired, I found a place to sit down. And not once—not the whole day—did it occur to me to wonder if I was welcome. It just didn't come up. The world let me *be*.

"And like I say, it was a day trip, but I'd brought an extra dose of potion just in case there was a problem with the bus back home. And then when it started to get late, I thought to myself, Why don't I stay the night here? And that's just what I did. I had my pick of hotels. *My* pick. I got a real nice room, no problem, and ordered up room service before I turned back into a pumpkin. Slept like a baby.

"And the next day I came home. It's probably good I only had the one spare dose of potion, or I might have stayed longer. Or I might have *not* stayed—I might have got on a different bus, kept going, north, west, wherever, stopping anywhere I pleased, until my money ran out. And just to know that I *could* have done that, if I chose to, feels like . . . well, like magic.

"And don't get me wrong," she said, suddenly conscious of how long she'd been talking, "I love the house too, I'd love to go on living there, but I'd give it up in a heartbeat for a few more days like that one, just a little more time of the world letting me *be* . . . Is that so wrong? You can understand, can't you?"

"Yes," Hippolyta spoke up. "I can." She reached across the table and put her hand on Ruby's, that sudden feel of human contact once more making Ruby want to swoon. And then she almost gasped, as she felt Letitia take her other hand.

"I don't know about this white lady business," Letitia said. "If the world only lets you be if you agree to stop being you, it sounds like you're giving up a lot more than you gain. You ask me, it's the house you should be fighting for. With real estate, you can live a better life *and* still see your own face in the mirror." Giving Ruby's hand a squeeze: "So what's the address, anyway?"

ANNUIT COEPTIS

⊹⊱⊰⊹

Quick." Bradley held the fire door open as George and the others hustled inside. When the door was safely shut again, he said: "OK, I can get you where you want to go, but it's a little tricky."

"Tricky how?" Abdullah said.

"We need to go to the subbasement. But most of the fire stairs, including this one, only go down as far as the basement, and even the ones that go deeper are no use—below the ground floor, the fire doors won't open from inside the stairwell. You can come out that way, but you can't get back in."

"So how do we get down there?"

"There's an elevator," Bradley said. "On this floor, it's on the same hall as the main morgue, which like I say is a little too busy for comfort. So we're going to go up to five, hospital administration. There shouldn't be anybody in the offices now. We catch the elevator there and go straight down."

"That doesn't sound too tricky," Abdullah said. "As long as we don't get lost upstairs."

"Don't worry, I know my way around. I could walk these halls in my sleep by now."

George wasn't worried about getting lost; he was worried about the return trip. They'd found a parking spot for Woody right outside this fire exit, and the sidewalk along this part of the building was poorly lit and largely devoid of foot traffic, which made it ideal for spiriting a body out undetected. But not if they had to run an obstacle course to get back here.

But then he flashed on Viola and thought, The hell with it, we'll find a way. I'll carry that cadaver on my shoulders if I have to.

They went up the stairs. The administrative level was a maze of branching corridors, but Bradley, true to his word, guided them to the elevator without difficulty. George did his best to memorize the route, using the names on office doors as landmarks.

To descend to the subbasement required a key, which Bradley produced from a ring on his belt. The elevator jolted into motion and everyone looked up at the floor indicator, tracking their progress. They passed through the intermediate floors without stopping.

At the bottom of the shaft, the elevator door opened on a cement-walled chamber that reminded George of the cube beneath the Winthrop House. But this space was lit by bare incandescent bulbs whose low wattage left shadows pooling in the corners. There was a fire exit on the right-hand wall, and facing the elevator was a heavy steel door, painted light blue, with the word STORAGE stenciled on it in red.

Bradley unlocked the blue door with another key from his belt. Beyond was a long corridor with doors on both sides. "Mostly old patient records in here," Bradley said, gesturing at the first of the left-hand doors. "Overflow from the basement storerooms. I got drafted into hauling boxes down my first week on the job. But what you want's up here on the right . . ." He stopped at a door marked COLLECTION, used another key to unlock it, and reached inside to flip on a light switch.

"OK," Bradley said. "This is where I leave you. Now, I got to lock that other door behind me when I go, so you won't be able to get back out that way—"

"Wait a minute," George said.

"—but it's all right, there's another set of fire stairs down the other end of this hall. Just remember you can't come back in once you go out."

"Where do those stairs go, though?" George asked.

"What do you mean, where? Up to the street."

"Where on the street?"

Bradley shrugged. "Hell if I know. But it shouldn't matter. Even if someone sees you leaving, they're not going to care, as long as you're not acting suspicious. And if you *are* acting suspicious, that's on you."

George looked to Abdullah for help.

"Here's the thing, Bradley—" Abdullah began.

"No," Bradley interrupted him. "Don't even finish that sentence. I told you already, I don't want to know what you all are up to here. You say you're OK with it, then fine, I'll trust you on that. But I do not want details. Now if you'll excuse me, I got to get back to my job. Try not to get your asses in trouble." With that, he stepped around them and went back up the corridor. They watched him go, listened as he slammed the door and locked them inside.

"All right," George said after a moment. "Looks like we'll have to improvise."

COLLECTION proved to be a chilly room lit by overhead fluorescents. There was no furniture, just a set of ten refrigerated body lockers in the wall opposite the door. Each locker had a small hook on the front; clipboards with forms hung from two of these, while the others were bare.

"Only two," George said. "Slim pickings."

"Looks like there's more in here," Pirate Joe said, stepping through an open doorway to the left and flipping another light switch. This room was larger and outfitted like a working mortuary: there was a big sink with a spray hose, a couple of wheeled steel tables for moving bodies around, and various other pieces of equipment. And arranged along two walls were over three dozen body lockers, most of which had clipboards attached.

"How do they get all these bodies, anyway?" said Abdullah. "People donate themselves to the medical school?"

"Some do," Mortimer told him. "But most of these are just what they call unclaimed. Folks without families, who die without anyone to bury them . . . What?" he said, seeing the curious looks the others were giving him. "We did dissections in dentist school. Can't be drilling in people's heads without knowing what all is in there. I remember the guy I learned anatomy on, he must've been some kind of hobo, the state his teeth were in . . . Say, is that going to be a problem?" He pointed to a stack of wooden crates in one corner, marked **CHAMPION CONCENTRATED EMBALMING FLUID**.

Pirate Joe and Abdullah both turned to George. "Winthrop's want sheet didn't say anything about embalming, did it?" Joe asked.

"No," George said, "but if they've been down here long enough to need it, we've missed our three-day window. Let's check the paperwork, see if it lists a time and date of death."

It did, and the news wasn't good. The most recently deceased of the cadavers had died almost two weeks ago, and some of them had been here for months. In growing frustration, George returned to COLLECTION. Here, things initially seemed more hopeful: according to the clipboard, the first corpse, one Robert Lee, had died of a heart attack on Friday afternoon. But when George opened the locker and slid out the drawer, he was disappointed.

"Chinese," he said. "Damn. With that name, I thought . . ."

"Yeah," Pirate Joe said.

Abdullah was examining the other clipboard. "This one's listed as Caucasian," he reported. "But it's a woman. Jane Doe."

"Let's double-check that," said George. "Maybe they got the sex wrong."

They hadn't got the sex wrong. George gazed at the dead woman, her face framed in brown curls, and tried to think of a way to salvage the situation. "What do you suppose would piss Winthrop off less?" he asked. "Waking up yellow, or a woman?"

"I'd go with Lee, if it were me," Pirate Joe said. "I don't think I could navigate being female."

"She's pretty, though," Mortimer put in. "And she's white."

But at last, reluctantly, George shook his head. "It won't work. Not either of them. Beggars can't be choosers, but Winthrop's no beggar. I got to give him exactly what he asked for."

He slid Jane Doe's drawer back into the locker and closed the door. As the latch clicked shut, a faint rumbling echoed down the corridor outside.

"That's the elevator," Pirate Joe said.

George looked at Abdullah. "Could it be Bradley coming back?"

"Not unless the Martians have landed," said Abdullah. "We better hide."

Mortimer looked nervously at the body lockers. "I'm not getting in one of those."

"The other room," Pirate Joe said.

They heard a key being inserted into the blue door. George closed the door to the corridor and locked it. He flipped off the light and followed the others into the embalming room. When Joe, Abdullah, and Mortimer had all found hiding places, he switched off the light in there too and stood against the wall just inside the doorway.

A sound of squeaking wheels came down the corridor and stopped outside COLLECTION. There was a rattle of keys; the door opened and the light came on again. George risked a peek through the doorway and saw a Negro orderly push a body on a gurney into the room. "Last stop, Mr. Armbruster," the orderly said. He picked up the clipboard that lay atop the sheet covering the corpse and hung it on the door of one of the empty lockers. George ducked back out of sight and listened as the orderly opened the locker and transferred the corpse from the gurney to the drawer. "You sleep tight now," the orderly said. He slid the drawer in and closed the locker and pushed the gurney back out into the corridor, turning off the light and locking the door behind him.

George waited until he heard the blue door open and slam shut again before turning the lights back on. Then he and the others went to see what the orderly had brought them.

"Guy looks like Dracula," Mortimer said, when the dead man's face was uncovered. Herman Armbruster, age forty-seven, had a prominent widow's peak, and the manner of his death—carbon monoxide poisoning—had turned his lips bright red and put a healthy pink glow in his cheeks.

"I'm OK with a vampire," George said, "as long as he ticks all the other boxes." He pulled back the sheet to examine Armbruster's chest. "No tattoos." Pulling the sheet back farther: "And he's uncircumcised."

"It's not like he had a lot to spare down there," Mortimer observed.

"Knock off the jokes," Abdullah said. "It's bad enough what we're doing here without you being disrespectful."

"I'm sorry," Mortimer said. "I'm just nervous. Can we get out of here now?"

"Yeah," George said. "Let's get him wrapped up to go."

They wound the sheet around Armbruster's body and put him on one of the wheeled tables from the embalming room. Then they rolled him down the corridor. When they reached the other fire exit, George had the others wait with the corpse while he ran up to see where the stairs let out. He returned moments later with an unhappy look on his face.

"No good?" Pirate Joe said.

George shook his head. "Ground floor exit's in the ambulance bay. There's no way we're carrying a body through there without getting noticed." He stared at the corpse, considering. "I think we're going to have to take him all the way up to five, see if we can find our way back to that other stairwell."

"What's through there?" Mortimer asked pointing.

Beyond the fire exit, the corridor continued a few more feet before ending at an unmarked door. Abdullah went over and tried the knob. It wasn't locked. A rush of moist hot air greeted him as he pushed the door open; beyond was a wider corridor with a vaulted ceiling, lined with pipes large and small.

"Steam tunnels," Abdullah said.

They'd entered at a bend in the tunnel, but the left-hand branch ended at a locked door after only a dozen yards. They took the straight path, stopping twice to lift the wheeled table over pipes that crossed the tunnel at floor level.

The air was swampy, and in no time they were all soaked with sweat. George didn't mind the discomfort, but he worried what this heat might be doing to the corpse. He'd just have to hope that Winthrop's seventy-two-hour time limit had factored in a certain amount of spoilage.

They came to another branch in the tunnel. This time it was the straight path that was blocked, by a tangle of crosspipes; they could have squeezed through, but it would have meant abandoning the table. Instead they turned left, and saw yet another branching point up ahead—this one a four-way intersection.

"What's that rule for finding your way through a maze?" Pirate Joe said. "Follow the wall on your left?"

"Stick to the same wall, anyway," George said. "But let's see what our options look like."

As if in response to this remark, the bulbs that lit the tunnel began flickering. Everyone stopped and looked up. The light grew steady again. The party continued forward, and had just reached the intersection when the bulbs flickered once more and went out completely.

A clink and a spark in the darkness. A flame sprang up; Joe raised his lighter overhead, using it to illuminate each tunnel branch in turn. As far as anyone could judge by the feeble light it cast, all three passages were equally promising.

"Left wall it is, I guess," George said.

"Maybe we should just go back," Mortimer offered.

"But then what?" said Abdullah. "You really want to haul this guy all the way up to the fifth floor?"

"No, of course not, but . . . What if we run out of lighter fluid?"

"I don't suppose anyone brought a flashlight," Joe said.

Everyone shook their heads, Mortimer looking embarrassed as he did so. "I didn't even think to bring my tool bag for this job," he said. "I'm sorry, George. I—"

"Quiet," Abdullah said, raising a hand. "You all hear that?"

From somewhere out in the darkness came a series of three sharp taps, followed by a long scraping sound.

"What is that?" George said softly. "Knocking in the pipes?"

Pirate Joe shook his head. "Doesn't sound like metal."

The sound came again: *Tap, tap, tap* . . . scrape. George closed his eyes, and an image sprang fully formed into his mind: the beat cop from Canaryville, rapping his billy club against the wall of the tunnel, then dragging the club's tip along the concrete. Which was absurd, but having thought of the idea he couldn't shake it, and when he opened his eyes and looked at his companions, he could see from their expressions that they'd all come up with their own scary notions of what it might be.

Tap, tap, tap . . . scrape.

"We need to move," Pirate Joe said.

"But which way?" said George.

"Well, we can't go back," Abdullah said. "Whatever it is, it's behind us."

"No, it's not," Joe said. He pointed down the left-hand passage. "It's coming from that way." Mortimer nodded agreement.

But George said, "No, it's coming from *that* way," and pointed down the right-hand tunnel.

They stood there, stymied, and then the noise came again, and their expressions all turned triumphant—You see?—before lapsing once more into confusion. And then, without further discussion, they began to move, straight ahead, following the one passage they all agreed the noise *wasn't* coming from.

At first they moved slowly, trying to make as little noise as possible. But the table's wheels, affected perhaps by the humidity, began to squeak like the wheels on the orderly's gurney, and realizing that stealth was not an option they sped up. Abdullah pushed the table from behind, while George and Mortimer trotted alongside, keeping it steady in the center of the tunnel, and Joe, in front of Mortimer, held up his lighter to give as much warning of upcoming obstacles as possible.

A low-hanging pipe loomed out of the darkness and they all ducked down, the corpse passing underneath with less than a foot of clearance. Then the tunnel bent right; they took the turn at speed, George flinging an arm across the body to keep it from sliding. When they'd straightened out again, they found this new section of tunnel had fewer pipes in it and seemed several degrees cooler.

A sudden draft blew out the lighter. Mortimer stumbled, cursing in the darkness, and Abdullah tried to put the brakes on. Too late: the table slammed into something and came to a dead stop, George once more throwing his arm over the corpse to restrain it.

A moment later, when the tunnel lights flickered back on, George was bent over the table practically nose to nose with Herman Armbruster. Straightening up quickly, George saw that the tunnel had come to an end at a set of concrete stairs, the table fetching up against the bottom step. He looked across the table at Joe, who was nursing a bruised elbow that he'd banged against a pipe valve, and back at Abdullah and Mortimer, both picking themselves up off the floor. Behind them, the tunnel was empty as far back as the turn.

The tapping noise had ceased. They listened for several moments but it didn't resume, so George returned his attention to the stairs. The steps ran up in a short flight to a landing before turning out of sight. It was definitely cooler here, with what felt like fresh air coming down from above.

George turned to Pirate Joe again. "Let's see where this goes."

"I'd like to come too," Mortimer said, but George and Joe were already climbing.

The stairs went up through two more landings, ending in a chamber with an eight-foot clearance beneath a hinged grate. Rungs were set into the wall. George climbed up and pushed the grate open, eyes widening. "You're not going to believe this," he said.

"What?" said Pirate Joe.

George hopped back down and moved aside. "See for yourself."

The grate was set into the sidewalk just a stone's throw from the fire door where they'd first entered the hospital. And right there at the curb, almost close enough to touch, was Woody.

"Huh," Pirate Joe said, looking up and down the deserted sidewalk. "What's that motto on the Great Seal? *Annuit coeptis*?"

"'Providence has favored our undertakings,'" George said nodding. "Come on. Let's get that body in the car before Providence changes its mind."

YOU'VE GOT NOTHING

⚜

The light above the stoop was on, but the townhouse's windows were dark. As the cab drove away, Ruby drew her pistol and Letitia slipped her wand from its velvet bag. Hippolyta had left the teleporter base unit back at the Winthrop House, but she'd brought both transport units with her as a precaution against Horace getting restless in her absence; she got out the one that was programmed with Terra Hiram's coordinates, showed it to Ruby, and explained what it was. "If things go bad, we can just huddle up, and I'll get us out of here."

"We're not running away," Letitia said firmly. She opened the gate and strode purposefully up the walk.

The front door wasn't locked. Letitia pushed it open and reached in to flip on the light as Ruby and Hippolyta came up behind her.

Right away, Ruby saw something was off. "Coat rack's missing," she said. Looking down the hall: "Kitchen table, too." She placed a hand on Letitia's arm and moved the wand aside so she could step past her.

The house had been cleared out. Most of the furniture had come with the place, but there were other items—like the cute little throw rug she'd found for the front parlor—that Ruby had bought with her own money, money she'd worked for. Braithwhite had taken it all.

She peered up the stairs, listening, then continued down the hall, pausing again at the kitchen doorway. "You hear something?" Letitia asked, but Ruby shook her head.

"No," she said, putting her gun away. "He's not here."

She turned on the kitchen light. The refrigerator was still there, but when Ruby looked inside, the jug of salvaged potion was gone. Turning to the stove, she saw that her favorite teakettle was missing too. Now that's just spiteful, she thought.

She went over to the basement door, thinking as she did that there was no point in checking. But she opened the door and turned on the lights and went down and stood staring at the oblong stain on the floor where the coffin had rested.

The basement refrigerator had been removed in its entirety, along with the filing cabinets and everything else that wasn't nailed or bolted down. The overwhelming emptiness of the space made the peanut butter jar sitting in the middle of the floor all the more conspicuous. Ruby went over and bent to pick it up. "What is that?" Letitia called from the foot of the stairs.

Ruby didn't answer. She held up the jar to the light to see if he'd left a note inside, but it was empty, as if he'd gobbled up the contents and licked the glass clean, the jar itself becoming the message: You've got nothing, now.

Ruby nodded her head in acknowledgment. Then her lip curled in fury and she flung the jar against the wall.

PART III

THE DESTROYER OF WORLDS

GITA

⟨⟩

Now I am become Death, the destroyer of worlds.

According to *THE ATOM SMASHERS!!!!!*, this line from scripture had flashed into J. Robert Oppenheimer's mind as he watched the successful Trinity bomb test. The first time Horace had read that, the meaning had seemed plain enough: Oppenheimer was Death, and the "worlds" were human lives, the doomed citizens of Hiroshima and Nagasaki.

But Rollo Danvers, whose corner grocery Horace ran deliveries for, had told him he had it wrong. To begin with, the scripture in question wasn't the Holy Bible, as Horace had assumed, but a Hindu scripture called the Bhagavad Gita.

"How do you know about Hindu scripture?" Horace asked.

"From a guy named Graham Banks," Rollo said. "I met him in England during the war, when I was working for the Quartermaster Corps. We got to be friends after he stood up for me and my buddies at this pub that didn't want to serve us. Graham grew up in India," Rollo explained, "and he'd come back to the home country to study theology at Cambridge. He was doing an English translation of the Gita as his thesis project when the Luftwaffe started bombing London."

The Bhagavad Gita, Rollo continued, was part of a much longer text, the Mahabharata, which told the story of a devastating war between the Kauravas and the Pandavas, royal cousins who'd fallen out over who should rule the kingdom. "Both sides call in allies from all over ancient India and beyond—we're talking millions of soldiers, almost all of whom end up dying in the end. They call on the gods for help, too. There's even this divine superweapon with a tongue-twister of a name—Pashupatastra—that's powerful enough to vaporize whole cities, or blow up the world if you ain't careful with it.

"So these two huge armies are lined up to fight, about to go at it, when Prince Arjuna, one of the heroes on the Pandava side, rides his chariot out to the middle of the battlefield. Arjuna's the deadliest archer in the world, and as he looks over the Kauravas' forces, he thinks about all the people he's about to kill—members of his own family, folks he used to call friends—and he starts to lose heart. He turns to his chariot driver, Krishna, and says, 'Hey man, I don't think I can do this.'

"But Krishna's not just some royal chauffeur. He's the human incarnation of a god named Vishnu who's come down to earth to restore the balance between good and evil, and he knows this war has to happen. So Vishnu puts the two armies on hold, and right there in the middle of the battlefield he gives Arjuna this long pep talk, and convinces him to take up his bow and fight. And the Bhagavad Gita, that's the record of their conversation."

"So what does Vishnu say to him?"

"He reminds him that the soul is immortal. Hindus believe that, the same as Christians and Muslims do. Your body can die, but your spirit—what Hindus call the Atman—that's eternal, with no beginning and no end."

"They got heaven and hell, too?"

"It's complicated," Rollo said. "Short-term, they got reincarnation: one life ends, you start another, in a new body. And there's an accounting, where the way you lived this life determines the hand you get dealt in the next—so if you commit too many sins, maybe you come back as a donkey, or a snake. But donkeys and snakes die too, of course, and if you learn your lesson you can turn things around for the *next* life . . .

Graham said one of the things he liked about Hinduism is that it's a lot more forgiving than Christianity. You always get another chance."

"And it just goes on like that?" Horace said. "One life after another, forever?"

"Not forever," said Rollo. "Long-term, the Atman's goal is to break out of the cycle of death and rebirth and go join Brahman, who's like, the soul of the universe. And part of making that break is coming to understand that the things of this world—things that pass away—just don't matter that much. Which is another point that Vishnu makes to Arjuna. He's like, 'Hey, prince, you're getting yourself all wound up over suffering and death, but even the worst suffering is temporary, and death, from the Atman's point of view, ain't even real.'

"Another thing he tells him—and this is where that Oppenheimer quote comes in—is that human beings aren't in charge of destiny, the gods are. When Vishnu says, 'I am become Death,' what he means is, 'I'm the one who decides when people die.' All the Kaurava warriors that Arjuna is destined to slay in battle, they're already as good as dead, because Vishnu has decided their time is up; Arjuna's just the weapon he's going to use to make it happen. But he's a god, he's got options, so even if Arjuna refused to fight, Vishnu would just find some other way to kill them. The only thing that would be different in that case is that Arjuna would have failed in his duty, which a good soldier won't do.

"So you can kind of see where Oppenheimer's head was at. He'd built a real-life Pashupatastra out in the desert, and the thought of all the people it was going to be used to kill made him sick at heart. But at the same time, the war was already happening, and America was going to see it through whether Oppenheimer played his part or not. And that meant a lot of people, including a lot of innocent people, were destined to die, because that's what war *is*. Even without the A-bomb, the Allies were already burning cities to the ground. Nothing Oppenheimer did or said could change that."

"So trust in the Lord, and do your duty," Horace said. "But isn't that . . . How is that different from, 'I'm just following orders'? I mean—"

"Yeah, I take your point." Rollo nodded. "And you're right—you *could* use Vishnu's words to justify pretty much any war crime you liked. That's the thing about scripture: the devil can quote it too. And I know there are people who think Oppenheimer is the devil. But I got to say, I feel for the man. I mean, *my* war? You spend your days loading cargo onto transports, the biggest dilemma you're likely to face is what gets priority, toilet paper or cigarettes. After D-Day, when I started driving trucks for the Redball Express, I did see some action, but even there, the one real firefight I was in, the guys I was shooting at shot at me first. A situation like that, you can't feel too bad about being the last man standing, especially when the dead guys turn out to be S.S.

"But the men who firebombed Hamburg and Dresden, knowing there'd be women and children on the ground? The generals who came up with that strategy? If they had any conscience at all, I imagine they might have needed a dose of scripture to live with themselves, after. And I'm not going to begrudge them. Because if they hadn't done that, the Nazis might never have given up—and for sure there would have been more of them shooting at me. And I'm glad I didn't get shot. I thank God for it."

There was more Horace might have said in response to this, but he'd decided to leave it there, figuring this was one of those cases where real-life experience trumped even the best abstract argument. One thought stayed with him, though: to take comfort from scripture, you actually had to believe in it.

But when Horace returned to his book and saw the photograph of Oppenheimer taken after the war, the haunted look in the man's eyes said that he'd never managed to make the necessary leap of faith. Like Horace, he must have feared that the Hindus had it backwards: God was the illusion; death was real; and the worlds that it destroyed were destroyed forever.

Which was a strange thing to be thinking after spending the night in a haunted house. But as Horace had argued to his mother, it wasn't *that* strange: Mr. Winthrop hadn't defeated death, as Jesus had, nor had he evolved beyond it, as devout Hindus hoped to. He'd just put it off, the way he might put off paying his taxes, sending lawyers and accountants to run interference with the IRS. But death, like the taxman, could afford to be patient. If it didn't get you today, there was always tomorrow.

Horace threw aside the blanket and sat up on the parlor couch where he'd slept. It was just past sunrise, and the Winthrop House was quiet. Letitia had come back alone last night around midnight and had told him that Hippolyta had taken Ruby home with her; when Horace asked why, and what was up with Ruby anyway, Letitia had demurred, saying that his mother would explain it all to him when she picked him up in the morning.

Horace wondered about that. After their adventure in Nevada, he thought he'd earned a spot as his mother's new confidant, but maybe that had only been temporary, and now that vacation was over she'd go back to being close-mouthed, not mentioning things that she thought would be troublesome for him to know.

He put on his shoes and walked out into the atrium, where Hecate regarded him with indifference. "Morning, Mr. Winthrop," Horace muttered, continuing on through the dining room to the kitchen at the back of the house. He poured himself a glass of milk and thought about how to occupy himself while he waited for his mother to come get him.

A draft stirred the air. Horace glanced towards the back hallway. If he was feeling courageous, he could go down the stairs to the basement and try to find that room that his mother had gone to, where, he gathered, it was possible to actually talk to Mr. Winthrop. Horace could tell him about the Bhagavad Gita and ask what it was like to be a ghost. The idea was intriguing, but the thought of blundering around in the dark under the house dissuaded him.

But there was another place he could go, not far away, that might suit the mood he found himself in.

Leaving his empty glass in the sink, Horace undid the locks on the kitchen door. He slipped out into the alleyway behind the house and started walking.

THE LAST PIECE

❊

Herman Armbruster's body now rested on a marble slab in Packingtown, awaiting the resurrection. The Freemasons had spent the remainder of the night drawing chalk circles on the warehouse floor and making other preparations for the ritual. With dawn breaking, they'd decided to head back to the Winthrop House to let Mr. Winthrop know they'd gotten what he'd asked for. But as George pulled up in front of the mansion, he saw that Winthrop had news to share, too.

"Up there," he said, pointing. "On the corner of the roof. You see that rusty chair? It's usually facing out, towards the lake. Winthrop told me he'd turn it around once he got the last piece of gear for the ritual."

"You sure nobody else moved it?" asked Mortimer.

"Letitia doesn't let tenants up on the roof. And even when she's out of town, you violate the rules of the house at your peril." George turned sideways in the driver's seat, eyeing each of them in turn. "Brothers, I know it's been a long night, but if Winthrop's ready to go, we *could* finish this up this morning . . ."

"I'm in," Pirate Joe said, without hesitation.

"I'll need to call in sick to work," said Abdullah, "but yeah, I'm in too."

"Mortimer?"

"I'm supposed to put in Deenie Anderson's braces today," Mortimer replied. "But I don't suppose she'll mind postponing. Just let me phone my office before we get started."

"You want us to wait here while you go inside?" Pirate Joe asked.

"You can wait in the car," George said. "But I'm going to drive around to the back door, first." Thinking of Mr. Fox: "I'd like to slip in and out unnoticed, if I can."

SCENE OF THE CRIME

❧

By the time George entered the Winthrop House through the un-locked kitchen door, Horace was two blocks away, standing at a corner bus stop that fronted on a four-lane avenue. This avenue marked the current extent of the housing turnover that had been triggered by Le-titia's arrival in the neighborhood several years ago. The homes on the opposite side were all still white-owned and -occupied, and the residents were determined to keep it that way; from where he stood, Horace could see the boarded-up shell of a cottage that had caught fire the day after a Negro family had come to view the property.

The bus hadn't been running on the Sunday afternoon when Celia was killed. She'd gone out walking after church, still in her Sunday best, carrying an issue of *Wild West Comics* that Horace had loaned to her. Why she had picked this particular spot to sit and read was some-thing only she knew, but there probably wasn't much to it. It was a nice day and the bench was unoccupied; why *not* sit there? If anyone from across the street had a problem with that, she wasn't the type to care.

Around that same time, a fourteen-year-old boy named Willy Prince had gone into a nearby drugstore. There were no other customers in the store, and seeing that there was no one behind the front counter either, Prince decided to help himself to the contents of the cash reg-ister. He'd just gotten the cash drawer open when the store's owner, an off-duty police detective named John Timmerman, had emerged from the back storeroom. Prince made a blind grab for the till and ran out of the drugstore with a fistful of bills. Timmerman went after him. A lengthy chase ensued, with Prince cutting through yards and hopping fences in an attempt to escape. But Timmerman, despite being twenty years older, managed to keep up with him.

Looking back up the street he'd just walked down, Horace could see a skinny yellow house with a pair of matching flowerpots on the stoop. Prince had been passing that house when Timmerman pulled out his service revolver and fired two shots. Later he would claim that he'd acted in self-defense. Prince had turned on him, he said, and appeared to be holding a weapon. But according to Ava Lewis, who lived in the house and happened to be looking out the window, Prince had only turned in response to the first gunshot; he'd dropped the stolen bills and was putting his empty hands up when Timmerman pulled the trigger the second time.

Prince wasn't hit by either bullet, but his feet tangled and he fell down and lay on the ground still trying to surrender. Timmerman began kicking him, only stopping when Miss Lewis came outside and yelled. At that point, Timmerman hauled Prince to his feet, forced his way into Miss Lewis's house, and used her phone to call for backup. A squad car came and took Prince away to the precinct station, where he was charged with resisting arrest and the theft of eight dollars.

Which would have been the end of it, if not for the matter of the two gunshots. One of Timmerman's errant bullets had struck a mailbox, dimpling the metal but otherwise doing no harm. The other had hit Celia Fox in the back of the head. It wasn't like the comics; the force of the impact did not send her flying off the bench. In fact, as her body relaxed in death, her head actually tipped backwards, making it look as if she'd simply dozed off. And so she remained, for nearly four hours, until a man out walking his dog noticed something strange in the way she was slumped and decided to take a closer look.

Horace squatted down behind the bench. The first time he'd come here, the day after Celia's death, he'd been disturbed to see streaks of dried blood on the back of the painted slats. He'd thought about wiping it off, but had feared that by doing so he'd be destroying evidence— and not just evidence of the crime committed here, but evidence that Celia had existed at all.

The blood was gone now, though. Not a trace remained, on the bench or the sidewalk beneath it.

He stood up and walked around to the front of the bench and looked back at Miss Lewis's house, mentally tracing the fatal bullet's trajectory. The geometry of it was maddening: if Timmerman had been just a few paces farther up the street when he'd fired, the shot would have been blocked by the corner of another house.

At the funeral, he'd asked his cousin Atticus whether Celia would have felt anything—whether she'd have known, even for an instant, that she was dying. Atticus had told him no; he'd seen people get shot in the head, in Korea, and they always went straight out, with no time to feel pain or fear. That should have been a comfort, but to Horace it became more nightmare fuel: that you could just be sitting somewhere, conscious and healthy and alive, and then a second later, with no warning, be gone. And if gone meant *gone*, not to heaven or some other afterlife, but *nowhere*, into *nothing* . . .

Horace turned and lowered himself onto the bench, sitting where Celia had been sitting. The back of his scalp started crawling, but he resisted the urge to look around and stayed facing forward, trying to imagine it, that split-second transition into nothingness. The destruction of a world.

Of course it was impossible. No one can imagine what it's like to cease to exist. It wasn't like falling asleep, because sleep is still something. Even when Horace couldn't remember his dreams, he always woke with the sense of time having passed, as if his conscious mind had been away somewhere and had just forgotten to take notes. But if death was noplace, there'd be no time there, and nothing to take note of. Nothing at all, forever.

"Yamaraja," Horace whispered, a mantra against his fear.

After Rollo had told him about the Bhagavad Gita, he'd spent some time at the library, researching Hinduism. The encyclopedias and other reference books he consulted contained a lot of contradictory information—another thing Hindus had in common with Christians, it seemed, was that they often disagreed about matters of faith.

One area of disagreement was exactly how long it took to reincarnate after you died. Some sources claimed it happened immediately, while others specified a waiting period—seven days, or forty days, or forty-nine days—before the Atman received its new body. The most interesting version of this that Horace had come across said that rather than spending the in-between time in limbo, your soul was summoned to the underworld to appear before the court of Yamaraja, the god of death. After weighing up your sins and your good deeds, Yamaraja would either grant you a forty-day stay in paradise, or sentence you to forty days in hell.

Now imagine if *that* were true: Celia's Atman ejects from her body like a pilot bailing out of a plane, to find itself surrounded by the Yamaduta, the demonic bailiffs of Yamaraja's court, whose appearance on this Chicago street corner would probably be more confusing than scary, as confusing as a flock of blond angels manifesting in the streets of Bombay. Confusing or no, though, there was no resisting their summons; the Yamaduta weren't the kind of cops you could run from.

Celia would have had her day in court by now, and either be enjoying her heavenly vacation or serving out her sentence (if the latter, Horace assumed that her punishment would be minor—forty days of clapping erasers and writing I WILL NOT TORTURE MY SUBSTITUTE TEACHERS). And then, in just a few weeks, she'd be alive again.

Horace wondered, if that *were* true, what the chances were that he and Celia might meet up again someday. Even if she were reborn in the same part of the world, it would be years before she'd be old enough to go walking around on her own. Assuming she came back human.

There was also the problem of recognition. Most people didn't remember having lived before, which raised the question of how the Atman could learn and grow without being able to recall past mistakes. One of Horace's reference sources tried to resolve this paradox by claiming that people *did* remember their past lives, subconsciously. Skilled monks and yogis could use meditation to access those memories directly, but even less enlightened people would experience the sensation of déjà vu, triggered by something familiar from a previous incarnation.

So maybe it would happen. Maybe one day, decades from now, Horace would encounter a woman—or a man—fifteen years his junior, and feel a sudden inexplicable flash of familiarity. Do I know you? Celia?

If only, Horace thought. He'd give a lot to know, or even believe, that such a thing might really be possible.

His musings were interrupted by a flurry of wings. A pigeon landed in the street in front of him and cocked its head in that way they do, this birdy side-eye coming across as mocking: Do I *know* you?

"Nice try," Horace said, as the pigeon bent to peck at a cigarette butt, "but there's no way Celia'd come back as dumb as you." This remark earned him another side-eye, but he leaned forward and waved his hand dismissively. "Go on, now! Shoo!" The bird took off and he watched it fly away, a wan smile on his lips.

When he lowered his eyes again, Celia was standing across the street in her old body, looking straight at him.

SOMETHING'S HAPPENED

❖

When Letitia sat up in bed, she could hear the Winthrop House elevator moving. It wasn't the sound that woke her. It was a sudden sense of doom, that feeling in your bones that tells you something's happened and the phone is about to ring with bad news. The last time she'd felt this way, her mother had just died.

She dressed quickly. When she came out on the atrium gallery, the elevator noise had ceased and the house was otherwise quiet. She stood with one hand on the banister and looked down at Hecate and said softly, "Mr. Winthrop? Is something going on I should know about?"

The statue couldn't speak, but Mr. Winthrop had other ways of communicating with her: ghostly thumps and knocks, as well as more aggressive displays of telekinesis. This time she got no response, which meant she could rule out an intruder, or any threat to the house itself. Whatever had her on edge must be something Mr. Winthrop didn't care about.

She went back past her bedroom and down the hall to Mr. Fox's room.

He wasn't dead. She could hear his loud snoring even before she cracked the door and poked her head inside. But the room had a rank smell to it that Letitia associated with a certain type of shut-in, people who'd lost the ability or the will to take proper care of themselves. Mrs. Wilkins's room smelled like that sometimes when her dementia got especially bad, but Mr. Fox had always been scrupulous about keeping his room clean and aired out.

We need to have a conversation, Letitia thought, looking at him sprawled on the bed. But not until he woke on his own; deep slumber was probably the only peace he knew these days, and it would be cruel to interrupt that. Her gaze shifted to the empty cot where Celia had used to sleep, and then to the crowded top of the dresser that stood against the wall between the cot and the bed. There, amid a collection of empty bottles, she could just make out the shape of a large revolver.

We *definitely* need to have a conversation, she thought.

The elevator started up again. She closed Mr. Fox's door and went back out to the gallery. The elevator stopped in the basement; she heard the distant rattle of the gate opening below her. "Hello?" she called down the shaft. "Horace? Is that you playing around down there?"

No answer. She hurried down the stairs and looked into the empty parlor. "Horace?"

Footsteps on the basement stairs. Letitia went through the parlor to the back hallway, but by the time she got there, the footsteps were already in the kitchen. The back door opened and closed. She raced to catch up, hearing a car motor rev outside. She opened the kitchen door and looked out into the alley and saw a red Packard station wagon— Woody?—speeding away.

What on earth?

She shut the back door and locked it, then returned to the atrium and looked up at Hecate with growing concern. "Mr. Winthrop?" Still nothing. "Are you asleep or something?" Maybe he's mad at me, she thought. But the silent treatment wasn't his style. When Mr. Winthrop got upset, he made the house jump.

She went into the parlor and picked up Horace's blanket off the floor. Now where did *he* get to? she wondered. If that was really George's car in the alley, she supposed Hippolyta might have been driving. But even if Hippolyta had decided to come get Horace at the crack of dawn, what would she be sneaking around the basement for? Not to mention that the teleporter base unit was still upstairs in Letitia's bedroom—it was hard to imagine Hippolyta leaving that behind a second time. You'd better call her, Letitia thought, draping the folded blanket over the back of the couch.

The doorbell rang.

"Now what?" Letitia said. As she went to answer it, the bell rang impatiently twice more. "Hold on, I'm coming!"

When she opened the door, Angus Rutherford was standing on the threshold like an angry goblin.

Before she could even blink in surprise, he punched her in the face.

WHAT ARE YOU DOING HERE?

⚜

Horace stared at Celia for about three seconds—long enough to be convinced that she was really there, and not just some daydream conjured up by his desire to see her alive again—and then his view was cut off by the sudden arrival of a bus at the stop. He jumped up and tried to wave the bus on, but it hadn't stopped just for him. The front door opened and an old man with a cane began making his way down the steps with agonizing slowness.

Horace ran around the back of the bus. Celia was no longer standing where she had been. He scanned the sidewalk frantically and spotted her moving away, headed in the direction of the burned-out cottage. "Celia!" he shouted, but she didn't look around.

The avenue, which had been quiet a moment before, was now busy with traffic. Horace tried to keep one eye on Celia as he dodged cars. By the time he'd made it across, she'd reached the cottage and gone up the steps to the little front porch. He called her name again and this time she paused, not looking at him but giving him a brief glimpse of her profile before she disappeared inside.

He skidded to a stop in front of the cottage a few seconds later and stared at the big sheet of plywood that had been nailed over the front door. A sign reading PROPERTY CONDEMNED was pasted to the plywood, and other, nastier messages were scrawled in graffiti around this. Horace felt a trickle of doubt, his mind doubling back to a winter's night two and a half years ago, when he'd stood outside another con-demned building and seen people who weren't really there.

Then he heard Celia laughing on the other side of the doorway and his doubt evaporated. He ran up onto the porch and shoved against the plywood. It didn't budge. Horace looked for a way to pry it open. The top and sides were nailed in place, but there was a gap of several inches along the bottom. He squatted and shoved his hands into the gap and pulled as hard as he could. The plywood gave, just a little—the nails on the lower-right corner were loose. He shifted his hands to get a better grip and something sharp bit into his right palm. A splinter, he thought at first, but then the sharp thing dug in deeper and sliced across his skin.

Hissing in pain, Horace yanked his hands out and fell backwards onto his behind and stared at the blood welling from the gash in his palm. "God damn it . . . Celia!" He lashed out angrily, kicking at the plywood, and heard, in response, the sound of footsteps moving away inside.

"Celia!" Balling his bleeding hand into a fist, he scrambled up and attacked the barrier full force, pounding and kicking at it, which accom-plished little beyond increasing the flow from his wound. Blood seeped between his clenched fingers, spattering the plywood and dripping onto the boards of the porch. At last he gave up, bruised and winded, and listened as the sound of his final blows echoed through the cottage.

The empty cottage, he thought, with a sudden despairing certainty. She was gone again, if in fact she had ever been here. A part of him didn't want to accept this—wanted to keep on hammering away until he got inside—but his returning sanity recognized that this would be futile. Worse than futile: if the neighbors hadn't noticed him already, they would soon, and then he'd have his own turn dealing with the police.

"Horace?" a familiar voice said behind him. Horace looked over his shoulder and saw Woody idling at the curb, with Abdullah and Mor-timer Dupree in the back, Pirate Joe riding shotgun, and his father at the wheel, leaning across Joe to call to him. "Horace! What the hell are you doing here?"

For a long moment Horace just stood there, dumbfounded, with no clue how to answer that question. Then he came down off the porch and held up his bloody hand. "You got anything I can use for a bandage?"

We got in late yesterday," Horace said, sitting in the back of the car with his hand wrapped in a handkerchief that Mortimer had given him. "I spent the night at the Winthrop House."

"And then what?" his father said. "You got up early and decided to get yourself arrested for trespassing?"

"I was just taking a walk. I thought I heard a cat trapped in that house and tried to let it out."

"A cat." George frowned, clearly not buying this. "Where's your mother? She at the Winthrop House too?"

"No, she went home last night. With Ruby," Horace added. "They *did* make it home, right?"

George cut his eyes away briefly before answering. "I don't know. We've been out all night."

"Doing what?"

"Hey," George cautioned. "I'm the one asking questions here . . . What are you and your mother doing back so soon? Did something happen?"

"You need to ask Mom about that."

"I'm asking you."

"It's not my story to tell," Horace insisted. "You need to talk to Mom."

George pursed his lips in frustration. "And Ruby? What's she doing at our place?"

"I don't know," Horace said. His face turned sullen. "Nobody tells *me* anything."

THE COWBOY

⚔

The blow knocked Letitia to the floor and left her stunned, in more ways than one. Living under Mr. Winthrop's protection, she'd become accustomed to being secure in her own house. She wouldn't have thought it possible for anyone—least of all a rival sorcerer—to lay hands on her here.

But now Angus Rutherford stepped unhindered over the threshold. Rather than continue his assault, he moved aside to make way for another white man.

This second man was tall and slender, and he was dressed like a cowboy in a white Stetson hat, brown suede vest over a blue denim shirt, jeans, and glossy brown boots. He wore a bolo tie around his neck, its braided black cord secured by a silver pendant inset with a black stone. Viewed obliquely, the stone appeared to be pure jet, but as the cowboy came forward, he raised his right hand and fluttered his fingers beside the pendant to draw Letitia's gaze. Looking straight at it, she saw that the stone's surface was more like a pool of oil, reflecting the light in a mesmerizing dark rainbow.

"Don't get up," the cowboy said to her. His voice was cultured and polite. "Stay calm. Don't call out."

The command to stay calm had no discernible effect—Letitia's heart was racing—but his other words carried more force. When she tried to scramble to her feet, her muscles wouldn't cooperate; she couldn't even prop herself up on her elbows. Her mouth opened and closed uselessly. In desperation she writhed on the floor, twisting her body and head around to throw a pleading glance for help at Hecate.

"I'm afraid that's no use," the cowboy said. "Hiram Winthrop has departed this house. So Mr. Rutherford assures me. I confess to being somewhat disappointed, as under other circumstances, the late Mr. Winthrop is someone I would very much enjoy meeting. But my business here today is with you."

Giving up the struggle, Letitia rolled onto her back again. She tried speaking in a soft voice: "What do you want?"

"To begin with, I'd like to know who else is in this house right now."

These words, Letitia realized, carried no force of compulsion either. "Nobody."

The cowboy smiled skeptically. "Just you, all alone in this great big house? I doubt that. It seems to me—" He broke off, hearing the unmistakable sound of a gun being cocked. He and Rutherford both looked up, and Letitia turned her head.

Mr. Fox was on the gallery, holding the revolver from his dresser. He rested his arm on the banister to steady it as he took aim at the intruders. "Get away from her," he said. "Before I put holes in both of you."

"There's no need for that," the cowboy said. His fingers moved beside the black stone. "Disarm yourself, sir."

Mr. Fox adopted a scornful expression, as if wondering whether the cowboy were crazy, but his scorn turned to dismay as his own hands betrayed him, carefully lowering the hammer of the revolver before tossing it aside.

"Very good," said the cowboy. "Now come down here and join us. Quickly."

Mr. Fox started to turn towards the stairs, but then, as the last word took hold, he placed both hands on the railing, vaulted over the banister, and dropped like a stone to the floor of the atrium.

❅ ❅ ❅

The cowboy had Letitia help Mr. Fox to the couch in the parlor. Once she was settled beside him, the cowboy ordered them both to remain seated. In Mr. Fox's case, this was hardly necessary, as he'd broken an ankle in the fall.

"Now," said the cowboy. "I will ask you again: Who else is in this house?"

"Nobody," Letitia replied, exactly as before. "Just us."

The cowboy studied her, as if they were seated across a poker table from one another. "I wish I could believe you. However . . ." He fingered the black stone. "I got this off a cunning woman in the Yucatan. It's a useful trifle, but limited in its powers. It can compel simple action—or inaction—but not truthful speech. For that I must resort to other methods, distasteful as I may find them."

Rutherford had gone back outside. Now he returned, wearing a heavily laden utility belt and lugging two metal suitcases, one large and one small. He set both cases down beneath the archway that connected the atrium and the parlor.

Turning to the small case first, he pressed a button on top near the front. The carry handle retracted and holes sprang open near the bottom of the case, four on each side. Jointed aluminum tubes sprouted from the holes, bending to form legs that lifted the case off the floor. Then the body of the case collapsed and reconfigured itself in a kind of mechanical origami trick, top and side panels folding, sliding, and shifting until the whole resembled a crude approximation of a spider. Another, larger opening appeared in the front, and a cluster of camera lenses emerged; mounted beneath these were a pair of chrome nozzles that might have been additional sensors, or weapons, or both.

The spider signaled its readiness with a chittering sound. "Search the house for other occupants," Rutherford instructed it. "Start at the top floor and work your way down. When you finish your sweep, switch to patrol mode. Go." The spider chittered again, then turned and headed up the stairs.

Rutherford now turned to the larger case. The activation process was similar, but this one transformed into a scorpion with the size and function of an attack dog. Its legs were thicker, square-edged brass pistons. Its tail was an articulated steel whip more than a yard long, tipped with a steel spike, and its claws were pruning shears, big enough to lop off a man's leg at the thigh. Rather than camera lenses, its sensory apparatus consisted of a single, many-faceted glass sphere, like a compound eye the size of a grapefruit, mounted on a metal stalk, and a series of bristling wires sprouting from its carapace that quivered in response to sound.

"Threaten," Rutherford told it, and it raised its claws and advanced on the couch, violently pumping its legs while the curved blades of the shears flashed open and closed. Unable to flee, Letitia and Mr. Fox leaned back as far as they could, burying themselves in the couch cushions, but the scorpion whipped its tail forward, stabbing at the air just inches in front of their faces.

"Thank you, Mr. Rutherford," the cowboy said. "That will do for demonstration purposes."

"Back off," Rutherford commanded, not without a certain reluctance. The scorpion obediently withdrew, backpedaling to its original position beneath the archway.

"Now then," the cowboy continued. "I assume you've already deduced who I am."

Letitia nodded, one eye still on the scorpion. "You're the man who owns the ranch. The one Mr. Red Pawn over there was double-dealing with."

"Yes," said the cowboy. "Though when I purchased the device from Mr. Rutherford, I had no idea there was a prior claimant. I am a respecter of other men's property and dislike being thought of otherwise. When I learned, belatedly, what Mr. Rutherford had done, I was very angry, and I have already informed him that he and I will not be doing business in the future."

"If you admit the teleporter isn't yours," Letitia said, "then why are you here?"

"Because you broke into my home and took something that didn't belong to you. The trespass I can forgive. It was rude, but understandable, particularly in light of Mr. Rutherford's behavior. If you'd settled for retrieving your lost property, I'd have no quarrel with you. But you got greedy—or perhaps you felt, having been stolen from, that you were entitled to steal in return. And that I cannot let stand."

"I don't know what you're talking about."

"I'm talking about the silver key that was kept in the same room where I had my driver put your teleporter. When I went out riding that morning, the key was there; when I returned several hours later to find my house burgled, the key was gone."

"Not with me," Letitia said. "Maybe your driver took it. Or one of your neighbors—I didn't bother to lock up on my way out."

"My neighbors know better than to steal from me," the cowboy said. "As do my employees."

"Maybe someone else, then." Eyeing Rutherford: "Someone with less sense."

"No," said the cowboy. "The thought did occur to me, but I know it wasn't him. You knocked out all of my men, but you missed my housekeeper. She saw a woman of your description come onto the property. She also saw you leave, accompanied by another colored woman and a colored boy. No one else came in or out before I returned, so if you didn't take the key, one of them must have it. The boy, I would guess. Young men have sticky fingers.

"So who is he?" the cowboy asked. "Does he live here with you? Does the woman? Are they here now?"

Letitia chose her next words with care: "Marvin and his mother don't live here."

"Where do they live, then?"

"I'm not going to tell you that. But I'll make you a proposal. If you let me use the telephone, I'll find out real quick whether they've got your key—and if they do, I'll see it's returned to you promptly."

"A reasonable offer," the cowboy allowed, "but I'm afraid it won't do. I'm going to need to speak to the boy—Marvin?—directly. His mother, as well. In person."

"That's not going to happen," Letitia said, adopting the same flat tone that Anthony had in Iowa. "I don't care what you do to me."

"I'm not going to do anything to you. Mr. Rutherford is. You understand, he's quite angry right now, because of the position his own foolish actions have put him in. And while I would say he has no one to blame but himself, he of course doesn't see it that way at all. He blames you. He would very much like my permission to hurt you. Are you sure you won't tell me where they are?"

"I'm sure," Letitia said. She turned to Mr. Fox, who'd spent the past few minutes looking dazed—partly by pain and fear, and partly by what was, for him, the unprecedented strangeness of this situation. But now his face grew resolute, and he nodded in agreement. "You cut and poke me all you like," he said. "I'll die before I help you hurt a child."

"There you go," Letitia said, turning back to the cowboy. "I'm right with Jesus, so you do what you've got to do."

The cowboy looked over his shoulder at Rutherford, and Letitia, feeling her bravado slip, braced herself for what was to come.

But instead of unleashing the scorpion, Rutherford merely nodded. "That should be enough," he said.

The cowboy reached into a pocket on the front of his vest and took out a small brass disk with a pattern of holes drilled through it. "Another trifle," he told Letitia, and handed the disk to Rutherford.

Rutherford unhooked a device from his utility belt. It was shaped like a telephone handset, but chunky, metallic, and cordless. He placed the brass disk over the device's mouthpiece, screwing it securely in place, then fiddled with a few dials and switches.

"You're sure this will be able to reach her?" the cowboy inquired.

Rutherford looked insulted by the question, but he nodded. "Her fingerprints were on the coin case, and she told me her name. That's more than enough for a trace." He handed over the device. "Press the green button to dial. It'll connect to whatever phone she's closest to. If you hear street noise in the background, that means you've got a pay phone, and you'll want to hang up—red button for that—so she doesn't get suspicious."

"Understood," the cowboy said. Turning back to Letitia and Mr. Fox, he commanded: "Total silence from both of you, now."

The phone was ringing. The cowboy pressed it to the side of his head, so that his lips were brushing the brass disk.

When next he spoke, it was with Letitia's voice.

MAKING CONNECTIONS

꧁꧂

Y ou worried about George?" Ruby asked, as she sat eating breakfast at Hippolyta's kitchen table.

"Not as worried as I would be if he'd learned to pick up after himself." When they'd gotten in last night, dirty dishes had been piled up in the sink—doing the math on those, Hippolyta could tell that George had been home the entire time she'd been away. And the four coffee cups and the half-eaten box of fresh doughnuts he'd left on the table said he'd had guests over yesterday. "I still think he's out with his friends from the Masons' lodge."

"Is it normal for them to stay out all night?"

"I wouldn't say normal, but it's happened before. I found this when I was cleaning up." She showed Ruby the map with the block in Packingtown circled. "That's George's handwriting."

"'Building 106,'" Ruby read. "You know what that is?"

"No, but I was thinking . . . Those gambling clubs where your daddy used to go to play poker, the mob ran those out of abandoned buildings sometimes, didn't they? Like old warehouses?"

"Sometimes, yeah . . . You really think George would be out gambling all night, though?"

"Not on his own. But if it's a bachelor party, or some kind of initiation . . ." Hippolyta shrugged. "I guess one reason I'm hoping it's that, is that if George is up to something a little bad, that might make things easier when I tell him Mr. Tunstall's trailer got blown up."

Ruby smiled. "Like, 'I forgive you if you forgive me'?"

"It's silly, I know . . ."

"No, it's not. But if that trailer cost as much as you say, you're going to want to hope that George either won big or lost big."

The phone rang. Hippolyta answered it. "Hello? . . . Hey, Letitia . . . Sure, I was planning on it, right after breakfast. Is— What?" Her expression grew confused. "Can you say that again? I think there was some noise on the line . . ." Her confusion increased, but she kept it out of her voice. "Sure, I can bring him with me. But what is this about? . . . OK . . . OK, sure, we'll be there as soon as we can . . . Oh, and before I forget, do you still want that sweater Tanya Robinson gave me?" Frowning at the answer to this question. "Sure, I'll bring that too, then. See you soon."

When she hung up, Ruby was staring at her. "Tanya Robinson's sweater? What was that about?"

"I think Letitia's in trouble," Hippolyta said. "She was real eager to have me come over to the Winthrop House. She said she had something important to tell me, something she couldn't talk about on the phone."

"She want me to come too?"

"No, she didn't even mention you. But she did ask me to bring Marvin."

Now it was Ruby's turn to look confused. "Marvin?"

Hippolyta nodded. "Something about the way she said it, I could have sworn she meant to say Horace. But it wasn't a slip of the tongue. It's like she was talking in code, like someone was listening in and she wanted to pass me a warning without them catching on."

"But who would that other person be?" Ruby said. "It can't be Mr. Braithwhite. He knows Horace's name, and he knows for sure that Marvin isn't here."

"I can think of someone else who might fit the bill." Hippolyta frowned again as she made another connection. "And the person I have in mind helped design the Winthrop House. Which means he might know a way to get past Mr. Winthrop's ghost."

"We'd better get over there, then," Ruby said. "You got a gun in the house?"

"Yeah, I do." Looking at the map on the table: "Be nice if George and his friends were here to back us up."

Footsteps rang on the fire escape. Both women turned to the window above the sink. "Oh, thank God!" Hippolyta said, seeing Atticus's smiling face looking in. She ran to unlock the fire escape door, but by the time she got it open another thought had occurred to her, and when Atticus tried to hug her she fended him off.

"Aunt Hippolyta?" said Atticus.

"What's wrong?" said Montrose, right behind him.

"Before I let you in," Hippolyta told them, "I've got to ask both of you some questions."

LET THEM GO

❧❦

When George turned the corner at the end of the block, he saw Hippolyta, Ruby, Atticus, and Montrose all piling into a cab. Rather than try to catch them, he took his foot off the gas.

"Pop, what are you doing?" Horace said from the back seat. "Honk the horn!"

"No, let them go," George said, speaking mostly to himself. "It'll keep things simpler."

"Keep *what* simpler?" Horace said.

But George didn't answer, only let Woody idle until the cab had pulled away.

George parked in front of the Safe Negro Travel Company. He and the other Masons went into the office to use the phone there.

Horace went upstairs to the apartment. He walked back to his bedroom and stashed the silver key in a cigar box that he used to store baseball cards and other treasures. Then he went into the bathroom and got cleaned up, bandaging his hand and changing into fresh clothes.

He came out to the kitchen to find something to eat and spotted the map on the table. He studied it, guessing, as his mother had, that this "Building 106" had something to do with why his father had been out all night. But what?

A clatter like shifting jackstraws drew his eye to the backpack that

Montrose had left behind on the kitchen counter. Horace went over to investigate, tipping the backpack forward as he fumbled to undo the buckle on the flap. When he lifted the flap up, Hecuba's skull was lying on top of the pile of bones inside, her hollow eye sockets seeming to peer straight out at him, like the orbs of the Blackwood death mask. Startled, he took an involuntary step back, and his grip slipped. The backpack tilted farther; he managed to catch it before it could fall off the counter and he caught the skull as well, but a dozen or so smaller bones slipped out and cascaded to the floor.

Horace shoved the backpack upright again and made sure it was stable, then stooped to gather up the fallen finger and toe joints. He'd just got them back in the pack when he heard the apartment door open. "Horace?" his father called.

"In here," Horace replied, securing the flap again. He turned around and saw a finger bone he'd missed lying on the floor. He ducked down quickly to grab it, and stuffed it in his pocket.

Then his father was standing in the kitchen doorway.

"Horace," George said. "I need you downstairs."

"What for?"

"I'm going out again. Victor Franklin's on his way over to mind the travel office for me. I need you to let him in when he gets here, then stick around in case he needs help."

"What are you going to Packingtown for?" Horace asked, nodding at the map on the table.

George pursed his lips and snatched the map up. "It's none of your business," he said. "Now come on, let's go."

Horace stared out the window of the travel agency office, watching his father and the others climb back into Woody. Pirate Joe offered a conciliatory smile as he pulled his door shut, but George didn't even look at him, just started the engine and drove off.

As soon as the car was out of sight, Horace went over to the drawer where his father kept the petty cash. He took what he needed and reached for the phone.

The cab was already waiting at the curb when Victor Franklin arrived. Horace opened the door and stepped past him with a perfunctory nod.

"Hey," Victor said. "Where you going?"

"Last minute errand for Pop," Horace told him. "I'll explain when I get back."

He climbed into the cab before Victor could ask any more questions.

PLAN OF ATTACK

⚜

There was a boarded-up tavern on the corner of the block where the Winthrop House stood. They had the taxi drop them off there.

"So tell us more about this Rutherford character," Montrose said when the cab had departed. "You know what kind of powers he has?"

Hippolyta shook her head. "He's an engineer. A gadget maker. I don't know if he can cast spells. But it's a safe bet he'll be armed." This last statement carrying a bit of an edge, as she was the only one in the party who didn't have a gun. Montrose had claimed the revolver in the apartment for himself, while Atticus had snagged the pistol George kept in his desk in the travel office. Ruby still had her .22.

"Who else is in the house?" Atticus asked. "Charlie Boyd's still away, right?"

"And Mrs. Wilkins," Hippolyta said nodding. "Mr. Fox is home, but he was pretty drunk last night, so he could still be passed out in his room."

"And Horace?"

"He's supposed to be there. But thinking about what Letitia said on the phone, I'm not sure Rutherford knows that. I think Horace might be hiding. So be careful what you shoot at."

"Right," Atticus said. "So Rutherford, Letitia, Mr. Fox, and maybe Horace. Anyone else?"

"Not unless Rutherford brought friends with him. For what it's worth, he didn't strike me as much of a people person. But you might want to keep your eyes peeled for booby traps."

"So how do you want to do this?" Montrose asked Atticus. "You got a key to the back door, right?"

"Yeah," Atticus said, "but I'm thinking the smarter play might be to go in through the roof."

"How you going to get up there?" Ruby said.

Atticus pointed to a dark line at the corner of the mansion. "I can shinny up that drainpipe."

"You mean *we* can," Montrose said.

"I don't know, Pop," Atticus said. "When's the last time you made a climb like that?"

"I'm sorry." Montrose turned to face him straight on. "Are you questioning my fitness after what we both just went through?"

"Pop—"

"Enough," Hippolyta said. "I can get you both inside, but only if you stop bickering." She brought out the transport unit that was programmed for Terra Hiram and explained what it could do.

"So we make a bank shot off the far end of the universe," Atticus said. "And end up where?"

"Letitia's bedroom. Unless Rutherford's found the base unit and moved it. You'll have to be prepared for that possibility when you click the button the second time."

"And you're sure it'll take both of us," Montrose said. Looking like he'd prefer to take his chances with the drainpipe.

"As long as you hang on tight to each other, yes."

"I'm coming too," Ruby said.

"What?" said Montrose. "No."

"No," Hippolyta agreed. She looked at Atticus. "You're going to give Ruby your back-door key. She'll go in that way. And I'm going up the front walk and ringing the bell to get Rutherford's attention."

"*No*," Montrose repeated.

"Listen to me," Hippolyta said. "My son's in there. Ruby's sister's in there. So we're not just going to wait out here and let you handle it. Either we all work together, hit Rutherford from every direction at once, *or*"—she held up the transport unit with her thumb poised on the button—"I can take Ruby in with me and leave *you* out here."

"That works for me," Ruby said.

"Foolishness," Montrose said scowling. "Goddamn foolishness."

But Atticus, in spite of his own misgivings, broke out in a grin. "Give it up, Pop," he counseled. "We're overruled." Nodding at his aunt: "We'll do it your way. But let's try not to get ourselves killed, all right?"

THE GOD OF DEATH

❊

George set the Stygian vessel in its designated circle. He gave the lid a clockwise turn to unseal it, then stepped back carefully, regarding the urn like a bomb that had just been armed. "Ready," he said.

Pirate Joe, diagram in hand, was double-checking the lettering around the other circles. "Looks like we're ready here, too."

"I still think we should tie his feet together," Mortimer said, staring at the body on the slab.

Winthrop's role in the ritual only required a voice, but other magical powers, such as telekinesis, involved the use of hand gestures, so after some discussion, they'd decided to put asbestos mitts on the corpse and bind its wrists together with rope. In a worst-case scenario, they hoped that this would at least slow Winthrop down for a few seconds. An added benefit to the precaution was that it offered a modicum of dignity to the late Herman Armbruster, whose genitals were covered by the mitts as well. But George didn't see the sense in tying him up further. "If it comes to the point where we're trying to outrun a dead man," he told Mortimer, "I'd say we're already done for."

They looked up at the skylight. "You ready, Abdullah?" George called.

Abdullah leaned into view above the missing windowpane and nodded. "Sound carries really well," he said. "I can hear everything from up here." He held up the gun, a big Colt .45, which George had produced from under Woody's driver's seat. "I'm going to pray I don't have to use this."

"I'm going to pray for that too," George assured him. "All right . . . Everyone take your places."

Click.

"Damn," Atticus exclaimed, as he and his father materialized on the beach at Terra Hiram. They both started at the sight of Scylla's deflated carcass, which Hippolyta had forgotten to warn them about. But the shock passed quickly, and Atticus had to suppress the urge to look around some more. "Time for jump two."

"Yeah," agreed Montrose, who was less enchanted by the alien seascape. "Remember to be ready in case we pop out somewhere unexpected."

They embraced again, stiffly, chest to chest, looking over each other's shoulders, gun arms curled around each other's waists. "On three," Montrose said. "One . . . two . . ."

Click.

The horn was the size of a bugle, but the noise it produced when George blew into it was that of a much larger instrument: a deep buzzing note that resonated in the bones, quickened the blood, and sent shivers across the skin. A sound to wake the dead.

He blew the horn three times. When the last note faded away, he crouched, set the horn on the floor, and picked up a piece of chalk and made two quick strokes with it, changing two of the letters in the circle that surrounded him. Beside him, Joe and Mortimer made similar alterations to their own circles.

All three men stood up again. George unfurled a scroll and read a long invocation, written in the language of Adam, which the circle now granted him the ability to read and utter. This was followed by a shorter, repeating chorus, which George voiced in a singsong; Joe and Mortimer echoed his words, at the same time striking long tuning forks that had been scribed with more of the magic letters.

The chorus was repeated seven times. By the second repetition, the room had begun to dim and the air grew noticeably colder. The sun still shone through the windows and the skylight overhead, but the energy of the incoming photons was being siphoned off and concentrated in the Stygian vessel. The urn glowed from within; viewed from the far end of the table, its steadily increasing brilliance formed a halo around the corpse on its slab.

The rest of the warehouse continued to darken. As the seventh repetition of the chorus reached its end, even the skylight faded into blackness, so that the shining corpse seemed to float in a void. Shuddering in the bitter cold, George lowered the scroll and looked down to see that the floor had disappeared beneath him, leaving nothing but the faintly glowing letters of the circle.

In the space of a heartbeat, everything was normal again. The light returned, and the summer warmth with it. George looked quickly towards the body, but it too seemed unchanged.

Then the corpse's right foot twitched. Its chest rose and fell, minutely at first, then more obviously, reanimated lungs drawing in deep breaths of air. Herman Armbruster's eyes opened and he began to laugh, a gleeful chuckle that made George want to run screaming from the building.

"Mr. Winthrop?" he said. "Is that you?"

The dead man sat up.

Having arrived safely in Letitia's bedroom, Atticus and Montrose disentangled themselves with care, mindful of creaking floorboards.

Atticus went over to the window and looked down into the alley, where Ruby stood waiting outside the kitchen door. He waved to her, then tapped his wristwatch and held up two fingers. Ruby nodded.

Montrose eased the bedroom door open. To his right, he could see the top of the stairs and the gallery extending beyond it. He heard footsteps pacing in the atrium below.

An angry white man's voice said: "Where the fuck are they?"

"Patience, Mr. Rutherford," said a second white man.

Letitia spoke up: "Hippolyta's probably having trouble getting a cab. Which makes it your own damn fault, for dumping her car out at that A-bomb site."

"Shut the hell up," the first white man said. Then he said something else that Montrose didn't quite catch, but whatever it was triggered a cacophony of pistonlike thumps, loud metal shearing sounds, and a whir like a chain being whipped through the air.

"Mr. Rutherford! Stop that!"

The machine noises ceased.

"This is bullshit," Rutherford said. "You should just let me kill them."

"Once I've regained my property, you may do as you like. But until then, Mr. Rutherford, you *will* control yourself . . . Now get that monstrosity of yours out of sight. I don't want it scaring off Mrs. Berry or her son before I have a chance to speak to them."

Montrose pushed the door shut. He handed his revolver to Atticus, who was standing next to him now, then went over and knelt down beside the bed.

"What are you doing?" Atticus whispered.

"Looking for the housewarming gift I gave Letitia." Montrose pulled a double-barreled shotgun from under the bed.

"Pop, you can't use that! The spread could hit Aunt Hippolyta."

"It's a risk," Montrose agreed, "but we might need the extra firepower."

He broke open the shotgun to make sure it was loaded, then checked under the bed again for more ammo.

Downstairs, the doorbell rang.

You want me to wait?" the taxi driver asked, not sounding enthusiastic about the prospect.

"No, thank you," Horace replied. "I don't know how long I'm going to be."

He paid and got out, nose wrinkling at the smell, which had been bad enough inside the cab. As he started down the alley, the taxi made a quick U-turn behind him and drove away.

Woody was parked in front of building 106. Horace glanced into the empty car and then tiptoed around it to press an ear to the warehouse's big double doors. He could hear voices inside, but they were too muffled to make out words. He took a few steps back and looked up at the roofline.

Then, continuing to move as quietly as he could, he went around the side of the building and started up the metal stairs.

Herman Armbruster's eyes were hazel; Hiram Winthrop used them to survey the rest of his new body. He bowed his head and studied his chest first, nodding approval at its status as a tabula rasa. The mitts and bindings on his hands got a quizzical look, but after determining by feel that he had all ten digits he didn't seem to care about being tied up. Shifting his hands to one side, he stole a peek between his thighs, here exhibiting his first sign of disappointment. But he shrugged it off and moved on, scanning down the length of his legs to his feet and wiggling his toes, which made him chuckle again.

At last, apparently satisfied, he acknowledged the presence of

George and the others. He raised his mitted hands. "If you're concerned about Onanism," he said, "I can assure you that I have neither the inclination nor the energy at the moment."

"No, Mr. Winthrop," George replied. "Those gloves are just to keep you from doing anything rash. Before we continue our business here, I need to have a conversation with you, about terms."

"Of course." Winthrop's smile grew cynical. "You want to sweeten the deal. Ordinarily I take a dim view of anyone trying to hold me over a barrel, but today I'm in an exceptionally good mood. So let's hear it. What more do you want? Money?"

"No, sir," George said. "I wouldn't trouble you for money."

"What, then?"

"I want your word."

"My word?"

"That you'll leave Chicago. That you'll leave my family and Letitia's family alone from here on out, and encourage your friends to do the same. We've had enough of the Order of the Ancient Dawn."

"Not *quite* enough," Winthrop noted. "Not until the cancer's out of you."

"True," George conceded. "But I mean it. When our business is done, I want you gone. And I want your solemn oath that, whatever you make of your new life, you'll do your best to refrain from evil."

Winthrop stared at him incredulously. "'Refrain from evil'? Are you joking?"

"I couldn't be more serious," George said. "I know our notions of right and wrong are probably very different. But you're an intelligent man. The concept of morality can't be entirely foreign to you."

"It isn't," Winthrop agreed. "But a moral man hardly needs to promise he'll be good. And if I'm the kind of immoral monster you apparently suspect me of being, why would you trust my word at all?"

"I've trusted it this far," George said. "Even a monster can be bound by an oath, if it's the right oath."

"I suppose. But who or what would you have me swear to? God? I don't believe in God."

"Maybe not by that name. But you do believe in power. The power that kept your soul intact after you were murdered. The power that brought you back here, to be talking to me right now."

"You mean 'magic'?" The dead man's lips twisted in a sneer. "There is no magic. This is science. An application of natural principles. And nature just *is*. It doesn't care about right, or wrong, or anything else."

"I believe that it does," George said. I have to, he thought. It's the only hope I've got here. "And I believe that if you ask it to bind you and hold you accountable, it will do so."

Winthrop went on sneering, but just for a moment he hesitated, and the barest hint of doubt came into his eyes. But he pushed past it. "Very well," he said. "I give my solemn oath to refrain from evil, and may the power that brought me back to life bind me and hold me accountable if I fail . . . Will that do?"

"Yes," George said, after his own brief moment of hesitation.

"Is that it, then? Or is there something else you want?"

"One more thing. My cure . . ."

"You'll have it. I've already promised you that."

"Not just for me, though," George said. "I'm not the only person facing a death sentence from cancer. There are thousands of others in this city alone. I—we—would like to help as many as we can. I'm not asking you to take part in that directly. But I need you to show us how to do it."

Winthrop's expression had reverted to incredulity. "So that's what this is about. You're a socialist."

"What?" George said.

"Like those fools who led my son astray. You want life to be fair. You think you can make it fair. But you're wrong," Hiram Winthrop said, "and I can't help you."

"What does that mean? Are you saying you can't teach us the spell?"

"I'm saying it won't do you any good. I could teach it to you, but it's useless for the purpose you intend. It's a simple procedure, really," Winthrop said. "Simple, but brutal: a blunt transference of life force. Whether you use it to revitalize dead tissue or repair a living body, that energy has to come from somewhere, and there are no half measures in the taking of it. For every life you would save"—and here he looked at Joe and Mortimer—"another must be spent."

"Hold on, now," George said. "You never said anything about—"

"No, of course I didn't," Winthrop said. "I'm not an idiot. I couldn't take the risk that you'd be too weak-willed to do what was necessary to survive—and I see now I was right to be cautious. You think you can have what you want without paying for it. You can't. That's not how nature works."

"Forget it, then," George said. "The deal's off." And he made to leave the circle.

But before he could take a single step, Winthrop flexed his hands inside the mitts. Then the mitts were gone, atomized along with the ropes that had bound his wrists. A wave of force rippled outwards, flowing down over the side of the table and across the floor, shifting the molecules of chalk, rewriting the lettering around the circles. George's feet—and Joe and Mortimer's, too—became rooted to the ground.

"No," Hiram Winthrop said. "We'll keep the deal. I can't go back to the house, and I'm not about to be stuck sitting on this fucking slab for another twenty years. So we'll do as we agreed. But I'm willing to hold up my end. You can still have your cure, if you want it."

"No." George shook his head, and it took every ounce of control he had to not look up at the skylight. "Forget it. Forget it."

"As you wish. But I'm taking what I need." He looked at Joe and Mortimer again. Sizing them up like options on a dessert cart. "It's a matter of indifference to me, which of you it is," he said finally. "I'll let you choose, Mr. Berry."

Shoot him, George thought. For God's sake, Abdullah. Shoot him.

"Come on," Winthrop prompted him. "I've been more than patient."

George looked at his friends: Pirate Joe standing dead still, in quiet resignation, Mortimer openly trembling, but still holding panic at arm's length.

There was only one answer he could give.

"Me," George said. "Take me."

"A man willing to die by his own principles," Winthrop said. "I could almost find that admirable, if it weren't so—"

A loud bang interrupted him. But it wasn't a gunshot. A box had fallen from the platform at the front of the warehouse.

"Who's there?" Winthrop said, turning his head towards the sound. George took advantage of the distraction to look up at Abdullah. But the skylight was empty.

"Who's there?" Winthrop repeated. "Show yourself." Now George looked towards the platform as well, wondering why Abdullah would have chosen to come inside—and hoping that he'd come up blasting. But the face that rose into view from behind a stack of crates wasn't Abdullah's. It was Horace.

"Oh God," George said. "No! Horace, ru—"

Winthrop waved a hand casually and once more the letters around the circle transformed, cutting off George's voice in midcry.

"Well, hello there," Winthrop said, looking at Horace with undisguised hunger. "*Young* man."

Please come inside," the cowboy said to Hippolyta, "and stand right over there."

She did as she was told, moving to a spot equidistant between the front door, Hecate's statue, and the foot of the stairs. Looking through the archway into the parlor, she saw Letitia and Mr. Fox sitting mute on the couch. The scorpion had been banished to the back hallway, but Rutherford was hiding just out of sight and stepped out as soon as he heard the front door close. Hippolyta did her best to act surprised.

"She didn't bring the boy with her?" Rutherford said to the cowboy.

"It would appear not. There's no one else out there." The cowboy walked around and stood facing Hippolyta. "Where is Marvin?"

"He didn't want to come," Hippolyta said. "Who are you?"

"We'll get to that in a moment," the cowboy said. "But first, please divest yourself of any guns or knives you have on your person."

"I'm not armed," she told him. "Who are you? What's *he* doing here? What do you want with my son?"

"All right," said the cowboy. "Let's talk about that . . ."

On the second floor, just out of sight beside the top of the stairs, Atticus stood with a gun in each hand. Carefully he leaned his head out. From his perspective, looking down, Hippolyta was farthest to the right, and the cowboy was a few feet to her left, standing in the open—an easy shot at this distance. Rutherford was going to be trickier: he was beneath the archway, only partially exposed, and given a second's warning he could duck back into the parlor. Ideally, Atticus would kill him first, then deal with the cowboy—but his every instinct was telling him that the cowboy was the bigger threat here.

No problem, he told himself. All you have to do is shoot them both at the same time . . . He pulled his head back into cover and concentrated, psyching himself up into a combat mindset, picturing what he was about to do as if he'd already done it.

He was just about to go when he was distracted by a scuttling sound coming from the elevator shaft. He looked to the middle of the gallery and saw a pair of wiggling aluminum tubes like spindly fingers poke out between the bars of the closed gate. The mechanical spider squeezed its body through the opening, dropped to the floor, righted itself, and turned in place, legs ticking like knitting needles, until its clustered camera eyes were pointed directly at Atticus. It reared back on its legs and began chittering in alarm.

Montrose stepped out from behind Atticus and swung up the shotgun, firing one barrel. The blast exploded the camera lenses and flipped the spider on its back. By the time it had come to rest with its legs askew, Atticus was in motion, pivoting around to the head of the stairs and bringing his own guns to bear.

There was good news and bad news. Alerted by the spider, Rutherford had chosen to step forward into the atrium and now presented a clear target. But the cowboy had turned to face the stairs and was holding up the black stone pendant, wielding it the way a vampire hunter would wield a crucifix. As Atticus tightened his fingers on the triggers, a strobing dark rainbow commanded his attention. Then the cowboy yelled "Stop!" and Atticus froze, triggers at half pull.

Montrose, still focused on the spider, saw Atticus stop moving but didn't understand what had happened. From where he was standing, he couldn't see Rutherford or the cowboy. Couldn't see the black stone. Given the way Atticus was poised, face fixed in concentration, he assumed it was some kind of standoff, with the intruders having drawn their own guns. "What is it?" Montrose said. "They got the drop on you?" He meant to whisper, but his ears were ringing from the shotgun blast and he spoke more loudly than he intended.

"That's an excellent idea," the cowboy said. "Get the drop on him."

Stepping back from the stairs, Atticus turned and pointed both guns at his father.

Pop?" Horace called to him. "Pop, you OK?"

No matter how hard he tried, George couldn't utter so much as a whisper in response. And his arms had become as leaden as his legs.

He couldn't gesture. He couldn't scream. All he could do was plead mutely with his eyes: *Run*.

"He's fine, for the moment," Hiram Winthrop said. "But I need you to come down here." Bracing his hands against the slab, and exerting considerably more effort than he'd used to break his bonds, he swung his new body around to face the front of the warehouse. His legs dangled over the side of the table and he leaned forward, perching like some obscene pale vulture that didn't quite have the strength to take wing. "Come here, boy."

"You go to hell," Horace told him.

"I can't come to you," Winthrop said. "But I can kill your father just by snapping my fingers." He looked sidelong at Mortimer. "I'll demonstrate with the little man, if you like."

Horace just stood there, fists clenched, breathing hard, poised between fight and flight.

Winthrop raised a hand, thumb and middle finger pressed together. "I'll count to five."

"No!" Horace said, putting his own hands up, palms out. He swallowed hard, then turned and started down the stairs, George dying inside as he did so.

On the warehouse floor, Horace hesitated again. His eyes darted around frantically and he lunged for a nearby shelf, grabbing a big pipe wrench which he brandished as a club. "Fair enough," Winthrop said, nodding magnanimously. He spread his arms wide, exposing himself in a pantomime of vulnerability. "Let's see how fast you are."

Horace steeled himself and advanced, club at the ready. As he closed the distance he tried to vary his stride, feinting left and right, bobbing and weaving in a manner that Winthrop seemed to find more amusing than threatening.

Winthrop let Horace get to within about fifteen feet. Then he curled the fingers of his right hand and an invisible force tore the wrench from Horace's grasp, spinning him around sideways as he tried to hold on to it. Horace watched the wrench fly away and then looked down in alarm as he realized he was still moving, his feet gliding along the floor as if it were greased.

Winthrop reeled him in. He seized Horace's flailing left arm with both hands and opened his mouth as if to gobble it down. Instead, tightening his grip, he began to recite a singsong chant in the language of Adam. A red glow appeared, shining between his interlocked fingers, and Horace grimaced in pain as he struggled to break free. Winthrop went on chanting, a look of bliss on his face now as his head tilted back and his eyelids went to half-mast.

Then his tongue seemed to stumble, stuttering to a halt in mid-verse. He shook his head and started again. But this time he only made it through a few syllables before once more sputtering to a stop. The red glow faded.

"Something wrong?" Horace said.

The lack of fear in his voice got Winthrop's attention. Winthrop looked him in the eyes; not liking what he saw, he tried to let go of Horace's arm, to free his hands for action, and discovered to his dismay that he couldn't.

Horace blinked, and blinked, and blinked again, and his irises changed from brown to blue. "Hello, Hiram," he said, smiling, and his voice was different too now. "Do me a favor, would you? If you see my father down in hell, tell him Caleb sends his regards."

He reached behind his back with his right hand and lifted the tail of his shirt to reveal the Colt .45 tucked into his waistband. In one fluid motion he drew the gun, cocked it, swung it around, jammed the muzzle up under Winthrop's chin, and pulled the trigger. In the fraction of a second it took for the hammer to fall, Winthrop's eyes went wide with terror. Then the top of Herman Armbruster's skull came off. The body pitched over backwards; the dead hands lost their grip and fell sideways, knuckles rapping and jiggling against the slab; the dangling feet twitched briefly and were still.

Caleb Braithwhite lowered the gun and stepped back, rolling his shoulders as if to work out a kink in the muscles there. When the reversion to his native form was complete, he looked down at himself, examining not his body but the clothes he was wearing. "Not a bad fit," he observed. "A little tight across the chest, but other than that, we could practically share a wardrobe." He raised his head and turned smiling towards the three Masons who were gaping at him. "Hello, gentlemen."

How? George mouthed.

"Ah," Braithwhite said. "Sorry." He waved a hand.

"How . . . are you here?" George said.

"That is a long and painful story, and I'd rather not spoil my good mood by going into it just now. Oh, and before you start worrying," Braithwhite added, holding up the Colt, "Abdullah's fine. You can go collect him from the roof when we're done here." He tucked the gun back into his waistband. "Now . . ." Grabbing hold of Herman Armbruster's ankles, he straightened out the legs and shoved, pushing the corpse across the table until the torso overbalanced and it toppled off the far side of the slab, tumbling to the floor with a loud thud. "So much for the great Hiram Winthrop," Braithwhite said, brushing his palms together.

George was still lost. "What are you *doing* here?"

"Taking advantage of an opening," Braithwhite said. "Not that it's my business, but you really should talk to your wife more, George. Hippolyta's been running errands for Winthrop for a while now. I got wind of it when she got in touch with a colleague of mine about one of the components used to construct that horn. After that, I started tracing her movements, and it wasn't hard to figure out what Winthrop was up to.

"But there was one item I knew he'd need that he couldn't ask Hippolyta for. She would never have agreed to steal a body for him. To undertake the ritual—and, in the process, to make himself vulnerable—Winthrop was going to have to find someone else, someone desperate enough to do almost anything, in exchange for a service that only he could provide. So I put my intuition to work and started thinking about who I could get to fill that role."

George stared at him. "What are you saying? Are you telling me that—"

"You don't have cancer," Braithwhite said. "Or at least," he amended, "to the best of my knowledge, you don't. When Dr. Blaylock gets back from the cruise I sent him on, you might want to schedule another physical, just to be sure. But I wouldn't lose any sleep over it."

The sense of relief George felt in that moment was so overwhelming he nearly fainted. But it was followed almost instantly by fury. "You son of a bitch. You—"

"I won't tell you that I'm sorry. These last two years haven't been fun and games for me, either, and if I'm honest, I was feeling a little vengeful." Braithwhite shrugged. "But that's water under the bridge now, as far as I'm concerned." Smiling again: "All is forgiven."

While George continued to fume, Braithwhite turned and walked to the head of the table and picked up the Stygian urn. He weighed it with both hands for a moment, then lifted it over his head and flung it down. It shattered explosively on the floor, sending up a plume of sparkling dust. Caught in a sudden draft, the dust spiraled higher, drawn up towards the missing pane in the skylight.

Outside, on the roof, someone sneezed.

Montrose, holding the shotgun with both hands, arms above his head, shuffled in a semicircle around his son, Atticus turning in place as he did so, keeping both handguns pointed at him. Atticus's expression made it clear he was acting against his will, and with his back turned to the stairs, he mouthed a warning to his father: "Don't look at him."

"Well now," said the cowboy, when Montrose was standing on the gallery. "How ever did you gentlemen get up there?"

"It's the fucking teleporter," Rutherford said. "The base unit must be up there somewhere." He looked at Hippolyta. "I'll be taking that with me."

"Only when I have my property," the cowboy reminded him. "You, sir!" he called to Montrose. "Please focus your eyes in my direction for a moment."

"That's OK," Montrose said. "I don't need to see your face. You all look alike to me anyway."

"Don't try me, sir. You can look at me, or I can have your companion blow your head off."

"Why wait?" Rutherford said. He pulled a snub-nosed pistol from a holster on his utility belt. "I'll blow his head off right now."

Back in the kitchen, what sounded like a whole stack of plates came crashing to the floor. This was followed by a string of gunshots that began in the kitchen and progressed through the dining room. Ruby stumbled backwards into view, holding her .22 in one outstretched hand. She tripped and fell, hooking the leg of one of the dining-room chairs with a foot as she went down. The chair spun around with a clatter and a spike on the end of a long steel whip pierced the wooden seat, lifting the entire chair up to be dismantled by a pair of metal shears.

"More company," the cowboy said. He circled around Hippolyta and walked towards the dining-room archway where Ruby now lay sprawled with the scorpion looming over her. "You wouldn't happen to know where Marvin is, would you?"

Ruby answered by flinging her empty .22 in his direction. As the gun hit the floor at his feet, the scorpion spun in place, orienting on the sound.

The cowboy stopped short. With the scorpion turned towards him, he could see that its visual sensor had been damaged: a lead slug was embedded in the glass ball with a dense web of cracks spreading out around it. As the cowboy considered the implications of this, he raised his right hand instinctively. The glass ball shifted on its stalk, attracted by the blurry motion of his fingers. Whatever the scorpion saw as it zeroed in on the black stone didn't seem to agree with it: a rising hum like a feedback whine emanated from within its body and it lifted its claws aggressively.

"Mr. Rutherford," the cowboy said, shying back, "would you please—"

The scorpion lunged at him, whipping its tail forward with blinding speed. The spike passed through the black stone, shattering it, and plunged deep into the cowboy's chest.

A shotgun boomed up on the gallery. The blast hit the scorpion in the side, striking something vital; it froze, claws open, on the verge of dismantling the cowboy as it had the chair. Instead the cowboy simply went limp, sinking to his knees with his head bowed, the brim of his Stetson resting against the metal tail still embedded in his chest.

And Atticus, freed from the cowboy's enchantment, whirled to face the foot of the stairs. But Rutherford had grabbed Hippolyta; locking an arm across her throat and pointing his pistol at her head, he wrestled her around, using her as a shield even as Atticus tried to draw a bead on him.

"Let her go," Atticus said.

"Fuck you!" Rutherford replied.

Hippolyta, unnoticed by either of them, reached into the pocket of her skirt.

In the parlor, Letitia got to her feet. Rutherford saw her moving out of the corner of his eye. "Stay back!" he warned, gesturing with his gun hand. As the muzzle of the pistol swung away from her head, Hippolyta opened her mouth and screamed all the air out of her lungs.

Then her thumb clicked the button of the transport unit in her pocket, and she and Rutherford disappeared.

❀ ❀ ❀

Braithwhite's voice floated up through the opening in the skylight: "Is that you, Horace? I had a feeling you might turn up here for real."

Horace, crouched on the roof beside Abdullah's unconscious form, leaned forward and showed himself at the skylight.

"Hey there!" Braithwhite looked up smiling at him. "Why don't you come down and join us? Don't worry, no one else is getting hurt today. I just need to discuss a few more things with your dad, and then we can all get out of here. But I'd prefer to keep an eye on you in the meantime."

Horace looked over at his father. George's lips were pressed tightly together and he was shaking his head no.

"Come on, Horace," Braithwhite said. "You're here because you wanted to be a part of this. So be a part of it."

Horace stood up. He stepped around Abdullah and went back over to the ladder and climbed down to the landing on the side of the building. The door there had been locked when he'd first come up, but now, as he descended, he heard the latch click.

He opened the door and a gust of air blew past his face, making him sneeze again. At the same moment he felt a twinge in his left ankle, as if the muscles there were cramping. He lifted his foot and shook it until the feeling passed. Then he went inside.

Braithwhite was still standing over by the marble slab. He'd taken the gun back out of his waistband and was holding it pointed at the floor. "Do me a favor, Horace," he said, as Horace stepped into view on the platform. "Hold your hands up where I can see them and do a slow turn around. I'm not trying to be rude, but I'm getting a funny feeling and I'd like to avoid any surprises."

Horace did as he was told. As he finished the turn, he felt something squirm in his pants pocket, but with his hands raised he couldn't do anything about it.

"All right," Braithwhite said. "Come on down here. But keep your hands visible, and no sudden moves, OK?"

Horace crossed the platform to the stairs. As he went to take his first step down, he felt the squirming in his pocket again, and a bolt of excruciating pain shot up from his left ankle all the way to his thigh. The leg collapsed under him, and then he was tumbling and sliding all the way down to the warehouse floor.

"Horace!" George cried out. He wanted to run to him, but he still couldn't lift his feet.

"You all right there, Horace?" Braithwhite called.

Horace didn't answer. He'd landed in a heap at the bottom of the stairs. As George watched him anxiously for any sign of movement, the light in the warehouse dimmed again, as if the sun had gone under a cloud. But the shadows were concentrated at the front of the warehouse, and as they grew and combined it became obvious that something else was going on. Braithwhite's eyes narrowed; he shot a look of angry suspicion at George, then scanned the walls behind him for an emergency exit. But the warehouse didn't have a back door.

A solid wall of shadow had engulfed the front of the building now. This darkness was warm, not cold, and waves of humidity emanated from it. The scent of manure from the stock yards was drowned out by the acidic smell of rotting vegetation. George heard the distant cry of a loon, the sound of lapping water, and a rhythmic chopping like a hand ax.

With no other way out, Caleb Braithwhite turned to face down the dark. "Horace," he said, struggling to hide the tension in his voice. "I don't know what you're up to here, but you need to come out where I can see you."

Uneven footsteps in the darkness. The shadows parted and drew back and Horace came down the center aisle, walking at a lean with an odd shambling gait that seemed to parody Braithwhite's bob-and-weave approach to Winthrop. Horace's left foot was turned out to the side and his knee bent in a way that looked both awkward and painful. But he showed no sign of discomfort. Drawing nearer, he focused his unblinking eyes on Braithwhite, his lips curved in a faint mocking smile.

"That's close enough," Braithwhite said, and Horace stopped obediently. There was something different about his face, George saw: a subtle furrowing of the muscles, accentuated by the dim light, that gave him the wizened look of a much older person. Then Horace spoke, and for the second time that day, George heard another person's voice coming from his son's mouth. A woman's voice.

"So here you are at last," she said, looking Braithwhite up and down. "The great Caleb Braithwhite, in the flesh . . . Huh. All these years I been dreaming of you, away up in the future making such a fuss, I expected something more impressive. Not a man dressed in boys' clothes. But then you aren't much more than a boy yourself, are you?"

Braithwhite received this with a brittle and wary expression. He wasn't often surprised, and knew it never boded well. But he made himself smile. "You have me at a disadvantage."

"You got that right."

The smile broadened. "And just who do I have the pleasure of speaking to?"

"Pleasure!" The old woman cackled. "You think you gonna charm me now? Don't waste your time. It's not our destiny to be friends, Mr. Braithwhite."

"Well, if you won't tell me who you are, at least tell me what you are," Braithwhite said. He glanced in George's direction. "Friend of the family? Member of the family?"

"You want to know what I am?" the old woman said, and the shadows gathered again. "I'm the ship that didn't sink. The broken bough that refused to fall. The fugitive in the night who stepped right every time, and the runaway hiding in the eye of the storm. I'm everything you tried to steal, but couldn't . . . And today? Right now? I'm the voice warning you back from the cliff you can't even see you're standing on.

"And I know you won't listen," she said. "You've been here before, and you were told, in no uncertain terms, that these folks want nothing more to do with you. But here you come again, with a piece of your hide already missing. Even a cat knows better than to sit on a hot stove twice, but you—you think if you just set your ass down a little different this time, you can make it all turn out the way you want it to. But I tell you now, that stubbornness is gonna cost you, and it's gonna go on costing you—today, and tomorrow, and tomorrow—until it costs you everything you have. And on *that* day? On that day, I'll be the one walking away in light, while you go down into the dark alone."

Throughout this recitation, Braithwhite had gone on smiling, trying to project an air of amused detachment. But the smile had grown increasingly strained, and now George, to his horrified fascination, saw red spots blooming on the front of Braithwhite's shirt.

"All right," Caleb Braithwhite said with a tremor in his voice. "That's enough."

"I can't tell you how many times I've said those very words," the old woman replied. "And you know what it got me?"

Braithwhite gasped and staggered back a step. The spots on his shirt merged into a single large bloodstain, and lines of red started rolling down the front of the fabric. He cocked the hammer of the Colt and swung the gun up and pointed it at Horace, aiming right between his eyes.

"Last chance," Braithwhite said.

"It is," the old woman agreed. Adding, with what sounded like genuine puzzlement: "Why won't you take it?"

Braithwhite pulled the trigger.

The gun exploded in his hand.

Even knowing it was coming and having some idea of what to expect, the abrupt transition to deep space was a shock. Of all the sensations

Hippolyta experienced in that instant, the one that left the most lasting impression was not the weightlessness, or the sudden absence of external sound, but the way that her tongue got cold, as the saliva in her mouth flashed to vapor in the vacuum and just as quickly crystallized as ice.

Angus Rutherford, caught completely unprepared, reflexively tried to hold his breath: the worst thing he could do under the circumstances. Agony ripped through his chest as rapid expansion of the air in his lungs caused the tissue to rupture. He convulsed, losing his grip on Hippolyta, and the two of them spun apart.

The region of space in which they floated was dominated by twin stars, one blue and one orange, like mismatched eyes set a few degrees apart in the firmament. The stars' light reflected off the surface of a nearby asteroid—nearby, but still unreachably distant without a jet pack or a rocket, and offering no safety in any event.

Dread eclipsed pain as Rutherford grasped the reality of his situation. Death was supposed to be only a temporary inconvenience for him, one that he'd long planned for. But his plan had a weakness: owing to the principles by which it operated, his soul-catcher had a limited range. It protected him anywhere on Earth, and even as far out as the orbit of the moon, if he should somehow chance to find himself there. But elsewhere in the cosmos, he was a skydiver without a parachute.

Hippolyta was drifting away from him. In desperation he flung out a hand and actually managed to snag a pleat of her skirt. But the victory was short-lived: as he tried to pull her back, she rotated on the fulcrum of his arm, and then both of her feet slammed hard into his chest.

They flew in opposite directions. Somersaulting across the universe, Hippolyta discovered that unlike Rutherford, she had no fear of dying here. The stars had never felt so close before, and even through her rapidly blurring vision, they were beautiful to behold. She could think of worse places to spend eternity, if she had to die.

But not today.

Click.

Braithwhite held his right hand up in front of his face and stared in disbelief at the blackened and bleeding stumps of his thumb and forefinger. A mewling started deep in his throat, rising to an anguished howl. He bared his teeth and charged. But Horace, still animated by the spirit of the old woman, moved nimbly out of the way. Braithwhite ran past him and kept right on running, dashing up the aisle to the front of the warehouse and shouldering the wooden doors open to escape into the alley.

When Braithwhite's howls had faded into the distance, Hecuba turned to George and Joe and Mortimer, and the energy that had sustained her thus far seemed to flag. "That's all I got for you," she said. "But *he's* just getting started, and you'd best be prepared when he comes back around." Focusing on George: "Tell your brother and your nephew I did my part. Remind them to do theirs."

She bowed her head and a tremor passed through the floor, blurring the chalk circles. Then Horace was back, standing on two good legs, but weak and on the verge of collapse. George, realizing he could move again, ran to catch him before he fell.

OAK WOODS

They laid Hecuba to rest in Oak Woods Cemetery on Saturday afternoon. The attendees gathered beneath the spreading oak tree that sheltered Lucy Turner's old plot and listened to Reverend Oxbow give the eulogy. He spoke of Joseph, who had made the children of Israel promise to carry his body out of Egypt, in effect pledging his own bones as a symbol of faith that God would one day guide them to freedom. And so too Hecuba: sending Nat Turner into an uncertain wilderness, trusting that God would lead him back out to bring the memory of the past into the future, even as the struggle for freedom continued. "And now it's our turn," the reverend said, "to carry on that legacy."

After the ceremony, the Prince Hall Freemasons and their wives set up a picnic buffet. People filled their plates and sat in groups on the grass to eat and talk, or wandered off to visit other graves.

Throughout the proceedings, Hippolyta kept a wary eye on Horace. So did George. In the wake of last Monday's events, they'd had a long and uncomfortable conversation during which the secrets they'd been keeping from each other finally came out. In a sense, Hippolyta had gotten her wish: there was enough blame on both sides that they could have just chosen to call it even. But they'd been angry with each other anyway, that anger fueled by knowledge of the terrible price their actions might have cost them. Nor had Horace escaped their wrath: today was the first time he'd been allowed out of the apartment since George had brought him back from the warehouse, and the only reason he was here was that they weren't ready to trust him at home alone.

Hippolyta was checking on the buffet when she noticed Horace standing over by the grave, staring at the hole as if he meant to jump in. Her brow furrowed and she started towards him, only to collide with George, who was headed the same way. Hippolyta was knocked to the ground, while George ended up with a plate of ribs on the front of his suit. They looked at each other in irritation, but any impulse to greater anger was short-circuited by the realization that they'd just reenacted their first meeting at the Smithsonian.

George helped Hippolyta to her feet and she got paper towels and cleaned the mess off his suit as best she could. Then they walked off to a quiet spot together, still keeping an eye on Horace.

"So," George said. "I guess we need to start sharing information more."

"Yeah," Hippolyta replied, "I guess we do . . . What? What's funny?"

George shook his head. "I never thought I'd be following Caleb Braithwhite's advice." He looked at her. "I am sorry, you know. For not telling you. But I was scared, and not just of the cancer. I was scared of being talked out of doing what I needed to do."

"I understand that," Hippolyta said. "Better than you might think."

"Getting the teleporter really meant that much to you?" No judgment in his voice, just honest curiosity.

"Yeah, it did. It does." She looked up at the blue sky. "To actually travel out there, not just stare at it through a telescope—I can't even begin to describe what that means to me. But when Mr. Winthrop told me it was possible, I just . . . I *had* to."

"OK." He took her hand. "OK, then."

"So," Hippolyta said, returning to earth. "Since you're in an understanding mood . . ."

George laughed. "Let me guess. You need a new car."

"I do."

"Well, I got good news on that front. I was talking to Joe, and he's got a friend who's looking to unload a used Buick. Same model Roadmaster as your old one, with only twenty thousand miles on it."

"Twenty thousand? That's practically brand new by my standards."

"I know. And I'll get it for you . . . But I need you to help me with something in return."

"Let me guess," Hippolyta said. "Mr. Tunstall."

He nodded. "We're going to have to reimburse him for the trailer. I don't see any way around that—he can't file an insurance claim without a police report. But it's not just a question of money. He's going to want an explanation, and I don't know what to tell him."

"Well, that's easy. Tell him I liked the trailer so much I decided to keep it."

This solution—so obvious in hindsight—caught George by surprise. But then he smiled. "That's perfect. He'll *love* that."

"I bet he'll give you a break on the price, too," Hippolyta said. "Especially once he sees the article I'm going to write for the *Guide*."

"OK," George said. "Looks like you're getting a new trailer to go with your new car. Papers for a trailer, anyway."

"I'm also going to need to build a space suit," Hippolyta said.

A boys' school?" Mr. Fox said.

"The St. Didymus Academy," said Montrose. "Grades nine through twelve."

"They need a substitute English teacher for the fall semester," Reverend Oxbow explained. "And Montrose tells me you used to teach high school English."

"That was a long time ago. Years." Mr. Fox leaned on his crutches and stared down absently at the cast on his ankle. "When my wife died, I lost my way for a while. Eventually I turned myself around again, for Celia's sake, but not in time to save that teaching job." Looking up:

"I appreciate that you're trying to help me, but no school is going to want to—"

Montrose put a hand on his arm. "Just hear the reverend out," he said.

"Don't let the academy's name fool you," Reverend Oxbow continued. "It's not some fancy boarding school. It was founded by a friend of mine, to help out boys who are in trouble. The students you'd be teaching have all had run-ins with the law or other serious problems, and a lot of them are from broken homes. So the fact that you've been through your own difficulties would be seen as an asset rather than a disqualification. And like I say, it's a substitute position—a one-semester commitment. But if it turns out that you're right for the job, and the job's right for you, it could become something more permanent. You could do a lot of good there."

"Of course," Montrose added, "you'd have to step up and lead by example."

Mr. Fox was silent a long time, thinking. Finally he said: "And it's just boys?"

"Yes," the reverend said. "There's a sister academy, for girls, but they keep them separate. Cuts down on distractions."

"And where is it?"

"Cincinnati. So you would have to relocate. But the job includes room and board."

"Relocate." Mr. Fox looked away across the cemetery. "That's hard."

"It's not that far," Montrose said. "And while you're away, I'll be coming here regular to tend Hecuba's grave. I can look after Celia for you too, if that helps."

Another long silence. But by the end of it, Mr. Fox was nodding.

I'm going to make another pass at the buffet," Anthony said. "You ladies want anything?"

"I'm good," Ruby said.

"I'll take another slice of that pecan pie," said Letitia. "Unless you think it'll make me too heavy for our flight later."

"Girl, you're a feather," Anthony said laughing. "I'll be back."

He walked away, Ruby breaking into a grin the moment his back was turned.

"Don't," Letitia said.

"Oooh, girl." Ruby waved her hand as if it were on fire. "You're a *feather*."

"Don't, I said." Letitia elbowed her in the side. "You be nice."

"I am being nice," Ruby said. "So is this for real?"

"It's something. I don't know exactly what yet. But I'm having fun."

"Well, good for you, then. I'm happy for you."

"Really?"

"Letitia! Why wouldn't I be?"

"I don't know," Letitia said. "You just seemed surprised, when I introduced him."

"Well, if I was, it's not because of him. I know I've been out of touch for a while, but I guess I just thought, with the two of you living under the same roof this whole time, that you and Atticus would have ended up together . . . Uh-oh!" Ruby said, seeing Letitia's reaction to Atticus's name. "Did I miss something?"

"No." Letitia shook her head. "Nothing bad like that. Atticus is a friend, and it's good to have him around."

"But?"

"He wants to protect people. Which is fine, if you don't overdo it, but Anthony . . . Anthony lets me fly the plane with him. The first time we were up together, he let me try, and not because I asked. He *offered* . . . And now tonight, when we take this little hop over to Detroit, he says he's going to let me handle the takeoff."

"Really?" Ruby said. "Is that safe?"

"He'll be sitting right next to me if anything goes wrong," Letitia said. "But he's not worried about it. And when I've learned enough to try landing, he'll let me do that too. He *trusts* me."

"Well then I really am happy for you. Maybe a little jealous, too."

"So what about you?" Letitia said. "You got a boyfriend?"

"Me?" Ruby laughed. "When would I—"

But before she could say any more, Anthony returned, bearing Letitia's pecan pie.

Horace was still at the graveside looking down at Hecuba's casket when his cousin came over to him.

"How you doing?" Atticus said.

"I'm not sure," Horace said, as if he'd been wrestling with the question. "You heard what happened? At the warehouse?"

"Uncle George filled me and Pop in, yeah."

"It's funny," Horace said. "You'd think being possessed by a dead lady would settle some of my questions about the afterlife. Turns out not so much."

"What was it like?" Atticus asked.

"I don't know if there's a word for it. 'Intimate,' maybe . . . I mean, not, you know, *intimate* intimate, but—"

"Yeah, I get what you mean."

"I couldn't read her thoughts," Horace said. "But I could feel her: The *way* she thought. The way she saw things. I could feel how different from me she was . . . And I know that's no real surprise. I mean, she was already older than me when Abraham Lincoln was born, and she's been dead longer than Lincoln was alive, so of course she'd be different, in all kinds of ways. But it's one thing to *say* that, and another to be like"—he held up his hands, meshed his fingers together—"like *that* with her.

"And she was strong, too," he went on. "That place in the swamp where she was laying all those years, she built up a lot of power there, somehow. It's how she was able to go toe-to-toe with Mr. Braithwhite. How she could still be here, at all. And don't get me wrong, it's good to find out that it's not just rich white men who can bend the rules, but I'm not sure how that applies to *my* situation, you know? Or to other people I care about. People without that kind of power. Does that . . . Am I making any kind of sense here?"

"Oh, yeah." Atticus nodded. "I know what you're trying to say." He thought a moment. "When I was in boot camp, I got to be friends with a guy named Derrick Campbell, from Jacksonville. We were real close, me and Derrick. Still would be, if he'd made it back from Korea. He was the first person I ever saw get killed in combat."

"They shoot him in the head?" Horace said.

"No. Here." Atticus put a hand on the left side of his chest. "He lived for maybe another minute, after, but there was nothing I could do besides hold his hand. I still play that back in my head sometimes, the way it looked when the light went out of his eyes. And I wonder: did that light *go* somewhere, or did it just, stop? And that's all tangled up with this other question, which is, Why him and not me? That bullet could have just as easily had my name on it. And one day, it will.

"But there were other things that happened to me in the war— stranger things, that let me know just how weird the world can be, and how little I really understand it. And then I come home to find more strangeness waiting for me right here. And you would *think*, some- where in all of that, I'd find something to help answer my questions about Derrick."

"But you didn't," Horace said.

"Not yet," said Atticus. "I haven't given up looking, though."

They both fell quiet for a moment. Then Horace said: "I've never heard you talk about the war like that before."

"Those kinds of war stories aren't for most people," Atticus said. "But I'll talk to you about it, if you want. Or about anything else that you think might help."

"OK," Horace said. "I might take you up on that."

Letitia and Anthony were discussing their Detroit plans when Ruby excused herself and struck out across the cemetery alone.

Earlier, during the eulogy, she'd noticed a colored man in a gray suit wandering among the nearby tombstones. Something about him had seemed off, but by the time the ceremony ended, he'd disappeared. Now she'd spotted him again, strolling along the bank of one of the cemetery's ponds. As she walked towards him, she realized what had been troubling her: one of his hands was darker than the other. This wasn't a skin condition; he was wearing a black glove on his right hand.

Ruby quickened her pace. The man turned away from the pond and stepped out of sight behind a small crypt. When Ruby got there, he'd vanished, but then he reappeared, coming out from behind a larger mausoleum some distance away. This game of hide-and-seek continued for several minutes; somewhere in the middle of it, she noticed that the man's hair had straightened and turned a light shade of brown, while the color contrast between his two hands had increased dramatically.

The chase ended at the Confederate Mound. Located in the southwest corner of Oak Woods, just north of the little Jewish cemetery, this was a mass grave containing the remains of several thousand Rebel soldiers who had died at the Camp Douglas prisoner-of-war camp during the Civil War. The United Confederate Veterans had erected a monument on the site, a tall granite column topped with a bronze statue of a glum-faced Confederate infantryman.

Caleb Braithwhite was sitting on the grass near the base of the monument, pretending to read, when Ruby caught up to him. She arched an eyebrow at the book in his hands: *The Ways of White Folks*, by Langston Hughes.

"So you're a comedian now?" she said.

"I'd never actually read him before," Braithwhite told her. "I thought I should give him a try, and the title piqued my interest. I can see why you like him."

He closed the book and set it aside. Ruby studied his right hand as he did this; it seemed intact beneath the glove. "I heard that you got your fingers blown off," she said.

"I did." Holding up the gloved hand so she could see it clearly, he whispered something, and the glove's thumb and forefinger collapsed, deflating like balloons. Another whisper and they filled out again; when he flexed them, the phantom joints moved beneath the leather in a way that appeared perfectly natural. "This is just a stop-gap, until I can come up with a more permanent solution," he explained. "I've developed a new interest in the healing arts."

"Between that and your Negro literature studies, I'm sure you'll be very well-rounded," Ruby said. "Now what are you doing here?"

"I came to bring you a peace offering." He reached into his suit jacket and brought out a small manila envelope.

"What's that?"

"A key to a post office box downtown. Every Monday morning, there'll be a package waiting for you with a full week's supply of the elixir."

Ruby felt her pulse speed up as if she'd been shot full of adrenaline, but she managed to keep her face impassive. "I'm not going to help you get *The Book of Names* back."

"I know that," Braithwhite said. "I never really expected you to."

"Then why did you show up on my doorstep like that, pretending to be Marvin?"

"Would you believe me if I told you that I wasn't entirely sure? I think I wanted to find out how long it would take you to see through my disguise. To remind myself what I saw in you. And you didn't disappoint." He smiled. "Peanut butter . . . That was good."

"You're just a crazy person, aren't you?" Ruby said.

"I am what I've always been: a man who knows what he wants, and how to get it."

"Well, you're not getting anything from me."

"I'm not asking for anything. The elixir is a gift. I know I disrupted your life, showing up the way I did, and I'd like to make amends."

"If you're talking about my job at the Lightbridge Agency, it's a little late for amends. I've been out a whole week without so much as a phone call. There's no way Miss Lightbridge is taking me back now."

"Oh, I wouldn't be too sure of that," Braithwhite said. "Miss Lightbridge hasn't hired a replacement for you yet. She hasn't even started looking for one. I think if you were to show up at the office, you'd not only find your job waiting for you, you'd probably get a raise in the bargain. And given what she now thinks she knows about your domestic situation, I believe Miss Lightbridge will be more open to your suggestions about expanding the agency's mission. The real question is whether *you* want to keep working with *her* . . ."

"No, Mr. Braithwhite," Ruby said. "The real question is what you're going to want from me."

"I told you, I'm not asking for—"

"Maybe not yet. But there's going to be a price, down the road."

"Ruby, I know you don't trust me . . ."

"Because you're not trustworthy!" she said, exasperated. "Why'd you even come back to this town? To get revenge? What for? You want *The Book of Names*? Find another damn copy! You've got money, and freedom, and now you even got your magic back. You could go anywhere in the world, do anything you like. Why come *here*?"

"I like Chicago," Braithwhite said. "I like the people. And my plans haven't changed. The destruction of Lancaster's lodge left behind a useful power vacuum, but the other chapters of the Order are still out there, still squabbling. If I can find a way to bring them together . . ." He raised his good left hand, fingers spread, then closed it into a fist. "Amazing things will become possible."

"Well, I don't want any part of that," Ruby told him. "You want to make amends to me? Fine. Forget the magic potion. Give me the townhouse. Sign over the deed, like you said you would."

"I can't do that."

"No, of course you can't."

"We had a bargain. You broke it."

"Yeah," Ruby said, "but that's not the reason. I couldn't afford to keep a house like that—not as Ruby Dandridge—but I could sell it for a whole lot of money. And then I wouldn't need Hillary anymore. Or you."

"You might not need Hillary," Braithwhite allowed. "But we both know you'd miss her. And there's no reason why you should have to. It's not wrong to want to be treated as a full human being. To want to be respected and taken seriously, without having to fight past artificial obstacles. To want to just *be*."

"No," Ruby agreed. "The sin isn't in the wanting. It's in what you do to get it."

"Maybe," Caleb Braithwhite said. "But maybe the key to redemption is in what you do *with* it. You asked me once what I would do, if I succeeded in unifying the lodges and making myself head of the Order. I told you that you didn't have to worry, that you and your people would be protected. And then you asked me what I meant by your people, and I said, 'The people you care about. Your family and your friends.' But I know there's another way to interpret the question—and I know it's not just your own family that you care about.

"Hiram Winthrop didn't believe that the world could be made fair. Neither did John Lancaster, or Angus Rutherford, or my father. Well, they're all with the dinosaurs now, and meanwhile the world *is* changing. You could help it change. I know you want to. And while you *could* do it as Ruby Dandridge, alone, I think you'd be a lot more effective—and happier—with Hillary on your side."

"With Hillary," Ruby said, thinking, Here it is. "And with you?"

"You think I'm evil," Braithwhite said shrugging. "As long as that's true, I know it's too much to hope that we could be friends. But we can still be allies. I'd like that. After all that's happened, I still admire you, Miss Dandridge . . . And I've missed you.

"Anyway, I'm going to leave this here." He placed the envelope on the grass. "If you don't want it, don't take it. The Sons of Confederate Veterans will be by tomorrow to clean up the site, and they'll dispose of it for you, if someone else doesn't grab it first. It's your call." He got his book and stood up. "But think about what I've said, Ruby. Think about it."

Then he turned and walked away in the sunlight, leaving Ruby to wrestle temptation on her own.

TO THE DREAMLANDS

꧁꧂

Abdullah came by the Safe Negro Travel Company just before closing. George was alone in the office, going over the proofs for the autumn edition of the *Guide*. He looked up smiling when Abdullah came in, but Abdullah didn't smile back.

"What's going on?" George said.

"You seen this?" Abdullah dropped a copy of that day's *Chicago Tribune* on the desk. The paper was folded over to a page 5 story headlined GAS MAIN EXPLOSION GUTS BUILDING IN DOUGLAS.

George didn't recognize the address, but it was close to the Douglas branch of the Travel Company. "Did someone we know get hurt?"

"No," Abdullah said. "It was a commercial building, and the explosion happened around two in the morning. Only person there was a night watchman, and he smelled the gas and got out before the blast."

"So why are you showing me this?"

"Because it's the same building I told you about a few weeks ago. The one my friend Errol worked construction on?"

George looked at him blankly. "I don't know what you're talking about."

"Yeah." Abdullah nodded. "I was afraid of that."

"Why don't you sit down?" George said. "Start over from the top."

Abdullah grabbed a chair and sat with his hands folded. "So, do you remember that day you called me, Joe, and Mortimer over to the temple and asked us to help you steal the body for Winthrop?"

"Of course I do." George smiled. "I'll remember that on my death-bed."

"And do you also remember coming by my house later that same day, to talk to me in private?"

The smile faded. "No. I can't say I do."

Abdullah nodded again. "When we met up to go to the morgue the next day, I got this weird feeling you'd forgotten all about it. It was on the tip of my tongue to say something, but we'd agreed we'd never speak of it again. Of course I didn't know, then, that I had to worry about running into someone who only looked like you."

"Abdullah. What the hell did we talk about?"

"*The Book of Names.*"

George leaned forward. "What about *The Book of Names?*"

"You wanted to know whether I'd actually burned it like I'd said I was going to. You were very apologetic about it. It wasn't that you didn't trust me, you said, but the question had been preying on you for a while, and now with the cancer and the business with Winthrop, you just wanted to put it to rest, so you'd have one less thing to worry about. I don't know, maybe I should have been more suspicious, but I'd kind of danced around the question earlier, at the temple, and I felt bad about it."

"Are you saying you didn't burn the book?"

"I tried to," Abdullah said. "Twice. Second time was at the tile factory where my brother works. They've got this ceramics kiln there that heats up over two thousand degrees. The book wasn't even singed. I tried other things, too: Tearing it. Cutting it. I even ran it through a wood chipper. It broke the blades. That's when I realized, I'd probably need magic to destroy it, and I didn't want to mess with magic.

"So I decided to get rid of it instead. Put it somewhere out of reach and just let everyone think it was destroyed. I thought about taking it out on the lake and dropping it in deep water, but I was worried that even if I weighted it down, it might get loose and wash up somewhere. Then I remembered my friend Errol. I called him up, asked what his next job was, and he told me about this office building that was going up in Douglas. I asked if I could be there the day they poured the foundation."

"And you buried it." George nodded at the newspaper article. "Under this same building."

"That's right," Abdullah said. "I went by the site earlier today. City's got it cordoned off, but you can see the blast crater from the barricades, and it looked to me like the gas explosion—if that's really what it was— was focused on the same corner of the building where I put the book. So if wasn't you I told about that . . ."

"It wasn't me," George said. He leaned forward again, peering closely at the photo that accompanied the article. "Jesus Christ!"

"What?" said Abdullah.

"The guy in this picture . . ." The photo showed a Negro man in a uniform standing in front of the shattered building. "'Night watchman Carl Brewer recounts his close call with death.' This is the same guy who was at the hospital."

"What guy?"

"The orderly. The one who brought Armbruster's body down to the morgue, just when we needed it." George shook his head. "Carl Brewer . . . Caleb goddamned Braithwhite."

Later that same night, Horace sat at the drafting table in his bedroom, chin in hand, gazing critically at his latest attempt to sketch the painting of the dreaming woman that had hung on the wall in the cowboy's house.

It was his third try, and from a purely technical perspective he knew there wasn't anything wrong with it. He had a strong visual memory and his technique was solid; but as with his previous drafts, the finished work left him dissatisfied on a gut level. This dissatisfaction, and his inability to pinpoint the cause, had been nagging at him throughout his weeks of home detention, even as he tried to focus on other things.

At first he'd thought the problem might be the change in medium. He was a drawer, not a painter. He liked the simplicity of just picking up a pencil and setting to work; even watercolors seemed fussy by comparison, and oil painting, with its cumbersome and expensive tool kit of brushes, palette, paint tubes, and turpentine was nothing he'd ever wanted to mess with. For his second attempt, he'd tried to cheat out the difference, using a full spectrum of colored pencils and pens. The result was impressive—some of his best work, really—but it still didn't satisfy.

For this latest draft, he'd made use of a trick he'd once read about in an art instruction manual. He'd done a series of preliminary sketches in which he isolated specific elements of the painting—the woman sprawled on her bed, the water pitcher and hand mirror propped on her nightstand—and blew them up, drawing them with much more detail than they would have, or could have, in the finished work. The idea being that when he shrank them down again, this added detail wouldn't be lost, but would be transmuted, subliminally, into a greater sense of vividness. It was an interesting exercise, and it did seem to have a positive effect, but it didn't solve the problem.

After staring fruitlessly at the drawing for a while, he picked up the stack of detail sketches and started flipping through them, pausing often to admire his own handiwork. When he got to the sketch of the woman standing naked on the balcony in dreamland, he broke out in a grin, reminded of the first nude he'd ever done. That had been in second grade, when the Reverend Oxbow's son, Reggie, had dared him to draw Betty Boop without her dress. The result, crude in both senses of the word, had earned him a hard smack on the back of the head and a trip to the principal's office when his teacher, Miss Vaughn, had caught him with it. Horace wondered what Miss Vaughn would make of this.

The next sketch was the dream city, the vast city of white towers spread out beneath the balcony. As he looked at it, Horace's expression turned serious again, and he nodded. This was it, he realized: the source of his discontent.

He hadn't got anything wrong. The problem, he saw now, lay with the original painting. The city's massed towers had been depicted with a shimmering, diaphanous mirage quality, a no doubt deliberate style choice intended to underscore the fact that this was dreamland. But Horace's enlargement of the cityscape, and his attempt to add at least a little more detail, had highlighted something less obvious: to the extent that they did have substance, the towers were all copies of one another. The same building, repeated over and over, in differing sizes but with only the most minor variations in outline. This too was no doubt a deliberate style choice—and a defensible one, given the subject matter.

But it wasn't a choice that Horace would have made.

That's not how *I* dream, he thought, with a pointed indignance softened by relief at having finally solved the puzzle.

He squared up the sketches with the finished draft and set them aside. Then he grabbed a fresh sheet of drafting paper and a charcoal pencil and went to work.

When he leaned back sometime later, the pencil had been reduced to a stub—he couldn't recall having stopped to sharpen it—and the paper was full. In place of the wispy city of cookie-cutter towers, he'd conjured up a dark metropolis, solid and rich with detail. It was anchored at its center by a varied range of stone and glass skyscrapers; extending down from these, like foothills from mountains, was a dense collage of smaller apartment buildings, shops, restaurants, libraries, movie theaters, parks, and crisscrossing elevated train tracks. Inside a walled cemetery, an oak tree spread its branches above a grave mound;

not far away, a young girl ran laughing to catch a bus. The sky above the city was a night sky, busy with celestial wonders: stars, planets, a crescent moon, a comet, and in the upper-right corner, a shining pinwheel galaxy whose spiral arms were reflected in the waters of a black lake below. And on the left side of the drawing, in place of the painting's balcony, was the open rooftop of a looming project building. An empty rooftop, for now—but he'd left room for a human figure.

That's more like it, Horace thought, surveying what he'd done. He set down the pencil stub and flexed his sore hand.

There was a light knock on his bedroom door. Horace flipped the drawing over, covering the stack of other sketches. He swiveled around on his stool. "Yeah?"

The door opened and his mother looked in. "Hey," she said. "I wasn't sure you were still awake."

Horace glanced at the alarm clock by his bed and was surprised to see that it was after eleven. "Just finishing up something."

"New comic?" Hippolyta said.

"Nah. Something different." Horace resisted the urge to cross his arms. "I'm not ready to talk about it yet."

"OK," his mother said. "So listen, you feel like getting out of the apartment tomorrow?"

"Yeah," Horace said, sitting up straighter. "Absolutely."

"Good. I was thinking of breaking in my new car with a little road trip."

"Where to?"

"Kalamazoo. I figured we'd have lunch with your aunt Ophelia, and maybe visit Grandma Lucy's grave. But really, it's about the drive. We can do some sightseeing on the lake shore. And there's this junkyard I want to stop at. Marine salvage."

Horace thought a moment. "You want to look for a diving suit?"

"Yeah. It's probably all wrong for what I have in mind—with diving, the pressure's on the outside—but I've never actually seen one up close. I'd like to take a look at the helmet, at least."

"Sure," Horace said nodding. "But you're right about the pressure. For space-suit parts, you probably want an airplane junkyard. A jet junkyard."

"Well, if you can find me an address for one of those, we'll go," Hippolyta said. "Now get some sleep—I want to get an early start tomorrow."

"OK, Mom."

After she'd closed the door, he took another long look at the dark city he'd created. Then he put it and the other drawings into the portfolio case he'd gotten for his last birthday.

He got undressed and sat on the edge of his bed and opened up his cigar box of treasures. He'd threaded the silver key on a loop of twine—a placeholder, until he could get a real necklace chain for it. He slipped the loop over his head and put the cigar box away and lay down and turned out the light.

Outside, in the distance, a police siren wailed. Horace thought about Celia. He thought about Hecuba, lying in the earth in Oak Woods—or maybe *not* lying there, maybe flying overhead even now. He thought about tomorrow.

Then curling on his side, and wrapping a hand around the silver key, he closed his eyes and drifted off to sleep.

ACKNOWLEDGMENTS

By the time I finished writing *Lovecraft Country*, I'd begun thinking about a longer story involving the same characters—one that would likely require several volumes to complete. But a lot of things had to go right to make that possible. I am grateful to my friends Nisi Shawl and Christopher Moore for their early support and encouragement; to Jordan Peele, Misha Green, J. J. Abrams, Ben Stephenson, HBO, and the incredible cast and crew of the *Lovecraft Country* TV series; to my agents, Melanie Jackson and Matthew Snyder; to my editor, Jennifer Brehl; and to Jonathan Burnham, Lydia Weaver, Matt Dissen, Nate Lanman, Jarrod Taylor, Ernest Lehenbauer, and Jeff Schwaner.

My wife, Lisa Gold, was indispensable as always.

My source for the legend of the third lost colony of Roanoke is Hugo Prosper Leaming's *Hidden Americans: Maroons of Virginia and the Carolinas*. The work of David Beers Quinn, Noeleen McIlvenna, and David La Vere offered useful additional historical detail and context. John Crowley's novel *The Solitudes* introduced me to the bounded cosmos of Copernicus and its transformation into an infinite universe. And H. P. Lovecraft, my imperfect muse, both chronicled and embodied the dread that infinite universe inspired.

ABOUT THE AUTHOR

MATT RUFF was born in New York City in 1965. An award-winning novelist known for writing in a wide variety of genres, he is the author of the college fantasy *Fool on the Hill*, the science-fiction satire *Sewer, Gas & Electric*, the multiple personality drama *Set This House in Order*, the paranoid thriller *Bad Monkeys*, the 9/11 alternate history *The Mirage*, and *88 Names*, a virtual-reality cyberthriller/twisted romantic comedy. Ruff's 2016 novel, *Lovecraft Country*, in which two black families confront both supernatural horror and the more mundane terrors of life in the Jim Crow era, was adapted as an HBO series by Jordan Peele, J. J. Abrams, and Misha Green.

Ruff lives in Seattle with his wife, Lisa Gold. You can learn more about him and his work at www.bymattruff.com.